LORI WILDE

Saving Allegheny Green

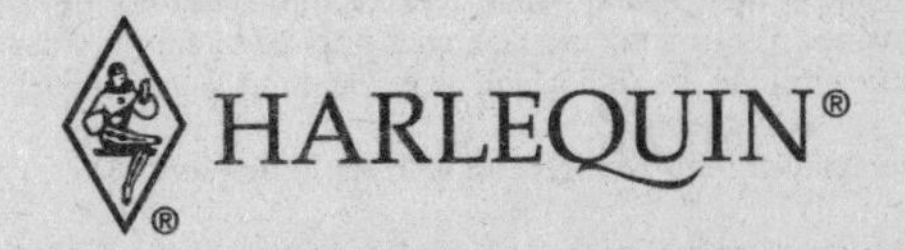

TORONTO • NEW YORK • LONDON
AMSTERDAM • PARIS • SYDNEY • HAMBURG
STOCKHOLM • ATHENS • TOKYO • MILAN • MADRID
PRAGUE • WARSAW • BUDAPEST • AUCKLAND

ISBN 0-373-83661-9

SAVING ALLEGHENY GREEN

This edition published by arrangement with Harlequin Books S.A.

www.eHarlequin.com

Printed in U.S.A.

To all the hardworking nurses at Campbell Memorial Hospital in Weatherford, Texas. You know who you are. Because of your loving hearts and expert care the world is a better place.

Acknowledgments:

A shout out to my online pals, Trish, Spike, Candy and Sarah, some of the funniest women I've had the pleasure to know. I appreciate the brainstorming.

And a special thanks to my editor, Kathryn Lye, who loved the book of my heart as much as I did. Thanks for taking a chance on Allegheny.

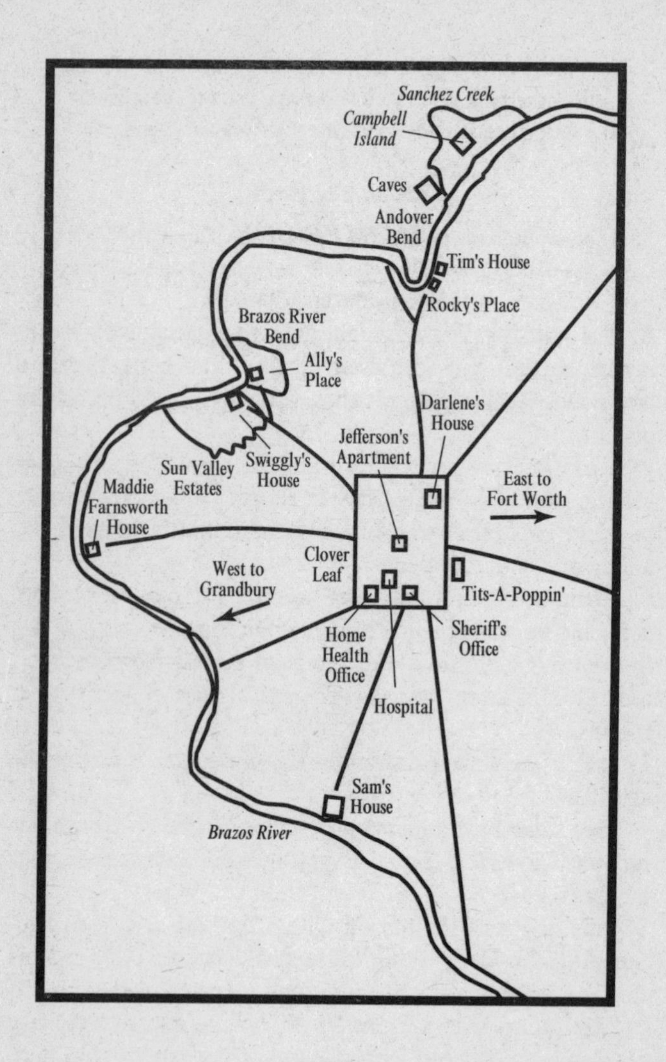

Sanchez Creek
Campbell Island
Caves
Andover Bend
Tim's House
Rocky's Place
Brazos River Bend
Ally's Place
Darlene's House
Jefferson's Apartment
Swiggly's House
Sun Valley Estates
Maddie Farnsworth House
East to Fort Worth
Clover Leaf
West to Grandbury
Tits-A-Poppin'
Home Health Office
Sheriff's Office
Hospital
Sam's House
Brazos River

CHAPTER ONE

AT TEN MINUTES after midnight on a muggy Saturday morning in late July, my kid sister, Sistine, shot her rat-bastard boyfriend, Rockerfeller Hughes, with a twenty-two caliber pistol.

Rocky and Sissy had been drinking, which was not an unusual occurrence. Particularly in Rocky's case. His favorite beverage of choice being a shot of Jack Daniel's dropped into a mug of A&W root beer.

Sistine didn't hurt him. Well, not much. There was blood, sure, and he was howling loud enough to rouse corpses, but in truth she shot him in the foot, and he was wearing steel-toed Doc Martens boots so it wasn't quite as awful as it sounds.

Still, it was a mess and some neighbor ended up calling the sheriff.

That's one bad thing about living in a rural river community like Cloverleaf, Texas. Everyone's got their nose in your business, 24-7.

Like any sensible person with a day job, I was in bed. Sleeping. Or rather trying to sleep. Between Rocky and his ragtag band of wanna-be musicians playing a miserable riff of "My Mama Didn't Raise No Ho" in the garage and Sissy screaming at a decibel far above top-of-the-lungs, I was finding it difficult to achieve theta state.

I had been struggling to restrain myself from intervening in their argument, having learned from experience meddling in Sissy and Rocky's battles was a fool's mission. But Aunt Tessa, dressed in a gauzy white flowing robe, à la Aimee McPherson, came running into my bedroom, her healing crystal charm bracelet jangling as she jumped around.

"Ally," she cried. "Get up. We need you. Rocky's been shot."

"Huh?" Pushing hair from my face, I sat up. The room was dark save for a shaft of moonlight spilling through the Home Depot miniblinds I had installed myself.

"Sissy shot Rocky. With your granddaddy's pistol. You better come quick. Someone's called the cops. Probably that sanctimonious televangelist next door, because I can *feel* the sirens."

Reverend Ray Don Swiggly, the latest Sunday-morning television huckster to make millions from spreading the supposed gospel, had recently built a palatial summer home on the edge of the Brazos River not far from our house. Being of the new-age persuasion, Aunt Tessa had vast theological differences of opinion with the good reverend and expounded on her convictions whenever anyone would listen.

I cocked my head, not wanting to get into a long-winded discussion about the Reverend Swiggly when there were more urgent matters at hand. "I don't hear any sirens."

"You will."

I let it go. With Aunt Tessa sometimes you just had to trust. It was easier than trying to figure her out. I threw back the covers, hopped out of bed and grabbed my practical terry cloth robe with the frayed hem. Okay, so I looked like a neglected housewife. Not everyone could pull off "flaky chic" like Aunt Tessa.

"Where's Mama?" I asked. "And Denny?"

"Your mother's in the pottery shack, I don't think she knows what's going on."

"Good. Keep her there. You know how she gets in a crisis." I gave Aunt Tessa the assignment not only to keep Mama from freaking out, but to give my aunt something to do. "What about Denny?"

"He's still sleeping."

"Are you sure?" Sissy's eight-year-old son had witnessed far too many of his mother's escapades.

"I'm certain. Come on." Aunt Tessa hustled me down the hallway.

We took the stairs two at a time then flew through the back door and out onto the stone walkway leading to the freestanding garage built years after the house was constructed. A million lights blazed and a knot of Sissy and Rocky's drunken friends—scraggly-haired young men and scantily clad women—clotted around the garage door.

I recognized Tim Kehaul. He was one of Sissy's many exboyfriends and the only guy to ever dump her. Tim had discovered rather late in life that he preferred strong, hard masculine muscles wrapped around him in the night to soft, feminine limbs.

Tim possessed a cherubic face, sensational cheekbones and thick bronze hair that curled tightly against his head like a cap.

"Ally." Tim shyly smiled. "Strange doings."

"Hey, Tim," I said, too distracted to really carry on a conversation or wonder what he was doing there.

Tim rarely came around since he didn't like Rocky, and Sissy hadn't forgiven him for taking up with his own sex. The fact that Tim and Rocky lived so close to each other in the same trailer park two miles upriver must have caused friction between the three of them. But I gave up asking questions about Sissy's tangled sexual history. Sometimes it's best not to know.

I elbowed my way through the crowd and hollered at Aunt

Tessa over my shoulder to take care of Mama before I plunged farther inside the garage.

Rocky lay on the floor, baying like a hound caught in a bear trap. His too-tight, blood-flecked Grateful Dead T-shirt had the neck slashed out in a deep V exposing an old scar criss-crossing his throat and more of his chest than I cared to see. For reasons that escaped me, Rocky always cut the neck out of his shirts.

Sissy sat with his head cradled in her lap, tears pouring down her face. "I'm sorry, Rocky. I didn't mean to shoot you," she wailed.

"Yes, you did. I'm having you arrested," he said through gritted teeth.

Thank God, maybe she'll break up with him.

I flicked my gaze over his body, searching for the wound and stopped at his feet. Blood oozed from the toe of his boot and pooled on the cement. Or rather, what was left of his boot. Bits of leather had gone flying and were stuck to guitars and drums. What a mess.

"Ally! Thank heavens!" Sissy exclaimed when she realized I was in the room.

"Your crazy sister shot me," Rocky whined. "Can you believe that?"

"Shut up. Both of you." I sank to my knees beside Rocky.

"Don't touch it!" He howled even though my fingers were nowhere near his blasted foot.

"You know I'm a nurse," I soothed. "Hold still so I can examine you."

"You might be a nurse but you're her sister and you hate my guts." He jabbed a finger at Sissy. "For all I know you'll make it worse on purpose."

"I admit it's a tempting thought," I said dryly. "If you'd rather bleed to death…" I shrugged and started to get up.

His face paled. “No. Wait. Don’t go. Is it really bleeding that bad?”

“I can’t tell until I take your boot off.”

“It’s going to hurt, isn’t it?”

“Like a son of a bitch,” I said cheerfully and loosened his laces.

“The cops are comin’!” Tim yelled from the yard and the next thing I knew engines were revving and the police sirens Aunt Tessa had predicted several minutes earlier screamed in the distance.

“Oh jeez, Sissy.” Rocky gazed balefully at my sister. “Run your hand in my back pocket and get out those joints. I can’t get busted for possession again. They’ll revoke my parole.”

“You brought marijuana into my house after I distinctly told you not to?” I shouted.

“It’s not your house, it’s your garage,” Rocky quibbled.

I jostled his foot. On purpose.

“Yow!”

“Sorry. My hand slipped.”

Rocky glared then turned his attention back to Sissy. “Come on, babe, get the joints.”

“Not if you’re going to have me arrested. You know I had every right to shoot you,” my sister told him.

“Sissy.” I frowned at her. “No one has the right to shoot anyone, no matter what that person might have done.”

“He’s got a wife,” Sissy muttered.

“What?” I glared at Rocky.

He looked sheepish. “It’s no big deal. I haven’t seen her in a year.”

“He’s lucky,” Sissy said. “I was aiming somewhere a bit higher but I missed and the bullet ricocheted off the clothes dryer and got him in the boot.”

Rocky rested a protective hand over his genitals. “Okay,

sweetie, baby. I was wrong. I'm sorry. I shoulda told you I was married when we started dating."

"Damn straight."

She's gonna dump him, once and for all. Praise the Lord and pass the ammo.

The sirens were getting louder. The crowd once assembled in my yard had vaporized.

"So get the joints out of my pocket, please." Rocky rolled calf eyes at Sistine and I knew she was falling for it. "I'll tell the cops it was an accident. I promise."

"Do you want me to flush 'em?" Sissy asked, rooting around behind him, frisking his bony butt. She came up with a crumpled baggy containing six fat hand-rolled marijuana cigarettes.

"Hell no, hide 'em in here somewhere."

My gaze caught Sissy's. "Don't you dare."

"Sheriff's Department." A commanding voice spoke from the open doorway. "Nobody move."

Law enforcement officials poured into my garage, guns drawn. They surrounded the three of us, locking us into some surreal, redneck militia melodrama.

We were screwed.

I caught my breath and glanced toward the door.

A tall, muscular man trod across the garage toward us. He looked like a Rambo-Terminator cross—hard gray eyes, jar-head haircut, service revolver strapped to him more snugly than a spare body part. The twinkling star on his chest revealed his identity.

Sheriff.

The famed former Marine MP, Sheriff Samuel J. Conahegg, as highly lauded in the *Cloverleaf Gazette.*

He'd been elected on the strength of his promise to scour the local government of corruption. His predecessor had run off with the county clerk, buck-toothed, knock-kneed Mavis Higgins—who was reportedly a real hottie in bed despite her uncanny resemblance to Olive Oyl—and two hundred thousand dollars of taxpayer funds.

Conahegg was known not only for his tendency to go for ride alongs with his deputies at any time without notice, but for his utter lack of mercy. Zero Tolerance was his middle name and from his ramrod-straight stance, I could believe it.

"What's going on here?" he asked, his voice a strange mixture of barbed wire and honey.

My heart did a crazy, swoony dance.

Why? I had no explanation. I'm not given to instant attraction to strangers. And most certainly not to domineering, uncompromising types.

His gaze took in Rocky with the shot toe and Sissy holding the bag of illicit weed. Then he looked at me. I shrugged and lifted my eyebrows.

Nobody said a word.

The sheriff turned to one of his men. "Call for an ambulance, please, Jefferson."

"Will do, sir." Jefferson sprinted from the garage.

"The rest of you can put away your weapons." Conahegg waved at the four remaining deputies. They obeyed his command, sliding their guns into their holsters while sending us malevolent stares.

"You." The sheriff flicked a finger at me. "What's your name?"

"Al…er…" My throat was as dry as a crusty gym sock. I tried to swallow. Twice. And finally got out, "Allegheny Allison Green."

"Is that your real name?"

"Don't blame me. I didn't pick it." I might be attracted to him but damn if I'd let him know it.

"What happened here?" He jerked his dimpled chin in the direction of Rocky's toe.

How to explain?

Rocky and Sissy were no help. Rocky had closed his eyes, feigning unconsciousness. Sissy peered assiduously at the floor, staring as if she did so long enough, that it would open up and suck her right down.

"He got shot," I finally answered.

"So it appears." Conahegg squatted beside Rocky. "Hurts pretty badly, does it?"

Rocky didn't move.

"Hmm," Conahegg mused, stroking his chin with two fingers and a thumb.

None of the stalwart deputies had spoken, or even moved. They stayed positioned at the ready, their faces expressionless.

"What I don't know," the sheriff continued in his oddly engaging tone, "is how he came to find himself toeless."

"A gun went off?" I ventured.

The sheriff jerked his head around and drilled me with eyes gone deadly sharp. "You're not that stupid."

Ulp!

He both complimented me and scared me in one breath. I had to give him a high mark for perceptiveness but a low score on charm. Still, something about him magnetized me in a way no man had in a very long time. Just my luck. I finally get the hots for someone and it's the kind of guy I could never get along with.

The sheriff shifted his body away from Rocky and toward me. Instant sweat popped out on my skin. I could feel it trickling down my neck.

"Let's start again, shall we?" Conahegg asked.

I nodded.

"All right." He paused to glance at his watch. "At exactly

ten minutes after zero hundred hours we received a report that someone was shooting off a gun at your residence."

He'd brought his military precision with him to his job as sheriff. You could see it in his posture, read it in his face. He was probably not an easy man to work for. He would demand perfection from his employees, and mete out just punishment if his orders weren't followed to the letter. He possessed an enigmatic power gleaned from years of hard self-discipline.

I shivered.

"We're outside the city limits," I pointed out, forcing myself to stop thinking about the strange pull I felt toward him. "It's not illegal to shoot a gun here."

"To discharge a weapon, no. But to shoot a person, yes."

"It was an accident," Rocky said.

Conahegg and I stared at each other again, our eyes striking like two flint rocks sparking off each other, before we glanced over at Rocky.

"Sh…sh…she didn't mean to do it," Rocky stammered.

"*You* shot him?" the sheriff asked me, a bemused smile flitting over his lips. It almost looked as if he admired me and for one short second I wished I had shot my sister's boyfriend.

"No." Rocky shook his head. "Her." He pointed at Sissy. "She was showing me her granddaddy's gun when she dropped it and the thing went off."

The sheriff reached over and gently pried the baggy of marijuana from Sistine's fingers. His gentleness with her surprised me. He touched her chin, lifted her face. "Is that true?"

Tears glistened in my sister's eyes. She shook like a kitten abandoned on the roadside.

"It's all right," he said softly. "You can tell me anything."

Oh, he was good. Too good. Sissy loved male attention and she'd go to the ends of the earth to get it. Although how he had sensed that about her I had no idea.

"Uh-huh," Sissy whispered. "It was an accident."

"What about this?" Sheriff Conahegg crushed the baggy of joints in his fist. "How did a nice girl like you get possession of a nasty weed like this?"

Sissy's gaze flicked from the sheriff to Rocky.

Come on. Tell him the truth. Rocky's the biggest pot hound in three counties.

Sissy took a deep breath.

We waited.

"I found it," she replied.

"You found it?" Conahegg shook his head, disappointed in her answer.

"Yes."

"Where did you find it?"

In Rockerfeller Hughes's back pocket!

"I don't remember." Sissy was studying a guitar lying on one side of the garage as if her life depended on memorizing every fret.

"Are you aware of the penalty for marijuana possession?"

"No." Her voice was barely audible. Sissy might talk tough and act tougher, but when she's in trouble she reverts to kid mode.

Silence ensued. You could even hear the frogs croaking down by the water. Conahegg rose to his feet and swept his gaze around the room.

The garage was unbearably hot. From where I sat crouched over Rocky's foot, the smell of fresh blood kept assaulting my nostrils and my knees ached from the cement floor.

"May I stand up?" I asked. "My leg is going to sleep."

He nodded.

I stood.

Or rather I tried to stand. My legs wobbled like rubber bands and I stumbled sideways into that hunk of granite passing for a human being.

Conahegg's hand went out to catch me.

The contact was electric.

No kidding. You read that clichéd comparison in romance novels and you assume it's an exaggeration. I mean, I'm a nurse for crying out loud. I touch people all the time. Save for static electricity you don't ever feel a jolt, a shock, a current.

Except I did.

And I had no clue why. It scared me. Big-time.

I jerked away. Fast.

"Are you okay?" he asked.

Oh, sure, other than the fact that you've fried all my internal organs, I'm peachy.

"Need to get the circulation back in my legs," I said, jogging in place, more to shake the sensation of Sheriff Conahegg's touch than to bring blood to my lower extremities.

"Ally?"

The sound of my name drew my attention to the garage door occupied by my mother, Aunt Tessa fluttering at her side.

"I tried to keep her in the pottery shed," Aunt Tessa explained, "but she heard the sirens."

Mama floated over, hardly noticing the sheriff's deputies with guns strapped to their sides. "Honey?" As always, she looked to me for explanation and reassurance. "What are these people doing here?" Her voice still held the sugary sweetness of her Carolina girlhood.

"Ma'am." Super Sheriff turned on his heel and held his hand out to Mama. "I'm Sheriff Conahegg and we received several complaints of disturbing the peace."

"Oh, dear." Mama pushed a wisp of graying brown hair back into the loose bun atop her head. "Why, I know you." She smiled. "You're Lew Conahegg's boy."

"Yes, ma'am."

"I remember when you wore short pants. Your father and

my husband used to have offices side by side on the courthouse square. Green's Green House and James Lew Conahegg, Attorney at Law."

Really? I didn't remember that.

"That's been a while," Conahegg said.

"I'm so sorry to hear about your father's passing."

"Thank you, ma'am."

"Well," Mama continued. "You'll have to excuse the noise. My daughter's boyfriend and his band like to practice here in our garage."

She waved a hand at the abandoned instruments. I was beginning to wonder if she'd even noticed Rocky lying on the floor, suffering from a gunshot wound inflicted by her youngest daughter. Mama had the amazing ability to focus upon only what she wanted to see and ignore the rest.

"So I've gathered." Conahegg nodded. He still held Rocky's bag of weed in his hand. As if he'd just become aware of that, he shoved the pot into his pocket.

"Goodness, Rocky," Mama said, finally catching on. She lifted up her long skirt and stepped over his injured foot. "What happened to you?"

"Accident, Mrs. Green."

"You've got to be more careful, dear. You weren't imitating those musicians on television who smash their guitars, were you? That's not a nice way to treat your instruments."

Everyone looked at me.

I shook my head. No point in explaining reality to my mother. I'd learned that a long time ago.

"Mama," I said. "Why don't you let Aunt Tessa take you inside and make you a cup of tea."

Mama brightened. "That sounds nice. Tessa?"

But as Mama spoke to her sister, a strange expression crossed Aunt Tessa's features.

"Ung!" Aunt Tessa cried out and all gazes swung in her direction. Her right hand went to her throat and her eyes stared vacantly ahead.

My heart sank into my shoes. No. Not now. Not a visit from Ung. Uh-uh. Please God.

Not in front of Conahegg.

But I was not to be the beneficiary of divine intervention. The gathered deputies watched in fascination. I'd seen it before. Many times. I admit, the first time you see it can be quite a show.

The expression on Aunt Tessa's face changed from empty indifference to lively animation. Her lips curled back, a combination smile and grimace. Her eyes widened until they seemed to encompass her entire face. Her nostrils flared. Her cheeks flushed with color.

"I am Ung!" Aunt Tessa growled in a deep voice.

Conahegg shot me a "what-in-the-hell" expression. I couldn't blame him. Aunt Tessa's transformation into her twenty-five-thousand-year-old spirit guide, a cavewoman named Ung, is quite a spectacle.

Aunt Tessa spread her arms wide. "I speak from spirit world. Heed warning." Her eyebrows dipped. She crooked a finger and lurched toward Rocky.

Reflexively, he raised his hands, shielding his face. "Get her away from me. She's creepy."

"The warning is for you!" Tessa-turned-Ung cried. "Much evil. Beware!"

Chills chased up my arm.

Granted, I don't often believe in Aunt Tessa's new age crapola but occasionally Ung will make a prediction that comes true. Of course, it's not much of a stretch to figure out that a dope-smoking, unemployed musician who cheats on his girlfriend with his wife and vice versa is going to end up in trouble.

The sheriff, who, by the way, had magnificent forearms, tugged me to one side. "What's this all about?" he whispered.

"You got me."

"Who is that woman?"

"My aunt."

The sheriff rolled his eyes. "Why does that not surprise me?"

"Are you disparaging my family?"

"Looks like they're doing the job all by themselves," he commented.

I planted my hands on my hips. Who did he think he was? I mean besides sheriff. He had the power to put us behind bars on one trumped-up charge or the other but he certainly didn't have the right to bad-mouth my kinfolk. We took enough guff off the locals. You expected more understanding from your elected officials.

"Hey, come on. Do something, man, get her off me," Rocky cried.

Aunt Tessa was hovering over Rocky's prostrate body, trembling from head to toe. "The evil forces are strong," she croaked. "Run. Run. Run for your life."

"That's enough!" Conahegg ordered and motioned for a deputy to intercept Aunt Tessa. "Where is that ambulance?"

As if on his command, the ambulance pulled down the graveled river road and into our yard, siren wailing and lights flashing.

Aunt Tessa crumpled in the deputy's arms, her face slack. On the floor, Rocky was sweating buckets and my idiotic sister sat rocking him in her arms and cooing into his ear. Some people never learn.

"What do I do with her, Sheriff?" the deputy asked. Aunt Tessa was dishrag limp, and she often stays that way for an hour or more after channeling Ung.

"I'll take her to bed," Mama said, surprising me with her

helpfulness. "Come on, Tessa." She took her sister's hand and guided her out the side door.

"We'll need statements from everyone involved," Conahegg explained at the same time as two paramedics trotted into the garage.

"Everybody else took off," Rocky said. "'Cept for my darling, Sistine."

Oh, brother.

"I'd never leave you, tiger," Sissy whispered.

No, but you'd shoot him in the foot, I thought rather unkindly.

There have been many times in my life when I could have sworn I was a changeling. When I was a kid, growing up with a head-in-the-clouds, fairy tale believing, troll-doll-making mother, a florist father who collected butterflies and a cave-woman-channeling aunt, I harbored sweet fantasies that gypsies had stolen me from my rightful parents—usually a practical-minded accountant and a devoted stay-at-home mom—and left me on the Greens' doorstep.

Although I never came up with a proper motivation for such rash actions on the part of these anonymous gypsies, I quickly determined my place in the scheme of things. I was in the Green family to take care of everything. To attend to the routine chores no one else seemed inclined to do like paying bills, holding down a steady job, cooking dinner, cleaning the house, washing the car, changing the lightbulbs. That sort of thing. If it hadn't been for me, the family would have unraveled long ago. Especially after Daddy died.

"I'd like you to come to the station with us," Sheriff Conahegg said to me.

"But I didn't witness the shooting."

He took me by the shoulder—that red-hot grip again!—turned me around, ducked his head and whispered in my ear.

"Maybe not," he said, "but you seem to be the only one in the place with a lick of sense."

I smiled. Swear to God I did. And flushed with pride. I *was* the only one with a lick of sense, but nobody in my family saw me that way.

In my bizarre-and-proud-of-it clan, I was known as the dull one. Ally would rather clean the dishes than strip naked and dance in the rain. Or Ally is such a snore, she has always got her nose stuck in a book instead of actually living. Or Ally doesn't have an artistic mind, she only cares about making money. My family never seemed to appreciate that because I did the boring, mundane things, they got to be eccentric.

The paramedics loaded Rocky onto the stretcher and trundled him into the back of the ambulance. Sissy begged to ride along but they wouldn't let her. She stood beside me, sobbing into her hands.

The deputies scattered, searching for witnesses to interrogate, leaving me and Sissy and Conahegg in the garage.

"Well, ladies," Conahegg said. "May I have the honor of escorting you to my squad car?"

CHAPTER TWO

"ARE WE UNDER ARREST?" I asked.

Conahegg's flint-gray eyes revealed no emotion. It would take a lot to get close to him. Had he ever been in love? I wondered for no good reason.

"No," he said and for one moment I thought he was answering the question I'd posed in my mind. "At least not yet. For now I'm simply detaining you for questioning."

What was I going to say? When an assertive man with a badge tells you he's taking you for a ride what choice do you have? To tell the truth, I sort of got off on his forcefulness. I'm used to being the one in charge, the leader, the boss. To find myself in the subordinate position was both thrilling and disconcerting.

"Just let me change." I flapped a hand at my bathrobe.

He nodded and I darted into the house, shimmied out of my gown and into blue jeans and a crisp white blouse. Okay, I admit it. I also stopped long enough to run a brush through my hair and roll on some lipstick. That's not a crime, is it?

Conahegg and Sissy were bent together in a huddle when I returned to the garage. I didn't like the feeling that zipped through me. Jealousy is not one of my usual faults.

"Ah," Conahegg said, straightening to his full height when he saw me. "You're here." The glance he flicked over my body was quick but I caught it.

And smiled to myself.

"Ready," I said.

We walked outside into the starry cloudless night. Warm, moist air wrapped around us like a soggy thermal blanket. The wind shifted and I caught the scent of honeysuckle mingled with river smell.

A copse of blue spruce and a six-foot stone wall separated our waterfront property from the house on the hill next door. Reverend Swiggly had recently completed the three-story Colonial affair reminiscent of Tara from *Gone With the Wind.* It was quite out of place on the Brazos where most homes were breezy farm styles like ours, functional A-frames or log cabin replicas.

The house was heavily guarded with a high-tech security system and motion detector floodlights. Clearly the good preacher did not wish to be ambushed on vacation by overly devout members of his flock seeking to kiss the hem of his thousand-dollar, tailor-made trousers.

Conahegg took Sissy's elbow and gently eased her into the backseat of the patrol car, a white and brown 2004 Crown Victoria. After she was inside he stepped away and motioned for me to join her.

Great. No reassuring hand on my arm. Wasn't that the story of my life? Men tripped over themselves for Sissy. Me, I had to fend for myself.

I climbed in and slammed the door a little too firmly. Okay, maybe I was a little miffed. It wasn't fair. I felt like a criminal and I hadn't done a damned thing.

"Buckle up," Conahegg said, before getting in and starting the engine.

I snapped my seat belt on. Sissy didn't. The ambulance was still wedged in the driveway between cop cars, the back doors hanging open. I spied one paramedic sitting next to Rocky taking his vital signs. The second paramedic was leaning against the ambulance filling out paperwork.

"What have I done?" Sissy whispered, flattening her face and palms against the window and peering dolefully at the ambulance as we drove past.

"It was an accident."

She shook her head. "I wanted him dead, Ally, you don't know half of what he's done."

"Shhh!" I laid a finger over my mouth and inclined my head toward Conahegg.

He shifted the car into second gear and started up the steep grade leading from our house to the main road above. A thick growth of underbrush and trees lined the gravel drive. In a flash something appeared on the road, taking us by surprise.

Conahegg trod the brakes.

Thump!

My head jerked forward. Sissy squealed, pitched off the seat and onto the floorboard.

"What happened?" I unbuckled my seat belt.

"I struck someone," Conahegg said.

"What?" I had to hand it to him. He sounded calm and in control. Not the least bit flustered. My kinda guy.

"A naked man jumped in front of the.car. I didn't see him in time to stop."

Simultaneously, we both leaped from the car. It was strange how we mirrored each other's movements. We left Sissy quivering on the floorboard, and ran around to the front of the patrol car.

Sure enough, a naked guy was rolling around in the gravel, clutching his knee and moaning, "Ow, ow, ow."

Tim Kehaul.

Conahegg and I crouched beside him. Our shoulders brushed lightly. Awareness jolted through me. I could smell his scent. All leather and Lava soap and he-man. I tried not to notice but it was like trying to ignore an elephant at a tea party.

"I was only doing five miles an hour," Conahegg said, "how badly could I have injured him?"

"Bad enough, motherf..." Tim started, but I clamped my hand over his mouth.

"Be cool," I told him. "That's the sheriff you're cussing at."

"Oh."

"Where are your clothes?" I asked.

Tim didn't answer.

"I'll get the paramedics," Conahegg said. "Don't let him move." He took off downhill.

A rustling in the bushes from where Tim had emerged drew my attention. "Who's there?" I called, the hair rising on the back of my neck.

More rustling, then the sound of feet slapping against asphalt. Whomever had been in the bushes with Tim, made it to the road. It didn't take a rocket scientist to figure out what had been going on in the thicket right outside my house. A little midnight delight.

"Who was with you, Tim?"

"Nobody," he muttered, clutching his knee to his chest. Tim was in good physical shape, I'll grant him that. Fine, firm body, well-endowed. Plenty of men who swung his way would find him attractive.

"Tim? Is that you?"

I turned my head to see that Sissy had crept around the car toward us. She had her arms crossed over her chest and she was shivering despite the heat.

"Go back to the car," I told her.

But as usual, my sister ignored me. She crouched beside Tim, reached out a hand to stroke the hair from his forehead. "My sweet Timmy."

"Sissy," Tim said, eating up the attention. "I never should have left you."

Thankfully, Conahegg chose that moment to return with a sheet, a paramedic and the deputy named Jefferson. Conahegg leaned over to cover Tim's naked body with the sheet, then straightened.

"Go with him to the hospital," he told Jefferson. "When he's released, arrest him for public lewdness."

"Hey, man," Tim protested. "That's such a gyp. You run over me and now you're arresting me."

"Think about that before you strip naked in public next time," Conahegg instructed.

We waited while the paramedics shifted him onto a second stretcher, then bundled him into the ambulance beside Rocky.

"Shall we try again?" Conahegg asked.

The remaining drive to the sheriff's department was uneventful. Conahegg ushered us through a back door and into his office, the sparse, unadorned space of a government employee.

Paperwork neatly stacked. Wanted posters tacked to the bulletin board. Everything gray and bland and impersonal. No plants or pictures. No curtains. Nothing fancy. Empty trash can. A desk. Three functional metal chairs. One behind the desk, the other two in front.

Apparently, to Conahegg's way of thinking, real men don't decorate. In that moment my dear little nurturing heart had the most irresistible urge to put a pot of geraniums on the sill, hang a bucolic pastoral scene on the wall and fill his desk with executive toys.

But clutter didn't suit Conahegg.

"Have a seat," he commanded, jerking his head at the chairs while he remained standing. I knew the ploy. He wanted to tower above us, keep the upper hand.

Sissy plopped down and I sat beside her, perching on the edge of the chair, poised to bounce up and face him eye to eye if needed.

Conahegg pulled the baggy of marijuana from his shirt pocket and dropped it on his desk. "Why don't we talk about the cannabis?"

"It's not my dope," Sissy said, petulantly protruding her lower lip.

Her case would have been better served if she had changed out of her Pantera T-shirt, put a scarf around her ebony-dyed locks and removed the matching black nail polish and nose ring, but my little sister had never come to me for fashion advice.

Conahegg said nothing for the longest moment, simply narrowed those steel-gray eyes and drilled them into her. "You're telling me you never toked a doobie with your boyfriend?"

It sounded quite odd hearing the sheriff use slang drug terms. I suppose I expected him to say "marijuana cigarette" like some cop on reruns. Perhaps the good sheriff was more worldly than I imagined.

Sissy started to shake her head.

Conahegg's mouth tightened.

"Well, maybe once or twice," she conceded.

"Once or twice?"

"Okay, so I smoke dope occasionally, what's the big deal."

I whirled on her. I knew Rocky smoked grass but I didn't think Sissy was that stupid. "The big deal is that you have an eight-year-old son who looks up to you as a role model," I let loose. "Are you a complete moron?"

Sissy flipped me the bird.

Conahegg raised a hand. "Allegheny, let me handle the interview, please."

"Fine." I sat back in my seat and folded my arms over my chest.

"Your family dynamics are not my primary concern." He glowered at me, then turned back to Sissy. He shook the baggy at her. "The weed could have been yours."

"I never buy it."

"That doesn't excuse your culpability."

Sissy thrust her wrists straight out in front of her. "Are you going to arrest me? Is that what you want? Then clamp the cuffs on me and get it over with."

I sighed. Sissy gets her melodramatics from Aunt Tessa.

"There's no need for that, Ms. Green." Conahegg cleared his throat. "I'm going to flush the marijuana down the toilet."

Sissy and I stared at him, the surprise on her face matching what I felt. What happened to Mr. Merciless Zero Tolerance? Not that I was complaining, mind you. But his easy capitulation took me unaware. Worried, I gnawed my bottom lip.

Was he planning something? I studied his face but got nothing. Maybe he wasn't as uncompromising as rumor had it. Maybe underneath that uniform beat the heart of a nice guy. The thought of what he might look like underneath his clothes got to me. My face heated and I had to look away.

"You're not going to throw the book at me?" Sissy whispered.

Conahegg cracked a smile for the first time since we'd entered his office. "I don't think that's necessary. Particularly when you have a young child at home under your care."

"What about the charge of unlawfully discharging a firearm?" I asked.

"Is the gun registered?"

"Yes. The pistol belonged to our grandfather. We use it for shooting the copperheads and rattlesnakes that come around the house."

"And does Rockerfeller Hughes happen to fit that description?"

"At times." I had to smile back. Conahegg looked like a real human being when he smiled and not some stiff-necked G.I. Joe with a badge.

"Both of you ladies, need to give me your statements and then you're free to go."

"Really?" Sissy breathed hard and for the first time I realized how much she'd been sweating possession charges.

"Really."

"Wow. Gee. Thanks," Sissy enthused. "You're not nearly as bad as everyone says you are."

I kicked her in the ankle.

"Ow!" Sissy scowled at me. "What was that for?"

"You figure it out."

We spent the next several minutes telling Conahegg how Rockerfeller Hughes came to be stretched out on our garage floor, a bullet lodged in his foot. When we got up to leave, Conahegg followed us to the door.

"Could I speak to you alone for a moment?"

I placed a hand to my chest. "Me?"

He nodded.

"Go ahead." I waved to Sissy. "I'll catch up."

She looked from me to Conahegg. "Okay, if you're sure."

Truth was, I shared her apprehension. What did he want to say to me in private that he couldn't say in front of my sister?

"Ms. Green," he said, after the door closed behind Sissy. "I wanted to make you aware that you are responsible for what goes on inside your household."

"Excuse me?"

"The marijuana. It was found in your home. Even if it doesn't belong to you, according to the law, you can still be held accountable. Particularly since you're aware that Mr. Hughes and your sister partake of an occasional joint."

There are definite drawbacks to being the sane, sensible

one. Mainly, you're held responsible for the crazy, unpredictable people in your life.

"You're saying I'm responsible for Sissy's use of recreational drugs?"

"In the eyes of the law, you should have turned them in."

"You want me to rat out my sister?"

"Or get her into rehab."

"Sissy's not a pothead."

"Oh? And I suppose you're not an enabler."

I hate that word. Enabler. Truly hate it. When you're the sort of person who takes care of your family and loves them unconditionally, the mental health care profession can't wait to slap labels on you. Why am I an enabler? Because I do the right thing? So much for Mr. Nice Guy. What I'd mistaken for understanding a few minutes earlier was actually condescension.

"And I suppose you're not an arrogant son of a bitch."

Conahegg's voice hardened, a vein at his forehead jumped. So, he was angry. Well, join the club. "Foul language is uncalled for."

"You don't have a family of your own, do you?" I accused, alarmed that I was still so aware of his body.

I read the papers. I also knew our new sheriff wasn't married and never had been. I knew he had come home to Cloverleaf after his father died. I also knew it was the first time that he had been back since high school. Not much of a son if you ask me.

"No, I don't."

"I'd rather be an enabler any day than neglectful of my family. You don't have to worry about enabling anyone because nobody gives a damn about you. Isn't that right, Sheriff?"

He lowered his head so we were eye to eye. My heart galloped. The saliva in my mouth dried up. Those eyes of his could wither a cactus. "Don't make me rethink my decision not to arrest your sister."

"Are you threatening me?" I eyeballed him right back. I wasn't backing down. I had a few nasty expressions in my repertoire, as well.

"Think before you speak, Ms. Green. Sistine could get as much as a year in prison."

"For a half-dozen joints? Don't make me laugh!"

"Haven't you heard? Parker County is now zero tolerance on drugs."

"Since when?" I asked. The man had a chin like a rock cliff. A very steep, very slippery, very dangerous cliff. So why did I have the urge to plunge my tongue along that treacherous outcropping?

"Since I took over." He stabbed his thumb into his chest. Was his hard-line stance supposed to make me hot and bothered? If so, to my complete embarrassment, it was working.

"So Parker County belongs to you?" I was literally breathing hard.

"That's right."

"I didn't vote for you."

"Too bad. I'm still here."

"If you've finished trying to intimidate me, I've places to be." I put my hand on the doorknob.

And he put his hand on me. On my shoulder to be more specific.

My knees liquefied into noodle soup. It was damned hot in here. Someone, please, turn on the air-conditioning, give me a fan, and while you're at it, how about a gallon of ice water?

"Let's get something straight," he said. "If I were intimidating you, then you'd know it."

"Excuse me." I tugged open the door but that pesky hand remained branded on my skin.

"Be careful what you say and do, Allegheny Green," he warned. "I've got my eye on you."

CHAPTER THREE

I'VE GOT MY EYE ON YOU.

His words echoed in my head. And, I really could feel his eyes on me. Burning, searing, scorching my backside.

I stalked away, determined not to wiggle. I held my head high, then realized to my chagrin I was going to have to ask Conahegg for a lift home. I turned and saw him in the doorway, one strong shoulder slouched against the jamb, a smug grin on his face, his car keys looped around his finger.

Did he have to look so damn sexy?

"Need a ride?"

Briefly, I closed my eyes and reached into the depths of my soul for patience. Oh, he knew what he was doing. I wasn't fooled for a moment. I stared at Conahegg and forced a smile. "If you please." My tone of voice could have frosted a dozen cakes.

"My pleasure." The corners of his lips twitched. He was clearly amused at my predicament.

The turkey.

I searched the corridor for Sissy but didn't see her. "Just let me get my sister."

"The ladies' room is around the corner." Conahegg pointed. "Try there."

"Thanks," I judiciously said. What I really wanted to tell him could have landed me in jail.

"I'll wait right here."

From the front of the building came the sound of an argument. In unison, Conahegg and I craned our necks at a man's raised voice.

"I have to see the sheriff. It's extremely urgent."

"Could I have your name, sir?" we heard the dispatcher ask.

Conahegg pocketed his keys and stalked toward the entrance in long-legged strides. Compelled by curiosity, and the fear my sister was somehow involved in the commotion, I followed.

We rounded the corner, Conahegg in the lead. We found a well-dressed man of about sixty standing at the front desk. A mousy woman maybe ten years his junior, stood beside him, nervously worrying her purse strap.

The man looked familiar, but I couldn't place him at first. His silver hair was swept back off his forehead in a glorious pompadour. His face was slightly flushed as if he'd either been drinking or had recently run a short distance.

He smelled of Yves Saint Laurent and something darker, mustier. His teeth were so perfectly white and straight, I figured that they had to be capped. He used his hands when he spoke, punctuating each sentence with flourishing jabs.

"I want to see the sheriff right now!" Both palms went up, slicing through the air faster than a ninja on Dexedrine. "As a taxpayer I should have carte blanche access to my elected officials, day or night." He spoke as if winding up for a Sunday-morning sermon.

Then I knew who he was.

The Reverend Ray Don Swiggly. And his wife, the very antithesis of Tammy Faye Bakker, Miss Gloria. Or that's how Swiggly referred to her on his weekly Sunday-morning, bible-thumping rampages.

I'd only caught the program because Aunt Tessa liked to

hiss and boo at the man while she ate breakfast. More than once his television effigy had sustained damage from flying Captain Crunch. Aunt Tessa had a fit when she had discovered the Swigglys had built the house next door to ours.

Miss Gloria was as dull as her husband was showy. The peahen to his peacock. She wore a shin-length brown print dress, sensible flat brown shoes, brown purse, brown hair worn in a tight bun at the back of her head, brown eyes without a hint of makeup—brown, brown, brown.

"I'm Sheriff Conahegg. How may I help you?" Conahegg stepped forward, all business, his hand outthrust.

Glad-hand was Swiggly's middle name. He pivoted and slapped his palm into Conahegg's.

"Well." Swiggly smiled. "You're the kind of public servant I'm pleased to meet."

"You have a problem, Mr.…?"

Swiggly looked surprised that Conahegg didn't know him. I could tell from Swiggly's expression that Conahegg had slipped into the "sinner" category.

"Swiggly. Reverend Ray Don Swiggly. Perhaps you're familiar with my weekly television prayer program—*One Step Closer to Jesus?*"

"Sorry," Conahegg said. "I attend local services on Sunday morning."

"Good man, good man." Swiggly pounded Conahegg on the shoulder. "Let me guess, Baptist?" Swiggly had formed his own offshoot of fundamentalist Protestantism which he had dubbed The Church of the Living Jesus.

"Catholic," Conahegg replied.

Swiggly drew back his hand as if he'd been introduced to the devil. "Well, long as you hear the gospel. That's all that's important."

"May I ask your business here, Reverend Swiggly?"

Swiggly puffed out his chest. "I have come to press charges against those no-count heathens that live next door to my brand-new summer home on the banks of the glorious Brazos river, built by the grace of God, praise his name. Amen."

"Pardon?" Conahegg frowned.

"He's talking about me," I whispered in Conahegg's ear. "Or at least my family, but he distracted himself and took a mental side trip down the Holy Roller highway."

Conahegg glared at me. "Why don't you go find your sister, Allegheny?"

Allegheny. Why did my name trip so easily from his lips? Why did it sound so lyrical even as he was chiding me?

Disturbed by these questions, I backed away but stayed in the immediate vicinity. Swiggly was putting on quite a show and I wanted to see what was going to happen next.

"Are you referring to the Green family?" Conahegg asked.

Reverend Swiggly sniffed disdainfully. "I don't know their names."

"We're the ones who called about the gunshots," Miss Gloria ventured, barely raising her head. "We saw you arresting some of them so we came down to file a formal complaint."

Swiggly placed a restraining hand on his wife's shoulder. "Miss Gloria, I'll thank you to let me handle the matter."

Miss Gloria ducked her head, stared at her feet and mumbled, "I'm sorry, Ray Don."

I wondered why she'd been dragged along on his misadventure at two o'clock in the morning. I felt sorry for the woman. She seemed so devoid of gumption.

"As I was saying," Swiggly continued. "These people have all-night parties even during the week, playing that devil music and throwing their garbage over the fence onto my lawn. Do you have any idea how much it cost to have three acres of Saint Augustine grass sodded? They're ruining it with beer and vomit and urine. And tonight they were shooting off guns. I'm fed up, Sheriff, and I want something done."

Conahegg nodded and let Swiggly rant. Since I wasn't a fan of self-righteous bitching, particularly when my family is the subject of said bitching, I figured I'd take the opportunity to search for Sissy.

The Parker County Sheriff's Department is not a big building. Maybe ten thousand square feet, not counting the jail facilities butted up against the main structure. There are four entrances to the place—one, the front door through which Swiggly and his wife had come. Two, the back entrance where Conahegg had brought us, accessible only with a key. Three, the doorway through the jail. And one more entrance through the small courtroom where prisoners were arraigned.

I knew the layout because I'd been here once before when Aunt Tessa was arrested for chunking rotten eggs at the Mayor during the Founders Day parade while in the throes of an Ung moment but that's another story.

It didn't take long to walk through the facility. I checked the ladies' room with no luck and ended up back at the front desk five minutes after I started. Conahegg and Swiggly were still deep in conversation about the evil Green family.

I waited until Swiggly halted his soliloquy to take a breath and I jumped in.

"Sorry to interrupt," I apologized. "But I can't find my sister."

Conahegg gave me his full attention which I found rather flattering until I belatedly realized he was simply desperate to find an excuse to get rid of Swiggly. So much for my natural charm.

"Do you think she left the building?" Conahegg asked.

I shrugged. With Sissy, who knew.

He frowned. "She shouldn't walk alone in this neighborhood."

Conahegg was right. The sheriff's department hunkers in the roughest part of town, which granted, in Cloverleaf isn't *that* bad, but it's where most crimes occurred.

Swiggly started talking again but Conahegg raised a hand. "Excuse me a minute, sir."

"Well…" Swiggly looked affronted. "I was talking to you first."

"I'm afraid something more important has come up." Conahegg took my arm and guided me out the front door. If I hadn't been so worried about Sissy I would have paid more attention to the strange sensations rioting through me at his touch.

"Do you think she would take off on her own?"

I shook my head. "It's twelve miles home."

"Would she hitchhike?"

"Yeah."

"Damn," he swore.

And then we both heard it. A distinctive moan coming from the patrol cars in the parking lot.

A soft feminine moan.

My stomach knotted.

Conahegg began to run.

We found Sissy crumpled on the ground in the fetal position.

"Sissy," I cried, struggling to stay my rising panic. "What happened?"

Conahegg bent and scooped her into his arms. When he raised her up, I could see her face in the light from the street lamp. Her right eye was swollen shut and her nose was caked with dried blood. My stomach lurched and I feared I was going to be sick.

You can't throw up, Sissy needs you.

"Ally?" She groaned and reached for me.

"I'm here." I squeezed her hand. "Right here."

It completely did me in to see my little sister beaten like

that. I started to shake and my head swam with empathy. "Where are you hurt, sweetie?"

"He punched me in the stomach."

"He who?"

"A man."

"Did you know him?" I asked.

Sissy didn't answer. I took that as a bad sign. She probably *had* known the guy. What a hellish night. First Rocky, then Tim, now Sissy. What was going on? Was there a full moon? Was Mercury in retrograde? Had the remaining Beatles reunited?

"Are you sick at your stomach? Can you describe the pain? How hard did he hit you?" I hurled the questions at her, desperately needing answers.

"Hush," Conahegg said softly. "You're upset, Ally." When had he started calling me Ally and why did it feel so nice? "Hush and let me take care of this."

I wanted to protest. To tell him that I was the one who took care of things in our family, and by the way he had no right to call me Ally. But he didn't even wait for me to tell him anything.

Conahegg started up the sidewalk, Sissy slack against his strong arms. I trotted along beside him, trying to keep up, my fingers laced through Sissy's.

Conahegg was at fault. If he hadn't brought us here, Sissy wouldn't have gotten beaten.

Immediately, I realized the unfairness of my accusations. I was thinking with my emotions. He'd simply been doing his job and if Sissy hadn't shot Rocky we wouldn't have been here, either.

Conahegg walked us through the station, ignoring Swigly who watched openmouthed, and took us out the back way to his patrol car. We drove to the hospital in two minutes flat. He hurried inside for a wheelchair and returned with three nurses.

They wheeled Sissy away and I started to follow but Conahegg stopped me.

"I'm sorry," he said.

"Yeah, well, so am I."

He put a hand on my shoulder. A gesture of support, commiseration. "I mean it."

"Why should you care?"

For a moment he hesitated. I tried to read the expression on his face but couldn't. "It's my job."

That wasn't the answer I wanted, but don't ask me what I expected him to say.

"I'll come back to question your sister after they're finished examining her," he continued.

"I gotta go." I pulled away from him. I had to get to Sissy and find out what she wouldn't reveal in front of Conahegg—the name of the man who'd beaten her and the reason why.

"Allegheny," he called out as I reached the pneumatic doors. I stopped and the doors opened, but I didn't turn around to look at Conahegg.

"Yes," I called over my shoulder.

"If she tells you anything I expect you to relay the information to me, even if it means implicating your sister in something illegal."

This time I did turn. "What are you suggesting?"

"I don't know what your sister is involved in, but I promise you I will find out who hurt her. And he will pay."

THE HOSPITAL RELEASED Sissy at 6:00 a.m. Conahegg had returned once to check on us and told me to call for a squad car when we needed a ride home, but I'd declined, having had enough of Conahegg and his crew for one day. I talked to an emergency room nurse I knew, Glenda Harrington, and she agreed to give us a lift, but she didn't get off until seven. We were stuck for another hour.

"I wanna see Rocky," Sissy whined. "Just for a couple of minutes."

"Sissy…"

"Ally, please."

"Are you going to tell me who beat you up?"

Sissy hardened her jaw, ran a hand through her spiky, midnight-black hair and looked away from me. We were sitting in the emergency room waiting area with two bleary-eyed drunks and an elderly lady who'd fallen fast asleep over her knitting.

"I don't want to talk about it."

"You knew the guy, didn't you?"

Sissy shrugged. "It's no big deal."

"Some thug bloodies your nose, blacks your eye, hits you in the belly and you tell me it's no big deal."

Who was my sister protecting and why? I wanted to take her by the shoulders and shake some sense into her but she'd been through enough for one night.

"Could we drop it?"

"Does it have something to do with your pal Rockerfeller Hughes?"

Sissy's expression confirmed my suspicions. The tip of her nose turns red when she lies. "You're wrong."

"What do you see in him, Sissy? He borrows money from you that he never pays back, he makes promises he doesn't keep. He does drugs for heaven's sake, and he's not even cute. I don't get it."

"You don't understand," she said. "How could you when you can't even get a man of your own?"

Ouch. Her comment hurt more than I cared to admit. The truth is, I haven't even gone out with a guy in over three years. My life is too busy, my past history with the opposite sex too shaky. Plus, I haven't found anyone who interested me. Until tonight. Until Conahegg. But why him? Why now?

"It's not that I can't get a man," I retorted. "I don't have time to date, not between taking care of you and Mama and Denny and Aunt Tessa. My social calendar is a little full."

"Nobody ever asked you to play martyr, Ally, but it's your favorite role."

"What's that supposed to mean?"

"Take it any way you want."

My pulse quickened, anger surging through me. Okay, the anger was born of hurt. I sacrificed so my family could survive, and I get accused of being a martyr. Nothing would please me more than if they'd take care of themselves and I could have my own life.

"I'm going to see Rocky whether you come or not." Sissy rose to her feet and swayed. I reached my arms out, prepared to catch her if she fell, but Sissy righted herself and headed for the elevators.

"Wait," I said. "I'll come with you. But we've got to be back here at seven to catch a ride home with Glenda or you'll have to find your own way home."

"Whatever," Sissy mumbled.

Whatever indeed. I was only five years older than my sister but right now, I felt like a hundred. Most of the time I had no idea where she was coming from. I imagine I confused her as much as she confused me.

We rode the elevator in silence. A man in a lab coat pushing an EKG machine got on. He smiled and nodded. I smiled back. Sissy stared unblinkingly at the elevator door.

We got off on the third floor. The day-shift crew had arrived. Groggy nurses carrying foam cups of bad coffee made their way to the report room. Since I occasionally worked here part-time on the weekends, I knew most of them. I smiled and called out greetings but kept walking, reluctant to stop and have a conversation. With my hand at Sissy's back, I pushed her down the corridor.

The door to Rocky's room stood ajar.

Abruptly, Sissy halted.

"What is it?" I snapped, still smarting from her martyr comment.

"Wait." She took a deep breath. "I'm not ready."

"Come on, you were so hot to see him." I plucked her shirttail between my fingers and hauled her through the door.

Big mistake.

Rocky was not alone.

Nor had we given him advance warning by knocking. If we had, perhaps the blonde in the bed might have stopped kissing him. As it was, Rocky and the blonde were welded together, arms around each other in a deep embrace, mouths joined hungrily as if they hadn't eaten in weeks.

Sissy stared in disbelief.

I got mad for her. My sister drives me buggy, but I wasn't about to let anyone else treat her badly.

"What is going on here?" I demanded.

Rocky and the blonde broke apart quicker than two dogs getting hosed.

"S...S...Sissy," Rocky stammered, not even bothering to address me. "What are you doing here?"

"She came to finish off the job," I said, unable to resist. "Where'd you put that pistol, Sissy?"

Rocky's arms flew up to cover his head. "Wait a minute, Sissy, it's not what it seems."

"Is she the one?" the blonde asked, shaking a cigarette from the package of Marlboro Lights she pulled from her pocket. She wasn't a real blonde, up close you could see her dark roots. Her face was pitted with old acne scars and she wore too much makeup in an attempt to hide them.

"No smoking," I said. "In case you haven't noticed, this is a hospital. And by the way, who are you?"

The bleached blonde shrugged and stuffed the cigarette back in the pack before jerking an oversize thumb in Rocky's direction. "I'm his wife. What's it to you?"

Ah, Mrs. Dirtbag.

I glanced over at Sissy. She was pale as a corpse. Except for the black eye.

Rocky had lowered his hand and was staring at Sissy, too. "Hey," he said. "What happened to your eye?"

Sissy didn't answer. Her bottom lip trembled. I had the strongest big-sisterly urge to tuck her under my arm and spirit her out the door.

"Come on, honey," I soothed. "Let's get out of here." I reached for her but she shied away and instead walked closer to Rocky's bed.

"I can't believe I ever thought I loved you," she said, her voice full of hurt.

"You, too?" the blonde snorted.

Sissy sent Mrs. Rocky the evil eye and the woman clammed up. "See this?" Sissy touched the black-and-blue ring beneath her eye. "The beating was meant for you."

"Huh?"

"You heard me."

"I don't get it."

"Your friend. The one you borrowed money from to make your demo."

"You *do* know the guy that assaulted you," I interjected. "Tell me his name, Sissy. I'll have Conahegg arrest him."

My sister paid me absolutely no attention. She was too intent on boring a hole through Rocky with her glare. "Your good pal gave me a shiner because I refused to pay your debt. He said to tell you this is a warning. That he's going to give you ten times the pounding if you don't have his money by Monday."

"Monday?" Rocky's Adam's apple quivered.

"I'm not taking any more beatings for you or from you, Rockerfeller Hughes," Sissy said, looking madder and braver than I'd ever seen her. I could barely contain myself from bursting into applause. "Next time, I'll tell him where to find you."

"Sissy…" Rocky whined.

"Oh, and for the record, I'm glad I shot you." Then Sissy whirled on her heel and marched out the door.

"Darlene," I heard Rocky ask the blonde as I hurried to catch up with my sister. "You got three thousand dollars I could borrow?"

CHAPTER FOUR

NO MATTER HOW I CAJOLED, Sissy refused to tell me the name of the guy who'd beaten her. She said it was none of my business. How's that for gratitude?

On Sunday, I worked the three-to-eleven shift in Labor and Delivery at the hospital. We had only one patient and she didn't deliver on our shift, which gave me plenty of time to snoop around and see what had happened to Tim and Rocky.

Tim, I discovered, had been treated the night before for a moderate laceration to the knee, then carted off to county lockup. Rocky was scheduled for a debridement of his toe early Monday morning but was being dismissed after the procedure.

I didn't go up to see him again, although there were a few things I wanted to tell him. Sissy had made me promise to stay away.

What did surprise me, however, was a visit from Conahegg.

My coworker and best friend, Rhonda Smithy, and I had medicated the plodding mother-to-be and left her with attentive relatives. We were unenthusiastically looking forward to our Lean Cuisine frozen dinners when lo and behold Conahegg appeared with a pizza.

"What are you doing here?" I asked, eyeing the pizza.

"Thought I'd see if you were hungry." He set the box down on the table.

"You expect me to believe you brought me a pizza out of the goodness of your heart?"

"Anyone ever tell you that you've got a suspicious mind?"

"All the time."

Conahegg grinned and ran his gaze over my body. It was a quick perusal but he was checking me out. I wished I was wearing something sexier than shapeless hospital scrubs.

"How did you know I was working at the hospital tonight?"

"I went out to your house."

"Did you need to speak to me about something?"

Conahegg's eyes darkened and he cast a glance at Rhonda.

Sharp as a hypodermic, Rhonda peered at her watch. "Oh, excuse me for a minute, I think it's time to change the IV on the patient in room one." She scurried from the lounge but not before giving me an exaggerated wink.

"Have a seat." I nodded at the chair Rhonda had vacated.

Conahegg sat, his long-limbed frame drawing my attention. Good gawd but the man was built. The quality of light in the room suddenly sharpened. I blinked in wonder. The fluorescent bulb flickering, surely. But I couldn't stop myself from staring at Conahegg.

"I think I know who attacked your sister," he said. "I drove over to see her but she won't talk to me. I get the feeling she's protecting Rockerfeller Hughes, but I don't know why."

"Me, either." I sighed. "Who do you think attacked her?"

"Loan shark by the name of Dooley Marchand. Do you know him?"

I shook my head.

"He works as a bouncer at the strip club out on I30. Your sister's boyfriend owes him a lot of money. Dooley doesn't like to wait for his due. We've arrested him before for working people over. One of my deputies saw him at the station right before your sister was beaten."

"Scumbag."

"I can't arrest him if your sister won't press charges. Could you talk to her?"

"Me?" I laughed. "She never listens to me." My Lean Cuisine dinged in the microwave. I gazed longingly at the pizza.

Conahegg opened the box. The aroma of garlic, onions and oregano filled the room. "Have a slice," he invited.

Pepperoni. My favorite.

"Is this a bribe?" I asked.

"Why, Ms. Green, what you must think of me."

If he only knew!

I took the pizza.

"Listen," Conahegg said, his eyes on my face. "The truth is, I wanted to warn you about Marchand. Don't mess with him. If you see him on your property call me immediately."

"Okay."

"I mean it." He laid one hand across the top of mine.

I froze in midchew. Holy Toledo, what the man could do to me with a single touch. To hell with Dooley Marchand. I was in danger of spontaneous combustion from close bodily contact with Conahegg.

"Hear me?"

I swallowed. Hard. "All right."

"And tell your sister to watch out for Mr. Hughes's wife."

"Oh? You know about Darlene?"

Conahegg's pupils widened. "I know about everything that goes on in town."

"I'll consider myself warned."

"Darlene Hughes has been in prison for the last thirteen months. Three weeks ago she was paroled."

I hated to ask. "What for?"

"Assault with a deadly weapon."

"Why am I not surprised?" I thought of the hard-eyed, bottle blonde with a penchant for Marlboros.

"She stabbed Rocky's last girlfriend in the neck with a rat-tail comb. Be careful, Ally, there's a lot of unsavory characters hanging around your sister."

Be careful? Did that mean he cared? Oh, why was I torturing myself? What was happening to me? I didn't pine over guys.

"I know," I said. Could he tell how I was feeling? Could he read desire in my face? Did he have the slightest clue that unflappable, sensible Allegheny Green was losing her perspective because of him?

He leaned forward. "Sissy is in over her head."

"What are you talking about?"

"Drugs."

"Oh come on. Aren't you exaggerating a bit? So she smokes some pot."

Conahegg shook his head. "I'm afraid it's more than that."

"I don't follow."

"We had the hospital do a drug screen on Hughes and it came back positive for cocaine as well as marijuana. We also suspect he might be dealing to supplement his career as a musician."

"What career? As far as I know he's never played professionally." I polished off the slice of pizza, dusted my fingers on a napkin.

"Exactly. How does he survive?"

"Mooches off Sissy."

"And your sister paints artificial nails for a living."

"When she's in the mood," I said.

"Not much money in part-time work like that."

I definitely didn't like where the conversation was headed. "My sister is not involved with drug dealers."

"How do you know that for certain?"

I didn't want to dwell on my sister and her problems. At

least not with Conahegg. I wanted to eat pizza and gaze into his granite-gray eyes and imagine what it felt like to be held in those strong, masculine arms. Great. Since when had I been reduced to romance-novel fantasies?

"How's Tim?" I asked, changing the subject.

"Tim?"

"You know, the naked guy you hit with your squad car."

"He posted bail."

"That was quick. Who sprang him? He's broke and he doesn't have much to do with his own family."

Conahegg shrugged. "I'm really not at liberty to discuss it."

"Oh."

So much for our chummy little conversation. I thought he'd come to see me but apparently he'd only been pumping me for information about Sissy and Rocky. Disappointment turned the pizza crust to sawdust in my mouth.

Conahegg got to his feet. "Enjoy the pizza."

"I will," I responded, feeling irritated with him. *If I have to choke down every last bite.*

He stopped at the door. My treacherous heart skipped a beat. Was he going to ask me out? Would I say yes if he did?

"Allegheny…"

"Please, call me Ally."

"Ally." He smiled.

"Yes?" I held my breath. Waited.

"You've got cheese on your chin."

"I HATE THAT MAN."

"You like him. A lot."

"I do not," I denied hotly a few hours later as I sat hunched over the computer signing out my charting. I was still smarting over the mozzarella on my chin incident.

The graveyard shift nurses had arrived, and they were in

the process of assessing our lone patient. Rhonda and I manned the phones and waited for eleven o'clock.

"You're obsessing, Ally." Rhonda blew on her freshly painted fingernails. Pretty in Puce, was the name on the bottle, as if it were physically possible to be pretty in puce. Rhonda was polishing her nails in anticipation of a midnight date, and I was still second-guessing Sheriff Sam Conahegg.

"What? Because I can't figure out what he's up to?" I said. I felt sheepish that for a few minutes I'd actually believed that Conahegg had come to the hospital simply to see me.

"He's pretty cute."

"He's okay." I shrugged.

Cute didn't begin to cover it. I thought of his flint eyes, those muscular thighs, that powerful voice.

Don't forget the arrogant attitude, I reminded myself. The cocky way he looked at me made me want to bop him over the head and pop him into my bed all at the same time. Rhonda, however, did not need to know about the last part.

Rhonda heaved an exaggerated sigh. "I swear, Ally, sometimes I think you're dead from the waist down. The guy's a major hunk."

"Define *major hunk.*"

"You're hopeless," she muttered. "Absolutely hopeless. If that màn doesn't melt your butter, it'd take a million years of global warming to thaw you out."

"Oh, all right. He's good-looking, I'll grant him that."

"And?"

"And nothing."

I didn't like liking Conahegg so much. Especially when I didn't know if he liked me or not. What was it about him that caused me to behave in the manner of a fifteen-year-old with a crush on the most popular guy in high school? Although as

I recall, in high school all the girls had had a crush on him, me included.

"Getting you to talk about men is like pulling snakes' teeth."

"Snakes don't have teeth."

"That's why it's so hard." Rhonda grinned. "Spill the beans. Is there chemistry between the two of you? You know, sparks."

"There's sparks." I glowered. "But not the kind you mean. He's opinionated and domineering and he embarrassed me."

And he flushed the marijuana down the toilet instead of arresting Sissy like he could have.

Okay, so he wasn't *all* bad.

"Come on, your last boyfriend was when…? College? Dang, Ally that was ten years ago!"

I was well aware of that fact. I was boyfriendless by choice, not happenstance. Guys clutter your life. Overall they weren't worth the headache. They either died on you like my daddy, or used you as a crutch like my old boyfriends, or disappeared on you like Rhonda's ex-husband, or cheated on you like Rocky did Sissy.

Yeah, okay, so maybe I had trust issues when it came to men.

"You're an attractive woman. You've got a great body and flawless skin," Rhonda went on relentlessly. "If you'd only wear a little more makeup and get a new hairstyle. That page boy might be functional but it's not sexy. Oh, and you might consider some blond highlights."

"I'm not going to bend over backward to attract some man."

"No? But you'll jump through hoops for your family."

"Rhonda, I don't have any choice. You know my mother. If I didn't manage her finances, she and Tessa would be in the poorhouse within a week."

"How do you know?" Rhonda busily applied a second coat of browny-purple-puke color to her nails. "Ever let 'em sink or swim?"

I stared at her appalled. "Of course not. That'd be like letting a baby play on the highway."

She snorted. "And your sister. Why doesn't that girl get a steady job and take care of her own son? Why do you have to be Denny's surrogate mother?"

"I love taking care of Denny," I protested.

"You should have a child of your own. A man of your own. A life of your own."

"I have a life."

"Oh, yeah? Never mind a boyfriend, when was the last time you even went out on a date."

"I don't need a man to complete me."

"You're not going to tell me that you believe in that stupid feminist slogan—a woman without a man is like a fish without a bicycle? What's that supposed to mean anyway?" Rhonda frowned and examined her nails with narrowed eyes.

"It's true. I have no need for a man."

Rhonda stuck her leg out at me. "Come on, pull the other one. Every woman needs a man. Unless of course she prefers another woman."

She was trying to get my goat and I knew it. I closed my eyes and battled the heat rising to my cheeks. "I have physical needs. Just like anybody else. But I know how to control myself."

"There's a fine line between self-control and shutting yourself off to your sexuality."

Rhonda didn't know what she was talking about. I had feelings. Lots of them. Thinking about Sheriff Conahegg brought a warm tingly sensation into the center of my body. An unwanted sensation.

Without warning my mind flashed to a startlingly clear image of Conahegg. Strong, dimpled chin. Sharp, intelligent eyes that missed nothing. Hard, honed body.

Electric shivers spiked my spine.

"Besides," I croaked, fighting to deny what was happening inside me. "Sex is overrated."

"You've never had an orgasm, have you?" Rhonda taunted.

"Shut up."

"You haven't! Oh my God, Ally. I had no idea. I'm so sorry." She got up and threw her arms around my neck, careful to keep her nails splayed outward.

I backed away, eager to extricate myself. "Please, it's no big deal."

"No big deal?" Rhonda was shaking her head and damned if she didn't have tears in her eyes. "You poor thing. I had no idea."

"Stop it." I didn't want her pity.

"You've got to quit substituting your family for a real life before it's too late. You're thirty-one and not getting any younger."

Thankfully, the clock chose that moment to strike eleven.

"I'll see you tomorrow." I sprinted for the door. I had to get out of here. Away from talk of Conahegg. Away from Rhonda and the overwhelming sympathy in her eyes.

ON TUESDAY MORNING, three days after Sissy shot Rocky, Joyce Kemper, the director of Cloverleaf Home Health Care, handed me two manila folders. "Here's your new cases. The first one is a knee laceration. You're to give IV penicillin for five days. The other patient is a twenty-seven-year-old male with GSW to the foot. Administer IV vancomycin once a week for four weeks and dress the wound thrice weekly."

GSW. Gun shot wound. My heart sank. Cloverleaf wasn't a big place. We probably didn't average one gunshot wound to the foot a decade.

I opened the top file and stared down at the name. My worst fears confirmed.

Rockerfeller Hughes.

"I can't take the case." I handed the file back to Joyce.

"What do you mean?" She stared at me blankly. In the five years I'd worked for Joyce I'd never refused a case.

"I know the man," I explained.

"Is he a relative?"

"No, but he's my sister's boyfriend."

"So?" She pushed the file at me.

"Sissy is the one who shot him in the foot. It would be a conflict of interest for me to take care of him."

"You didn't shoot him. What's the conflict?"

"Come on, Joyce, have a heart."

"Ally, there's no one else to send. Yvette's swamped. She's got twenty-five patients to see this week. You only have sixteen. Marcie's out on maternity leave and Kayla's on vacation. You lose by default."

"You could do it," I pointed out.

Joyce looked at me as if I'd lost my marbles. Joyce was far beyond pleasingly plump and she was loath to move her girth any more than necessary. "I have to run the office."

"Felicity can handle things for the amount of time it would take you to give Hughes his antibiotics and change his dressing." I waved toward the outer office where the secretary sat.

"Absolutely not. It's your territory. In fact, your other patient lives in the same trailer park." Joyce glowered.

I folded my arms over my chest. "You don't understand. I despise the guy."

"And you don't understand. Take the case or you can find yourself another job."

I shook my head. Surely, I had heard her wrong. She was willing to fire me if I didn't go see Rockerfeller Hughes?

"I'll switch with Yvette."

"She's gone to Zion Hill for the day. She won't be back

until five. You can switch with her for the duration of his treatment but for today, he's yours." Joyce waved the file in my face. She bared her teeth and shook her jowls like a bulldog.

"Oh, fine." I snatched the file from her hand. "But if I end up killing him, then you're responsible."

"Thank you, Ally." Joyce's voice was pure NutraSweet.

I stormed from the office wondering which god I had offended to get this crap assignment.

Sissy had come home last night with hickeys tracking up and down her neck. To my disgust she said that she and Rocky had made up and he'd promised her he was going to divorce Darlene.

I had fought the temptation to get a gun and finish Rocky off so I wouldn't have to hear for the one millionth time what a wonderful person he was for not pressing charges against her. This from the sleazebag who'd turned Sissy on to drugs, encouraged her to quit her job to sing with his band and who, upon occasion, took the back of his hand to her face.

Trying my best not to think about my sister, I got in my car and looked at my other patient file and discovered I'd been given Tim Kehaul, as well. While Cloverleaf is not huge, it's not *that* small. Population seven thousand or thereabouts. What were the odds of me getting two of Sissy's boyfriends to make home health visits to?

Rocky lived in a trailer park in Andover Bend. A particularly redneck community where the average IQ score hovered somewhere around my shoe size. Most of the people who lived there supplemented their welfare checks and unemployment income by fishing and raising vegetables to sell at a community roadside stand.

The road into Andover Bend was a narrow, one-lane affair. After a couple of miles the asphalt petered out where the county turned the road over to the development. I passed several shotgun shacks with dirty-faced kids playing in the yard. Dust billowed behind my tires.

I wondered if they'd dismissed Rocky from the hospital with a saline well instilled in his arm or if I'd have to start one myself. The idea of prodding Rocky with a large bore needle was not entirely unpleasant.

Rounding the curve, I blew past the nine-hole golf course which was better maintained than most of the residences. Tanned guys with bellies overlapping their belts and beers clutched in their hands, maneuvered golf carts around the fairways.

The clubhouse was next and the community swimming pool, filled with kids on colorful floatation devices and mamas at poolside reading, tanning and gossiping.

Then the road arched toward the river. The farther I went, the grungier the houses grew. The area flooded frequently and since no one could afford to build to code, they couldn't buy flood insurance. Water-level stains ringed the buildings, some waist high. The vehicles, parked in the driveways and on patches of bare lawn, were almost exclusively pickup trucks. And aged ones at that.

I crossed a small bridge so low to the ground it almost touched the water. Here, the Brazos looked swampy and brackish. Not like the healthy branch that flowed past my place.

The posted speed limit was twenty-five miles per hour. I slowed. I was in no hurry to see Rockerfeller Hughes or go into his disgusting house but eventually I rolled to a stop outside a clump of about thirty trailers that had seen better days.

I decided to visit Tim first. Rocky could wait.

Tim's trailer was the best in the bunch and that wasn't saying much, but at least his grass was trimmed and there were no rusting vehicles in the yard. He even had curtains in the window, and his front porch steps looked sturdy and reliable.

I parked and turned my head to peer directly across the road at Rocky's house. In contrast to Tim's double-wide, Rocky owned a tiny repo job teetering precariously on cinder blocks right at the river's edge.

His dilapidated truck was parked nose in against the house. The windows were screenless and there was no underpinning around the bottom of the trailer.

Beer cans and whiskey bottles were stacked like a shrine to alcohol consumption right next to a rusted burn barrel. There was one tree in the whole yard. An old oak with a half-dozen dead branches that needed pruning.

I'd never been inside Rocky's trailer, although I had come to pick Sissy up here one night after she called me, crying. She'd been standing by the road when I'd arrived and kept her face turned away from me.

It wasn't until we'd gotten home that I'd seen the bruise on her cheek. She'd been smart to hide the marks from me. I would have called the cops on Rocky right then and there and she knew it.

What was it about my little sister that made her such a loser magnet? Rocky wasn't the first, well…rocky relationship she'd had.

She'd always been something of a wild child and from the age of fourteen had engaged in risky sexual behavior. I preached to her about AIDS and other sexually transmitted diseases until I was blue in the face. It took me a while to catch on that the more I preached the more promiscuous she became. Finally, I stopped commenting on her sex life. But I never stopped caring.

"Oh, Sissy," I whispered. "When will you ever learn?"

I let the engine idle, pretending I wanted to hear the last of Eric Clapton's "Tears in Heaven" on the radio, when in reality I wanted to avoid getting out of my car.

I collected Tim's file, along with the doctor's orders and my bag of antibiotics and IV supplies. I made sure I had Betadine and alcohol preps.

When I could avoid it no longer, I climbed out of my trusty Honda and headed toward Tim's trailer.

I knocked at the screen door.

And waited.

I knocked again and fidgeted, shifting my weight, tucking my supplies first under one arm, then the other.

Nothing.

I checked my watch. A little before noon. He should be awake, even if he was feeling bad.

Clearing my throat, I knocked again. "Tim," I called out. "It's Allegheny Green. Home health sent me out to check that knee and give you some antibiotics."

No answer.

I opened the screen and knocked on the front door. It swung inward at my touch.

"Tim?" I stepped forward and stuck my head around the door.

The room was dark, the curtains drawn.

"Hello?"

Nothing.

I took a deep breath. The place smelled funny but I saw no garbage in the trash can. The kitchen was clean, no dirty dishes or food in the sink.

"Tim?"

My voice echoed in the empty room.

With a staggering sense of dread, I moved farther into the house. I set my supplies on the bar and inched down the narrow hallway paneled in dark particle board. The first door on the right was a bathroom. No one in there.

That left the two bedrooms. With the closed doors.

"Tim?"

Suddenly, I found it hard to breathe. My chest tightened. I only knew one thing. I did not want to open that door.

I rapped on it gently with my knuckles. "Tim, it's Ally Green."

Not a sound. Not a peep. Not a whisper.

The hair on the back of my neck rose.

I reached for the knob.

Forget it. Leave. Go. Tell Joyce he wasn't home.

But I didn't move. I stayed. My hand growing sweaty on the knob.

My heart pounded in my ears.

What's the matter, Ally? You're not Aunt Tessa, you don't have visions. Open the damned door.

And so I did.

The bedroom was even darker than the rest of the trailer. Pitch-black in fact. Like the bedroom of a night-shift worker who keeps foil on the windows. My fingers fumbled along the wall, searching for the switch.

Light flooded the dreary room with shocking intensity.

I blinked.

And then I screamed at what I saw.

Tim's naked body dangling from the ceiling.

CHAPTER FIVE

HAND OVER MY MOUTH, I stumbled through the house and out to my car, struggling not to toss my cookies. The bright, beautiful day was a shocking contrast to the dark tragedy I'd witnessed.

Taking several slow deep breaths, I lowered myself into the front seat, picked up my cell phone and dialed 911.

I waited.

The sun beat down. Sweat plastered my floral print uniform top to my back. I pushed my bangs from my forehead and waited. I closed my eyes but when I did, I saw Tim's body slowly rotating from the end of the rope and I quickly opened them again.

I'm a nurse. I've seen a lot of grisly things. But I'd known Tim. He'd spent time at my house.

My stomach roiled. I got out of the car and paced the lawn with my hands folded across my chest. I glanced over at Rocky's trailer, saw his bedroom curtain move and knew he'd been staring at me. Cocking my head, I studied the window and I wondered if he'd seen anything going on at Tim's.

I'm not sure what I was thinking. I mean it was pretty clear Tim had hung himself. It wasn't murder, but then why would Tim kill himself? Depression over getting arrested? Surely not. It hadn't been that big a deal. Then again, I realized how little I knew about Tim and his inner life. What seemed inconsequential to me might have been earth-shattering to him.

I nibbled a fingernail. Honestly, I was a little numb.

Feeling vulnerable to Rocky's scrutiny, I got back in the car. Ten minutes later, when the patrol car rolled to a stop beside me, my knees were still quaking. I had rested my head against the steering wheel, steeling myself for what lay ahead. Therefore, I didn't notice that the deputy walking around my car was no deputy.

Knuckles rapped against the window and I jumped like a skittish cat at Fourth of July fireworks.

Sheriff Conahegg pantomimed rolling the window down. I did better than that. I swung open the door and got out.

Damn, he looked handsome with that badge pinned to his chest, and that gun hanging on his hip. Nonsensically, he made me feel safe and I realized I was glad to see him.

I leaned against my car. He stood so close I could feel his body heat. His gray eyes held mine. Was it concern for me that widened his pupils? Was I reading more into his gaze than was there? Since when had I started trying to second-guess Conahegg's emotions?

He touched my shoulder, a gesture of condolence. But it felt like so much more than that. His eyes—oh, those enigmatic eyes that gave away nothing—stayed fixed on my face. "I'm sorry," he said, "that you had to find the body."

"Hazard of the job," I said, trying to make light of a very serious subject. If I didn't stay detached from Tim's suicide, I would have to fling myself into Conahegg's arms and beg him to hold me close. "I've seen bodies before."

"You're pretty tough, Allegheny." Admiration tinged his voice, slightly curved his lips.

I had the goofiest urge to smile. Conahegg was proud of me.

Two more cruisers glided to a stop, sirens cutting off in

midwhine. At the appearance of the other officers, Conahegg's countenance changed. He straightened, stepped back, removed his hand from my shoulder.

And most telling of all, he dropped his gaze.

I felt robbed, cheated, relieved.

Talk about mixed messages. Talk about conflicting signals. I was sending them and receiving them.

"Did you spot any vehicles leaving the scene, Ms. Green?" Conahegg asked. His tone was distant, his words clipped.

"No."

"Pass anybody on the road?"

I shook my head.

"Anyone on foot."

"No again."

He said nothing.

"Do you need for me to go back inside?" I asked, squaring my shoulders to gather my courage, struggling hard to be all business, too.

Conahegg's mouth flattened in a noncommittal expression and he motioned his crew toward the trailer. "No. It's best if you stay out here. But don't go anywhere. I'll be back to talk to you."

"I've got another patient to see in half an hour." I glanced at my watch.

"Call your office and get someone else to do it," he snapped, making me wonder if I had imagined his earlier compassion.

Overall, he had the personality of a steamroller and he was obviously accustomed to having his edicts followed with unquestioned loyalty, but his badass attitude made me want to rebel.

"I'm sorry," I said. "My patients always come first."

"Tim Kehaul was your patient."

"Tim Kehaul is dead. My responsibilities are to the living."

"Stay put." He raised a finger of warning. "Don't make me take you into custody."

"You wouldn't dare." I lifted my chin and wondered why in the hell I felt so jazzed. It was the same sort of adrenaline rush I got during a code blue. Nervousness born of inexplicable excitement that I didn't know how to alleviate. What in the hell was wrong with me?

His eyes met mine, hard and unreadable. "Try me."

I resisted the childish urge to stick my tongue out at him. His men circled the house. One of the deputies stepped up on the front porch and peeled back the screen door. It creaked loudly.

"Needs WD-40," I said inanely.

"Sheriff's Department," the deputy hollered after knocking on the inner door, which was still standing open as I had left it. "We're coming in."

"There's nobody inside the house except Tim," I told him.

"Procedure," Conahegg answered. "You never know for sure."

I knew for sure, but who was I to argue with an ex-marine with a very big gun?

"Stand over here," he commanded, ushering me off Tim's property without actually touching me, until I was standing in the middle of the dirt road. Strange, but it seemed as if I could feel that muscular arm at my back, pushing me along like a broom at a piece of dust.

Why the man intrigued me while punching my buttons at the same time, I could not say. I only know I had never been so aroused and yet so irritated by anyone. I wanted to kiss him and kick him in the behind at the same time.

Jeez Louise, what's wrong with you? Now's not the time to get warm and fuzzy over Conahegg. There's a dead body inside that glorified tin can. A body who happens to be your sister's ex-boyfriend.

Besides, Conahegg wasn't my type. I preferred tender men who read poetry and studied art, not steel and iron types with piercing dark eyes that could drill a hole straight through you at a hundred paces. I wasn't a glutton for punishment.

And yet, I couldn't help but watch him stalk back toward the trailer house, his butt encased so finely in that formfitting uniform. When he disappeared inside, I finally looked away.

One of the deputies started roping yellow crime scene tape around the perimeter. I tugged my cell phone from my pocket, extended the antenna, punched in the numbers then broke the news to Joyce that she'd have to finish my visits for the day since I was apparently being detained by the sheriff for the duration of the afternoon. Joyce wasn't too happy, but hey, it wasn't my problem.

Minutes passed. The sun continued to beat down and I was awash in sweat. Nice. A fly kept buzzing around my head and no amount of swatting seemed to persuade him to find a more receptive landing place. I began to walk around to outdistance the fly and that's when I noticed that several people had gathered outside their trailer houses, necks craned in my direction.

Great. I was a one-woman freak show. Uncomfortable with the perusal, I glanced away. But it didn't do any good. One of the neighbors ambled over.

"How-de-do." A middle-aged, overweight man with a face like a boiled ham came to stand beside me, his thumbs tucked under the straps of his triple XL overalls, a matchstick stuck in the corner of his wide mouth.

"Hello." I gave him a tight smile.

"What's a goin' on?" He had a Jethro Bodine drawl and small curious eyes.

"I'm not at liberty to say."

"Is that little gay boy in trouble with the law again?" Matchstick inclined his head toward the patrol cars. "I heard he got arrested for runnin' around nekked in the bushes up where the rich folks live in Brazos River Bend."

So I was considered rich? I cast a quick glance at Matchstick's patched overalls with the ketchup stain on the bib and figured, yeah, according to him, I probably was wealthy.

"Yes ma'am. There's been some strange going-ons over there."

"Like what?" I asked, deciding to use the Andover Bend grapevine to my advantage. Who knew? Matchstick might hold the key to Tim's suicide.

Matchstick relished his role as keeper of the trailer park gossip. He rubbed one ear pensively, building the tension. "I don't work you understand. Hurt my back at the gravel pit in '97. Haven't been able to even pick up my grandkids since. My wife, Lindy Sue, she has to support us. We can't make it on my disability. She cooks at Heavenly Acres retirement center in Cloverleaf."

"Uh-huh."

"Anyway, I got time on my hands and nothing much to do with it 'cept keep an eye on the neighborhood. I'm head of the community crime watch program," he exclaimed proudly.

I scanned the dilapidated trailers and wondered what kind of pathetic criminals would steal from these poor folks.

"That young'un, Tim, he was a good boy even if he did like to ride the baloney pony," Matchstick said. "If you know what I mean."

Unfortunately I did and I really didn't appreciate the image Matchstick's words brought to mind.

"But he had all kinds a weirdos coming to visit. I kept an eye on 'em. Never can be too careful."

"That's true," I murmured. "Did you see anything unusual in the last day or two?"

The man stopped to ponder my question. He removed the matchstick from his mouth and scratched his head with it. "Hmm, let me think."

"I saw sumptin'." The voice startled me.

I turned to find a woman about my age wearing a faded housedress and sponge rollers in her hair standing directly behind me and Matchstick. In an age of hot rollers and curling irons I didn't know people still wore sponge rollers. A couple of toddlers were wrapped around her legs and from the looks of her distended belly, she had another bun in the oven.

"You did."

She nodded. "They had a fight over there last night. Way late. I was up with my youngest." She placed a hand on the head of the child to her right. "Marianne had a bad cough and couldn't sleep. I brought her out on the porch so she wouldn't wake Alfred, my husband. He hasta get up early to drive the school bus."

"I didn't hear nothing about no fight," Matchstick grumbled, obviously unhappy to have my attention usurped by the woman.

"Who are you referring to?" I asked.

"Tim," she said. "And that big blond guy."

Big blond guy? Who was that?

"Do you know the man's name?"

She shook her head. "No. He's not very friendly. I tried to say *hi* a couple of times when I was out workin' in the yard but he never said *hi* back. I wondered what Tim saw in him."

"How do you know they were lovers?"

The woman blushed and glanced down at her kids. "I saw them," she whispered.

"Saw them?"

"You know—they was holdin' hands, kissin'. Other stuff, too."

"Er…how did you see them?" I asked.

Her blush deepened. "I went over to borrow a cup of sugar one night. I was making strawberry pie and Tim had left his front door open. They was in the living room goin' at it."

I looked at Matchstick. "Do you know the blond guy?"

"Saw him once or twice. He looked like one of them professional wrestlers."

"You never spoke to him?"

Matchstick shook his head. "He had one of them deformed ears like a boxer. What do they call? Some kind a vegetable."

"Cauliflower?"

"Maybe." Matchstick frowned. "Though it coulda been cabbage."

Other neighbors came forward and began to offer their opinions and theories. But I didn't learn anything more about Tim and his mysterious lover. The conversation degenerated into a dissertation of how best to cook cabbage. Matchstick smacked his lips and sucked on the match extra hard when he talked about how Lindy Sue fried cabbage with black pepper and onions.

After what seemed an eternity, Conahegg finally came back outside.

He shooed the neighbors away and told them he'd send deputies over to talk to them, then he hustled me aside. He shook his head over Tim's untimely and undignified death, then surprised me by clamping a hand on my shoulder and asking, "Are you all right?"

I nodded. "Tim was a nice guy. Why would he want to kill himself? Do you think it had anything to do with getting arrested the other night?"

Conahegg gave me a strange look and removed his hand.

"And why would he hang himself in the nude? Surely he wouldn't want to be found that way," I continued.

"I don't believe that it was intentional," Conahegg said.

"Beg pardon?"

"Put two and two together, Ally."

Suddenly the answer hit me. Rope. Neck. Naked.

I felt my hairline heat and knew I was blushing. "Oh," I muttered. "Autoerotic asphyxiation."

Conahegg nodded. "That's my guess, but of course we investigate any unexplained deaths as homicides."

I might be a country girl but I'm not naive. I'm a nurse for crying out loud. I went to college for four years. I learned about sexual perversions in abnormal psych class. At least in theory.

"Can I go?" I asked, thoroughly embarrassed that I'd been so slow to catch on. Conahegg must think me an unsophisticated hick.

"I've got a better idea."

"Oh?"

"Why don't I take your statement over a soft drink in an air-conditioned diner? The heat's made you cranky."

I wanted to say no. I didn't really want to be alone with Conahegg, but the idea of a tall Dr. Pepper over crushed ice was too much temptation for this sweaty, small town girl.

"I'm buying," he said.

That cinched the deal. "Okay. My car or yours?"

"Why don't you follow me?"

And that's how I ended up sitting across from Conahegg at the Dairy Queen several miles up the road from Andover Bend. The lunch hour had passed so we were the only ones sitting at the red plastic booths.

It felt weird being there with him. Like regular roadside travelers stopping in for a thirst quencher. Like normal folks with normal conversation, not a sheriff and a home health nurse discussing a suicide victim.

"You want something to eat?" Conahegg asked, steepling his fingers in front of him.

I shook my head. "Finding a dead body is kind of an appetite killer."

"Yeah." He nodded.

I took a long suck through the straw of my Dr. Pepper, savored the sweet, syrupy taste.

Conahegg had ordered coffee, but he wasn't drinking it. Avoiding my eye, he took a pen and notepad from his pocket.

"Tell me about finding Tim's body."

Were we only going to talk about the business at hand? No mention of the strange attraction surging between us? Probably a good idea. Ignore the bomb on the kitchen table and maybe it'll disappear on its own.

I cleared my throat and verbally rehashed my steps for him. I was careful to stick to the facts and keep my opinions to myself.

Best to steer clear of emotions.

"How well did you know Tim?" Conahegg asked when I finished.

"Sissy dated him for eight months about two years ago. Actually, Saturday morning, the day you ran over him, was the first time I'd seen Tim in over a year." I toyed with the paper from my straw.

Conahegg scrawled in his pad. "Did he have any enemies that you were aware of?"

"Tim was a friendly guy, but he was gay. You know as well as I do that small towns and homosexuals don't always mix."

He nodded. "Can you think of any reason why he might kill himself?"

"Sorry. I didn't know him that well. You might talk to Sissy. I think she still kept in touch with him."

"I'll do that," Conahegg said. "I'll call you if I have any more questions."

"All right."

He pocketed his notepad. "You can go."

"That's it?"

"Yes."

"Gee thanks," I said, realizing I sounded sarcastic and not really sure. "I appreciate the Dr. Pepper."

"You're welcome."

I got to my feet, and hurried to my car. I pulled out of the Dairy Queen parking lot and turned down the street, trying my best to get the image of poor Tim Kehaul off my retina and the thought of Sam Conahegg off my mind.

I was more traumatized than I realized when I stopped at the intersection that led to the highway and my leg started jumping when I pushed in the clutch.

I felt shaky clean through my stomach, the way you do when your blood sugar hits rock bottom. I should have let Conahegg buy me a Beltbuster but the thought of food nauseated me.

With rising trepidation, I drove home. How was I going to break the news to my sister that her gay, ex-lover was dead?

CHAPTER SIX

SISSY'S CAR WASN'T in the driveway and for that small favor I sent up a prayer. But Mama's little 1965 rainbow-colored Volkswagen Beetle, the only car she'd ever owned, was parked beside Aunt Tessa's chili-pepper red Mustang convertible and a brand-new powder-blue Cadillac El Dorado that I didn't recognize.

I let myself in the back door. Strains of Yanni poured from the CD player. Candles flickered along the mantel, scenting the air lavender. From the back room I heard muted voices.

That explained the El Dorado. Aunt Tessa had a customer.

I took a Dr. Pepper from the fridge and plopped down at the kitchen table to massage my temples. Closing my eyes, I pressed the cold can to my forehead.

I wondered what Conahegg was doing. Had he gone back to Tim's trailer? Was he in his office? I doubted he'd gone home. Thinking about him was becoming as contagious as a case of the chicken pox. No matter how hard I tried to put him from my mind, he kept coming back like a bad itch.

I decided he was probably still at Tim's trailer. Again I visualized finding Tim's body. I shuddered.

What had gone through Tim's head those last few moments of consciousness? Had he had the most mind-blowing orgasm imaginable?

Blech. I didn't want to know.

Footsteps sounded in the hall, along with murmured voices. Aunt Tessa appeared in the doorway. I was surprised to see Reverend Ray Don Swiggly's wife, Miss Gloria, trailing behind her, dressed as nondescriptly as she had been that night at the sheriff's department.

Hmm. Apparently her husband wasn't meeting *all* her spiritual needs.

Aunt Tessa looked pale as she always did after a reading. The blowsy chartreuse caftan she wore accentuated her natural pallor. She rarely went out in the sun and when she did it was with gloves and long sleeves and a wide-brimmed hat.

"Take these," Aunt Tessa said, drawing a pair of crystal earrings she bought at the five-and-dime for two bucks a pair, from her pocket. She prescribed them for her clients experiencing emotional pain. Combined with her readings, the crystal earrings were supposed to induce healing. Me, I never bought into it. Then again, who knows? Faith is a powerful thing.

Aunt Tessa pressed the earrings into Miss Gloria's palm. "Wear them every day for two weeks."

"Thank you," Miss Gloria mumbled, head down. She handed Aunt Tessa a fifty-dollar bill which my aunt tucked into her cleavage. "You've been a big help."

"My pleasure." Aunt Tessa nodded.

The other woman turned for the door, spying me for the first time. "Oh."

"Hello, Mrs. Swiggly," I greeted her.

"Uh." She couldn't look me in the eye. "Hello."

"We met in the wee hours of Saturday morning at the sheriff's department," I reminded her. "I'm Allegheny Green."

"I remember," she murmured. "Nice to see you again."

"I hope Aunt Tessa helped you with your problem."

Miss Gloria's eyes widened. "Oh, no. You're mistaken. I

don't have a problem. Your aunt was asking *me* about my religion."

What? I stared at Aunt Tessa. She vigorously shook her head.

"Okay," I responded, not knowing for sure what was going on here. "Would you like to stay for supper?" I waved a hand at the stove. "I'm going to make tuna casserole."

"No," Mrs. Swiggly said, then repeated herself. "No. But thanks for the invitation. I must get home. Ray Don will be wanting his supper, too."

"Bye." I raised a hand.

The woman bustled out the door and I turned to Aunt Tessa. "Whoa! Don't tell me you're thinking about converting to the Church of the Living Jesus?"

Aunt Tessa shot me a dirty look and snorted. "Don't be ridiculous."

I jerked a thumb at the back door. "What was that about?"

Gleefully, Aunt Tessa rubbed her palms together. I could tell she considered it quite a feather in her cap that Miss Gloria had sought her expertise. "The woman was embarrassed to come to me. She insisted on the proselytizing story to cover the fact she wanted her cards read and swore me to secrecy." Aunt Tessa sank into a chair beside me. "Lord, that woman's got a lot of problems."

"Like what?"

"Come on, Ally, you know I can't violate client confidentiality."

"You're not a priest, Aunt Tessa, nor a psychiatrist."

"In many cases I assume the role of both," she said.

"But you hate Swiggly. How come you're giving readings to his wife?"

"She paid fifty bucks."

"It could be a put-on. You know, she could be trying to gather ammunition to use against us."

Aunt Tessa shook her head. "You didn't see what the cards told me about her, Ally. The woman is very messed up."

"Is it her husband?" I asked. "Does he cheat on her? Let me guess, he's diddling the church secretary. You know the old classic story." I couldn't resist chuckling.

"I'm not discussing it." She pointed her chin in the air. "It's obvious you don't respect my profession, I suggest we change the subject." When Aunt Tessa turned haughty it was a sure bet you weren't going to get anything out of her.

"Wanna soda?" I asked, defusing her indignation before it expanded.

She nodded and without getting up, I swiveled my torso toward the fridge, opened the door and hauled out another Dr. Pepper. I popped off the top and passed it to Aunt Tessa.

I wasn't quite sure if my aunt was really psychic or simply believed she was. She wasn't a fraud, at least not intentionally. Sometimes her predictions came true and sometimes they didn't, but she did possess uncanny insight into human nature. That, I believed, was her real talent.

Then again, if Aunt Tessa was so perceptive maybe I could ask her about Conahegg and me. Like what were the chances we'd ever get together?

"Something's wrong," Aunt Tessa stated.

"Is your Dr. Pepper flat?"

"No, there's something wrong with you."

I met her eyes, which darkened with concern. Before she could read me, I looked away. "Nothing's wrong with me."

"Bad news," Aunt Tessa said.

"How do you know?"

"When you're worried you get these little lines around your mouth. Just like your father used to."

I reached up and fingered the corners of my mouth. "You're right. It's bad news."

"Is it about a patient?"

"Yeah. But it's more than that."

Aunt Tessa's hand flew to her chest. "Someone's dead."

I nodded.

"Anyone we know?"

I nodded again.

Aunt Tessa inhaled sharply. "Let me see if I can determine who."

"It's Tim," I said, not inclined to play guessing games.

"Tim? You mean Sissy's ex-boyfriend? The one who decided he was gay?"

"Yes."

"But how? When?" Her hand crept from her heart to her throat and her eyes widened.

"It was an accidental suicide." That was a polite way of explaining his undignified demise.

"Does Sissy know?"

"Not yet."

"Oh my gosh, who's going to tell her?"

I knew I'd be the one to have to tell Sissy. I'd known it from the moment I'd found Tim's body. What would Aunt Tessa do, I wondered, if I told her she'd have to break the news? Probably go into Ung mode and hibernate.

"I'll tell her."

Aunt Tessa placed her hand over mine. "You're an angel, Ally. A direct gift from God."

Funny how my mother and my aunt always complimented me when I took care of the unpleasant things in their lives. But they were my family, how could I begrudge them? They'd come to depend upon me so completely it was impossible to pull the rug out from under them. Like it or not, I was the caretaker. Always had been. Always would be.

Inexplicably, I longed for a man to lean on. A strong masculine presence to take care of everything. I shook my head, surprised at my own thoughts.

"Listen, don't tell Mama, at least not yet," I said.

"This is a very bad thing."

"Tell me about it."

"And I have the strangest feeling it's not as it seems," Aunt Tessa said.

"Where's Denny?" I asked, anxious to change the subject.

"He's upstairs watching television."

The back door opened and Mama came in from the pottery shed, smelling of plaster, paint and turpentine. She carried a cardboard box in her arms.

I got up to take the box from her and set it on the table.

"Thank you, Ally," Mama said. "You're home early."

"Yes. Bad day. I'll tell you about it in a bit." I nodded. "Do you know where Sissy went?" I picked an apple from the fruit bowl and polished it against my shirt.

"What do you think?" Mama held up a ceramic troll doll and two different colored tufts of cotton. "Green or pink for his hair?"

"Pink. His whole outfit is green."

"You're right." She nodded.

"What about Sissy?" I bit into the apple and pulled out a chair for Mama. It was hot in the pottery shed and her hair had come loose from its chignon and lay flat against the back of her neck.

"I believe that she went to see Rocky," Mama murmured and sat down, that familiar faraway expression in her eyes.

For most of my life my mother has been out to lunch. When I found out she had been quite the hippie back in the sixties, I wondered if too much experimentation with drugs had affected her powers of concentration.

But the truth is, everyone on my mother's side of the family is a little off center. First, there's Aunt Tessa. A cave-woman-channeling tarot card reader who'd been through four husbands and lived in sixteen foreign countries before coming to stay with us after Daddy died. Then there's my Uncle Charlie, who's a charming Shakespearean actor with a penchant for kleptomania. He's currently serving five to ten in Huntsville for "borrowing" a Jaguar from a dealership showroom.

My mother's father had been a circus performer. A fire-eating sword swallower. I never met him. He died in a rather grisly circus accident before I was born. Nobody talked about it much.

And grandma was reputed to have been an herbal healer and a good witch. The kind you go to for lucky talismans and love potions. I do remember her. She was small and had a naughty twinkle in her eye. She liked to gossip about the neighbors and their health problems.

I used to sit on a stool in her kitchen and watch her cook up crazy things in big vats. Poultices and headache cures, restorative elixirs and impotency remedies. She never baked cookies or raised flowers in her gardens like regular grandmothers. When you think about where they came from, you can't really blame Mama and Aunt Tessa for being so weird.

I laid my hand on Mama's and waited for her to give me her attention. It took a while. When Mama is off in her magical, mystical world of trolls and castles, fair maidens and dashing knights, it's often hard to pull her back.

She looked up and blinked at me over the top of her reading glasses.

"We have got to do something about Sissy," I said.

"Allegheny." A stern note crept into her voice. She didn't believe in butting into her children's lives, even when she *should* be butting in. "Your sister is a grown woman."

"Rocky is a bad influence on her."

"It's not our place to tell her who she can and can't date." Mama's gaze slid sideways toward the troll, her fingers tightening on the porcelain figurine. I could see she was aching to slip back into her world and away from mine.

"Why not? We care about her. We love her."

"Allegheny, we don't learn when people lecture. We only learn from our mistakes."

It's really hard to get my mother to see reality. Usually, I don't even try. But sometimes Sissy will listen to Mama. She never listens to me.

"He's got her smoking pot."

Mama leveled me a look. "I smoked pot when I was young."

Yeah, I was tempted to say, *and look what happened to you.* "Not when you had kids," I said instead. "Sissy is responsible for Denny. She needs to be held accountable for her actions."

"Sometimes you can be very harsh, Ally. I don't know where you get that from. Your father was so kind and caring and I don't judge people. What's made you so hard?"

Her words stung. I won't deny it. Hard? Harsh?

"I only mention it because I care about Sissy and I don't want her to get into trouble." I smashed my lips together. I would not cry.

"Leave her be, Ally," my mother said. "Just leave your sister be."

"Fine."

I got up and slung my uneaten apple into the trash can on my way out the door. I was still dressed in my mauve scrub suit and white lab coat but I didn't care. I stalked away from the house and down the hill toward the river.

I reached the river's edge and stared out across the water. I swallowed several deep gulps of air and watched as a sand crane skimmed the water searching for one last meal before bedding down for the night.

When had I become the enemy?

Maybe Rhonda was right. Maybe it was long past the time when I should let my family sink or swim.

Why don't you hightail it out of here? the rebellious voice in the back of my mind whispered. The voice I never listened to. *You could leave. Get a job as a traveling nurse. Take off and see the world. Like you've always dreamed of doing.*

I bent to pick up a stone and skipped it across the water. It splashed four times before sinking into the middle of the Brazos river. My father would have been proud. He'd taught me to skip stones and he loved the river with his heart and soul. He had passed that love on to me. It's the reason why he willed me the house. He knew no one cared about the place the way I did. He also knew I'd provide for everyone.

"Ah, Daddy." I sighed.

He'd been dead for almost sixteen years but I never lost that tight awful knot somewhere dead center within my heart. He'd been the only sane thing in my insane childhood. He'd been the cement holding our bizarre little family together and when he died, he'd passed that torch on to me.

I closed my eyes, remembering the end. His body had been completely ravaged by cancer. I'd only been fifteen but I'd stayed out of school to be with him.

Mama had been hysterical, unable to cope. The doctors had kept her so medicated she'd stumbled through the next few years in a total daze. With one of his last breaths, Daddy, his frail body no more than flesh-covered bones, had taken my hand in his.

"Promise me you'll take care of your mother, Ally. And Sissy, too. They'll never make it without you." He squeezed my fingers. "Promise me, so I can die in peace."

"I promise, Daddy."

I'd made that vow with the most solemn of intentions. And I'd kept my promise. Ah, the old triple threat, duty, honor and guilt. What powerful motivations.

Don't forget fear, the voice in the back of my head piped up.

Fear? I wasn't afraid of anything.

And yet the question nagged. Was I afraid to let go of my family? Was I afraid to be alone, to fashion my own life? Was I actually using their dependency as an excuse, hiding behind it so that I didn't have to face the truth?

Was Allegheny Green afraid of not being needed?

The idea was startling, disturbing and I didn't want to consider it anymore.

I hitched in a deep breath and opened my eyes. The sun was hugging the horizon in a vivid splash of orange and pink. I smelled honeysuckle and the odor of fish.

Home.

I parked my butt in a lawn chair on the dock, and watched the perch come up to feed, blowing bubbles on the water's green surface. I heard the back door creak and footsteps padding down to the river.

"Aunt Ally?"

Glancing up, I saw my nephew, Denny, standing in the twilight. He was a cute kid with big brown inquisitive eyes and a chocolate-colored cowlick that insisted on flopping over his forehead no matter how much hair gel he slathered on it.

"Hey there." I held out my hand to him. He sauntered over the dock's planks and let me pull his lanky body onto my lap. It wouldn't be long until he would resist such closeness. I knew that and I savored his warm, slightly sweaty body pressed against mine.

We sat for the longest moment, staring out across the river, breathing together as the stars began to speckle the sky.

"Are you mad at Mom?" he asked.

"I'll get over it."

"I hate that Rocky fella."

I smiled at his unintentional pun. "So do I."

"When Mom's with him she forgets about me."

No matter what my opinion of Rockerfeller Hughes might be, I had to be diplomatic when dealing with an eight-year-old. The poor kid had never known his real Daddy. Hell, Sissy wasn't even sure who the father had been.

"Your mother never forgets about you, Denny. She loves you very much."

"Yeah? Well if she loves me so much how come you're the one who packs my lunch and drives me to school and takes me to the dentist?"

"Denny, I like doing those things. I like taking care of people. That's why I'm a nurse."

"I wish my mom liked taking care of people the way you do, Aunt Ally." He leisurely swung his foot, kicking me lightly in the shins.

"Your mom is good at other things besides taking care of people."

"Oh yeah? Like what?" Denny challenged, turning his head so he could see my face.

"She's a good singer. And a good dancer. Don't you two have lots of fun when she turns up the radio and dances around the living room with you?"

"She doesn't do that much anymore. Not since she started hanging out with fart-face Rocky."

"Denny," I said. "Don't talk like that."

"Why not? Mama says fart and worse." He folded his hands into his armpits so that his arms looked like wings.

"Your mother shouldn't say such words, either."

"I know."

What was one supposed to do with a wise kid? I had no idea. I only wished my sister would grow up and realize what a treasure her son truly was.

"Aunt Ally?"

"Uh-huh."

"You won't ever go away will you?"

"Of course not." I looked down at him, guiltily remembering that a few minutes earlier I'd been contemplating escape. "What makes you ask that?"

Denny shrugged. "I heard Gramma telling Aunt Tessa you need a boyfriend."

"Well, even if I did have a boyfriend, I wouldn't leave you."

"But what if you got married and had kids of your own? Who would take care of me and Mama?"

"I'd never marry someone who wouldn't let you and your Mama live with us."

Denny made a face. "I don't want you to ever get married."

"Don't worry about it, champ. If I ever get married, it's a long ways off."

"Aunt Ally? Can I ask you a favor?"

"For you, anything."

Denny took a deep breath. "You know my Junior Adventurers troop is having a campout the weekend after next."

"Yes."

"Mama said she would go but now she says she can't."

"Oh, Denny, I'm so sorry." Fresh anger at my sister welled inside me.

"Will you do it, Aunt Ally? We need another grown-up to help chaperone or they're going to call off the trip."

"Why sure, Denny. I'll be happy to. I'll switch my work schedule at the hospital with Rhonda."

"Really?" He beamed.

"Sure."

He hugged me. "You're the best aunt in the whole wide world."

Unexpected emotions crowded my throat. I ruffled his hair. "Come on, let's go inside. The mosquitoes are nibbling you up and it's time to start dinner."

Denny followed me into the house, a pensive expression on his face. I knew that he was worrying about his mother and his own future. We were a lot alike, my nephew and I. Both worriers, both willing to take on the weight of the world.

I wanted to tell him it wouldn't do any good. That no matter how much you worried bad things still happened. But who can tell an eight-year-old something like that?

Instead, I shook off my own gloominess and took Denny by the hand. I wasn't afraid to be alone. I'd made my decision a long time ago. I belonged here. On the river. With my family. The people who counted on me. There would be no trips to foreign locales. No boyfriends and no marriage. No matter how I might dream that it could be different, there simply wasn't enough room in my life for Sam Conahegg.

CHAPTER SEVEN

I WAITED UP UNTIL midnight for Sistine to come home. Finally, I dozed off in the rocking chair in the living room, Mama's hand-crocheted afghan thrown across my lap. The back door creaking open jerked me awake a little after 2:00 a.m.

The low-watt kitchen venti-hood bulb illuminated Sissy in silhouette. She crept into the house carrying her thick-soled, sling-back pumps in one hand and her purse in the other. She wore one of those barely there tank tops like the female characters on a *Friends* re-run and a spandex skirt that didn't cover her thighs.

Reaching over, I clicked on the floor lamp.

Sissy squinted, raised her arm to block her eyes. "Hey, sergeant, cut the light, you're blinding me!"

"Where have you been?" I asked, trying not to sound like a nagging parent but failing miserably.

She'd been drinking. I could tell by the too bright sheen in her eyes. Her mascara had smeared, causing her to look like a raccoon. "None of your beeswax."

"Very mature, Sistine. Want to tell me how you got those hickeys?"

She wagged her tongue at me, showing off her gold stud. "Jealous?"

"Were you with Rocky?" I asked, an awful feeling slithering through me.

"What if I was?"

"I thought you were finished with him." My frustration knew no bounds. I wanted to throttle my sister for her stupidity and idly wondered if Conahegg would arrest me.

The notion of Conahegg and handcuffs generated immediate sexual imagery. I'd love to cuff him to the headboard of my bed, strip him naked and trail a feather oh so slowly over his body. The thought of the strong, imposing sheriff completely within my power rocked me with a shudder that dove clean through my pelvis.

"Rocky's changed, Ally," Sissy said, shattering my scorching daydreams and bringing me back to grim reality. In that instant I understood why Mama spent so much time in her fantasy world. It was fun.

"Changed?" I blinked. Back to big-sister mode. Forget about Conahegg. Forget about handcuffs. Forget about bondage and feathers and orgasms.

"He told me that getting shot in the toe gave him something to think about," Sissy continued. "It made him realize how much he loves me."

"Excuse me?" I shook my head. The vestiges of my flights of fancy completely dispelled. "The man caused you to be beaten by a loan shark, Sistine Eileen Green. Have you forgotten about that? Your bruises haven't even faded."

Sissy waved a hand. "It was a misunderstanding."

"Stop!" I held up a palm. I couldn't absorb anymore. Sissy back in Rocky's arms. "What about his wife, Darlene?"

"He's divorcing her, then we're going to Vegas to get married."

"Sissy, don't let him play you for a fool."

"Can't you be happy for me?"

"Sit down." I rubbed my face with my hand. "I have something to tell you."

"Don't start ragging on me, Ally."

"Sissy, this is important." I pointed at the sofa. "Sit."

"Screw you, you're not my mother."

"I've got bad news and it has nothing to do with Rocky. Please, have a seat."

"Let me guess," Sissy sneered. "You got passed over at work for employee of the month."

I'd meant to tell her about Tim in a delicate manner but my self-destructive sister was making diplomacy impossible. "Tim Kehaul is dead," I said bluntly.

Sissy blinked at me as if she hadn't heard me.

"Your ex-boyfriend committed suicide."

Then just like that, her knees buckled and she crumpled to the carpet. Dang. Hadn't I told her to sit down?

I leaped from the rocker, ran to her side and braced her with my arm. "I'm so sorry."

"Tim?" She whimpered. "Dead?"

"It was an accident."

Sissy frowned. "But I thought you said he committed suicide."

"He did. Except not on purpose."

"I don't get it."

I explained what had probably happened and Sissy began to cry.

"Shh," I soothed, brushing her hair with my fingers. "It's all right. Shh."

"Poor Tim." She sobbed.

"I know."

Her shoulders shook and she leaned against me.

"You were with Rocky, right? Didn't you see the patrol cars at Tim's place?"

"I met Rocky at Zydeco's," Sissy said, referring to a trashy country-and-western bar located at the Parker County line in an area known as Whisky Corners, which consisted of Zydeco's, a strip club called Tits-a-Poppin', a Majestic liquor store, a bingo hall frequented by the blue hair set, a massage parlor professing to specialize in Rolfing and three cut-rate gas stations renowned for watering down their petrol.

"What was he doing out of the house?" I asked. "He's supposed to be recuperating."

"He had cabin fever."

"Please, tell me you're not serious about marrying Rocky," I begged.

"Well…"

"Think of Denny." I clasped her hand. "Think of yourself. You could do so much better, Sissy. Don't sell yourself short."

"Rocky says he's got a surefire way to make a lot of money," Sissy blurted.

"Even if it's true, there's more to life than money, Sis. What about love?"

"What about it?"

"Do you love Rocky? Does Rocky love you?"

She shrugged. "I loved Tim and look what happened." The mention of his name brought fresh tears. "No one ever treated me as good as he did. Then he turned gay on me!"

"Tim didn't turn gay, Sissy. He was always gay. He just happened to come out of the closet while he was dating you." I took a deep breath. Analyzing my sister's choices was beyond my expertise. She needed professional help. "It's late and we're both tired. Why don't we talk tomorrow?"

Sissy nodded and I helped her to her feet.

"I do know of one young man who loves you very much, Sissy."

"Who's that?" She looked at me expectantly, eyes wide. The sad thing was, she didn't even realize who I was speaking of.

"Your son."

THE NEXT MORNING I hit the gym before work, tackling the StairMaster to relieve some of my frustration over Sissy. An hour later, exhilarated with exhaustion, I started for the showers only to stop in my tracks as I passed the weight room.

There, in all his half-clothed glory, was Conahegg hefting barbells over his head.

Like a kid drawn to a cheap carnival ride, I sidled over to him. "Hi. Hello. I didn't know you came here."

Conahegg simply grunted and lowered the weights. He inhaled, then exhaled. "Hey," he finally said.

I couldn't seem to stop my gaze from skittering out of my control and attacking him. He wore a red muscle shirt and black cotton shorts. I think he had on Nike runners but to tell the truth I didn't pay much attention to his feet.

There was not an ounce of fat anywhere on his body. And his forearms! God, what forearms. There ought to be a law against such perfection.

I wanted him. With a physical hunger unlike anything I'd ever known. My hormones must have been out of whack. Estrogen overload. That had to be the answer. By nature, I was not a lusty gal. I did not drool over movie stars or gaze longingly at the backsides of handsome construction workers. I did not throb for romance novel heroes nor did I daydream of riding rugged cowboys.

But there was something about Conahegg that floated my sexual boat. And no matter how hard I tried, I couldn't seem to deny my obsession.

You're a sick, sick puppy, Allegheny Green.

It's okay. It's all right. No harm in fantasizing. As long as he doesn't know how you feel, everything is hunky-dory.

But if I didn't put my eyes back in my head soon he was going to figure out my secret.

His gaze flicked over me. Steady. Controlled. Yet deep inside those gray depths I saw something else. Something that wasn't the least bit steady or controlled. Something primal, something elemental. Something that made my toes curl.

"Well," I said awkwardly, flapping my white towel around like a flag of surrender. "I saw you here and wanted to come over and say hi."

Inwardly, I cringed. How inane!

He smiled. Just the tiniest bit. "Hi."

"Didn't mean to interrupt your workout." I was shifting my weight, nervous as a grasshopper in a pen full of chickens. "You have fun."

One corner of his mouth lifted a little higher.

"I better be going. See ya. Bye."

Then I zoomed away.

If someone had asked me to take a ride on the space shuttle leaving for Mars, I would have jumped at the chance. Instead, I threw myself into the shower and blasted the cold water.

Take that, you oversexed ninny.

A few minutes later I changed into my scrubs and sneaked out the back door of the gym, desperate to avoid Conahegg.

I stopped by McDonald's for coffee and a breakfast burrito to help calm me down before heading to my first appointment.

By seven-thirty, it was already hotter than the day before and I ended up turning on my air-conditioning along with the morning show on Q102. I took farm road 413 off highway 51 and drove past rolling ranch land to a small frame farmhouse dropped in the middle of ten acres, eight miles out of town.

Miss Maddie Farnsworth was my favorite patient. She'd once been my fourth grade homeroom teacher. She should have sold her house and moved into Cloverleaf long ago but Maddie had her own way of doing things.

She'd come to need my services by way of a fractured hip

and a nasty nosocomial infection. She'd been released from the rehab hospital two weeks earlier and had been healing nicely but still had to receive antibiotics to stem the tide of methicillin-resistant staph aureus circulating in her blood.

Because she'd never married and had no children, Maddie lived alone, but she was never lonely. An obsessively cheerful woman, she'd spent forty-five years in the Cloverleaf school system. She knew everyone in town and everyone knew her. Her former students, members of her church and other friends dropped by on a daily basis to keep Maddie informed on current events in Cloverleaf. Plus, she had an addiction to the telephone, which she happened to be on when I arrived.

I knocked on the door, announced myself and walked on in.

Maddie beamed and waved at me from her wheelchair. "Gotta go, Evie, my favorite nurse is here. Call me back in an hour." She switched off her cordless phone and rested it in her lap. "Good morning, sunshine," she welcomed.

Sharp blue eyes peered at me. She hadn't changed much over the years. A little thinner, her shoulders a little more stooped but she still possessed a quick wit and a keen mind.

I smiled. "Morning, Maddie."

She'd been a strict but fair teacher and I'd long ago forgiven her for making me stand at the front of the class with gum stuck on the end of my nose. I'd violated one of her ten commandments. Thou shall not chew gum in Maddie Farnsworth's class. The consequences of ignoring the rule were a humiliating experience but she had broken my gum habit.

"You look tired," she announced. "Francie dropped by with poppy seed muffins and a pot of green tea. Would you like for me to heat you a cup in the microwave?"

"No, thanks, I just finished my coffee."

"Coffee? Honey, that stuff revs you up. You need to calm down."

Calm down? Could she tell my pulse was still racing from my encounter with Conahegg? How? Did I have that "I wanna get laid" look about me?

"I need revving up," I lied. Anything to dispel the notion that Conahegg had done anything to increase my core body temperature.

"Pah! You're too young to be tired."

"I had a rough day yesterday," I murmured, suddenly realizing I needed a little sympathy, a little mothering. Something I rarely got at home.

"I heard." Maddie clicked her tongue. "So sad about young Tim Kehaul."

"You know about that?" I arched an eyebrow. She never ceased to amaze me.

Maddie nodded. "I even know you were the one to find his body. Can't hide anything from me."

That was true. She knew everything about everybody in Cloverleaf and the surrounding area.

I sat on the couch beside her wheelchair, opened my bag and began to remove the medical supplies. Syringes, heavy-duty antibiotic ointment, gauze, a vial of vancomycin, alcohol preps, Betadine wash, sterile drapes, IV tubing, normal saline.

Maddie had zero veins, so instead of dismissing her with a saline well as they normally did, the hospital had put in a subclavian catheter. It was my job to keep a hawk eye on the insertion site for any signs of an infection developing there.

"I knew that boy was headed for trouble," Maddie sighed.

"You did?"

She unbuttoned the top button on her lace blouse and I spread out the drape under the subclavian catheter sewed into her neck vein. I'd never seen Maddie in a nightgown. She was always up and dressed whenever I arrived, her hair combed, her lipstick on.

"He had such a gambling problem." Maddie shook her head.

"He did?" News to me. "We're still talking about Tim?"

She nodded. "I imagine that's why he hung himself, poor boy—got so far into debt he couldn't get out."

I didn't tell her about the autoerotic asphyxiation theory. She was seventy and I didn't want to shock her.

"He really got bad after they legalized horse racing in Texas. Before that he was limited to driving to Shreveport or his annual trip to Las Vegas."

"How do you know?" I asked, as I prepared her subclavian catheter for the treatment.

"I have my sources," she said cagily. "And I remember all you kids. None of us changes much. Tim always liked to take a gamble. So did your sister, Sistine. You always played it safe. Quiet, calm, serious."

"What about the time I chewed bubble gum in your class? That wasn't playing it safe," I said, grasping at straws as it dawned on me that Maddie was right. I had been dull my entire life.

She smiled. "Well, there is a spot of rebel deep down inside you."

I beamed. It's pathetic, I know. I wanted to cling to the hope that yes, I could be wild if given the opportunity. Then I surprised myself by asking, "Did you ever have Sam Conahegg as a student?"

"You know Sam?"

I could have bitten my tongue off. Why couldn't I stop thinking about him? It wasn't as if I didn't have enough stuff to worry about.

"We recently met. I barely remember him from high school. He was a senior when I was a freshman." And he'd been the son of one of Cloverleaf's prominent citizens, while I'd been the girl with the kooky family from the wrong side of the river. I'd known from the beginning that Sam Conahegg was out of my league.

Maddie nodded. "He graduated valedictorian. Did you know that?"

"I'd forgotten."

"Hard worker. And one of the brightest pupils I ever had the pleasure of teaching," Maddie mused. "But things weren't easy for Sam."

"What?" I pricked up my ears. Do tell.

"Sad." Maddie clicked her tongue.

"In what way?"

"Lew Conahegg was a drunk. Used to beat the boy. You didn't know that?"

I shook my head.

"Oh yeah. Lew hid his dark side from the public, but he showed it to his family. His wife, Sally, Sam's mother, was pitiful. She bent over backward trying to please Lew. Course nothing she did suited him. What do they call it? Codependent?" She stopped to haul in a breath. "Sally smothered poor Sam. Always fussing over him. When he was in my fourth grade class she sent a note forbidding him to go outside in the winter, even on pretty days. She packed his lunch with crazy health food—tofu and brown rice and organic vegetables—long before it was popular. She walked him to school every morning, was there every evening to pick him up."

Ah, so that explained why Sam had left Cloverleaf, joined the Marines and never looked back. He'd been trying to escape. So why had he come home?

"He's another one with a responsibility complex," Maddie said. "You two are peas in a pod."

"What do you mean by a responsibility complex?" I frowned.

She waved a hand. "Don't take it the wrong way, Ally. You

both have this need to take care of things. To be in control. There are worse flaws. But because of your like temperament you two wouldn't make a good match."

"Who said anything about us making a match?"

Maddie's eyes twinkled. "Sam's got his hands full as it is."

"What do you mean?" I added the vancomycin to the small bag of saline solution and hooked it into Maddie's catheter.

"Big problems in the sheriff's department."

"Oh, that leftover stuff from Sheriff Jameson's administration."

"Yes and more."

"More?"

"Trouble's brewing."

"What kind of trouble?"

Maddie shrugged. "I've heard rumors that someone in his department is selling the drugs they confiscate from drug busts."

"You're kidding?" I stared at her.

"It's only a rumor, mind. But it's going to destroy Sam's run as sheriff if he doesn't find out who's behind the thefts and put a stop to it."

"Maybe he should ask you who's doing it," I said.

Maddie grinned. "How would I know that?"

I started Maddie's IV drip. After that, I checked her blood pressure and pulse, then had her turn to one side so I could change the surgical dressing on her hip.

"Goodness," she said. "It's nine o'clock. Time for my program. Would you hand me the remote, dear?"

I gave her the television remote control and sat down on the sofa to wait for her IV to finish.

She snapped on the television set and turned it to the Religious Channel. "I missed his Sunday broadcast," she said. "But they repeat it on Wednesday mornings at nine."

"Who?"

"Why the Reverend Swiggly, of course."

"You watch his program?"

"Oh, my yes! Ever since I broke my hip and haven't been able to attend local services. Have you ever seen him? He's so full of fire and emotion. I was tickled pink when I heard he was building a summer house on the river."

"Right next door to me," I mumbled.

"Really? I didn't know that."

"Yep."

"I suppose you heard about his heart attack."

"He had a heart attack? When?"

"Why last night, dear girl. Really, Ally, you've got to start paying more attention to what goes on in your community."

Maddie watched Swiggly strut across the stage. He ranted and raved. He praised God. He sang. He pounded his fist on the podium. He broke down into tears. He put on a pretty good show if you went in for that sort of thing.

The program ended at about the same time Maddie's antibiotic treatment did. "Sweetie," she said. "Could you get me my purse."

"Sure."

I brought her purse to her. It was almost threadbare, the pockets bulging with coupons and tissues and pictures of gap-toothed children from years gone by. She pulled out a checkbook.

I didn't mean to be nosy but I was hovering around her chest closing up the subclavian catheter and I saw her making out a check to Reverend Swiggly for two hundred dollars. I couldn't believe it. Miss Maddie lived on a teacher's pension. She couldn't afford that kind of tithe.

"Surely you're not sending him that much money?" I asked. I looked around at Miss Maddie's tiny abode and thought of the fortress Swiggly had built on the river. And that was just his summer home.

"Mind your own business, Allegheny Green," she said in a polite, but firm tone.

"He's a huckster, Maddie."

"He gives me comfort, child. Now hush."

Properly chastised, I gathered up my things and headed for the door.

"Will you drop this in the mail on your way out?" Maddie asked, sliding the check into an envelope and licking it closed.

"Sure, Maddie." I sighed. "Whatever you want."

CHAPTER EIGHT

"GOT ANOTHER NEW PATIENT." Joyce dropped the file on my desk and waddled toward the coffeemaker.

Somehow, I'd made it to Friday without any more excitement in my life. I paid the bills, did my daily stint at the gym and got a haircut. For some unknown reason, that had absolutely nothing to do with Sam Conahegg, I even had my hairdresser put some gold and auburn highlights in my mousy brown hair. I liked the change.

I even went grocery shopping and almost bumped into Conahegg. I was cruising down the frozen foods aisle and wheeled past a man with his head poked into the freezer. His cart was filled with artery-clogging junk. Frozen pizzas, French fried potatoes, fish sticks. Clearly, he needed someone to mother him whether he knew it or not. I shifted my gaze to the man.

And recognized the backside.

Conahegg.

I actually whispered, "Yikes" under my breath, took off at a dead run and managed to get around the corner of the aisle by the time I heard the freezer doors pop closed. I didn't even finish my shopping, just went straight to the checkout counter. I couldn't figure out why I hadn't simply said hello and walked on. Maybe it was lingering embarrassment over the awkwardness at the gym. Or maybe it was because I'd had an overwhelming urge to make him a decent meal.

The deal was, I wasn't sure how Conahegg felt about me. At times I was certain he was interested in me as a woman. I'd seen him perusing my body with fascination. But I also got other vibes from him and I'm not sure what it meant.

Since I'm being honest, let me say that I've been confused by what's been happening in my life. My sister shooting people in the toe. My patient committing suicide by autoerotic asphyxiation. An unfriendly televangelist moving in right next door. My own inexplicable sexual awakenings. It was a lot to absorb in a week's time.

And I'd become really dissatisfied with my life of late. I was tired of being everyone's mama but I didn't know how to act any differently. I kept telling myself that my attraction to Conahegg was a symptom of my restlessness not the cure. But my body was in full-blown denial about that.

"Ally?" Joyce called my name. "You hear me? You got a new patient."

"You already gave me two new patients," I protested, snapping back to the present.

"Yes, but one died and besides, the new patient lives right next door to you."

"Huh?" I flipped open the file. Reverend Ray Don Swiggly. I groaned.

"Yep. The televangelist. They let him out of the hospital yesterday evening. Straight from the ICU home." Joyce shook her head and her jowls quivered. "Don't know what health care is coming to. He had the heart attack on Tuesday night. The guy's got great insurance and they still toss him out after only three days."

"It is a shame," I agreed.

"Go see him first, will you? His wife's already called twice and it's only eight-thirty."

"What's she calling about?"

Joyce crinkled her nose. "I get the impression the good Reverend is something of a handful."

I remembered meeting Swiggly at the sheriff's department, his rantings imprinted on my brain. "Great," I muttered.

I stepped outside into the sweltering July heat and made a beeline for the Honda. I cranked the AC full blast and turned the radio to an oldies Motown station. "My Girl" wafted from the speakers.

I sang along off-key at the top of my lungs struggling to psych my mood for dealing with Swiggly. Mentally, I reminded myself that I'd become a nurse to help people and that I enjoyed my job.

Most of the time.

Over the course of the last few months my discontent had grown. An "is-this-all-there-is-to-life" sort of sensation gnawed at the back door of my soul.

I wanted adventure. I wanted excitement. I wanted romance.

I wanted Conahegg.

I wanted him the way a child wants a cookie. A child doesn't care about gaining weight or rotting her teeth or ruining her supper. She sees a cookie and she goes for it.

I wanted to consume him in one greedy bite and lick my fingers afterward. I wanted him without consideration for any consequences. I wanted to smell his scent on my skin, taste his tongue in my mouth, hear his voice as he called out my name in the heat of passion.

To hell with one cookie. I wanted the whole frigging jar.

But the cookies were locked up behind a badge and I was growing weak with hunger. Did I have the strength to battle for what I needed?

"Stop this, Allegheny. You're only making things worse." I shook my head and forced my attention on the road.

Cloverleaf is three-fourths surrounded by the Brazos River.

It sits like a hub, eight roads fan out into spokes. Seven of the roads lead to the river. The main avenue cuts east toward Interstate 20 and Fort Worth. I took highway 51. If you keep going for seventeen miles, you'll run into Granbury. If you take a right after the first bridge you'll run into my house.

By way of the river, Swiggly's house was right next door to ours, but by road the entrance to his place was a good half mile away since we lived in separate subdivisions.

Instead of taking the turn off into my addition, Brazos River Bend, I traveled south and took the exit into Sun Valley Estates.

Swiggly's swanky community was a far cry from both my middle-class neighborhood and the low-rent abodes of Andover Bend. These expansive houses sprawled across three-acre lots and boasted perfectly manicured lawns. Doctors and lawyers and pilots had summer homes here. CEOs and computer software consultants and electrical engineers built retirement mansions along the riverbank. Mercedes and sport utility vehicles and Lexus sedans were parked in the yards. Most of the residents owned elaborate boats that cost more than my annual salary.

When I arrived at Reverend Swiggly's house, I had to be buzzed in via locked gate. I parked behind Miss Gloria's El Dorado under the shade of a sheltering elm and walked up a newly poured cement walkway to the front door. The doorbell chimed out some warped Muzac and belatedly, I recognized the old gospel hymn, "Lamb of God."

The door swung open revealing a Mexican woman dressed in a long black skirt and white blouse topped with a sunflower-decorated apron.

"Hi," I greeted her, assuming she was the maid. "I'm Ally Green, Reverend Swiggly's home health nurse."

She bobbed her head and stood to one side.

"What's your name?"

She seemed surprised that I would ask. "My English—" she smiled shyly and ducked her head "—it not so good."

"It's a lot better than my Spanish," I said to put her at ease. "I'm going to be around a lot and I don't want to holler, 'hey you.'"

White teeth flashed in her brown face. "Esme."

"That's a beautiful name."

Esme had placid, nondescript features. She could have been anywhere from thirty-five to fifty with her thick black hair, threaded with gray strands, plaited into one long pigtail down her back. Clearly, she was accustomed to keeping a low profile, like Gloria Swiggly.

"Please." Esme wiped her hands on her apron. "You come inside."

I stepped over the threshold. Esme closed the door behind me and the resounding click echoed high into the cathedral ceilings. Immediately my eyes were assaulted by row upon row of religious paintings lining the endless hallway.

Jesus on the Cross. The Last Supper. Moses on the Mount. Noah and his Ark. Jesus on the Cross again, different painting, different artist, same message. Mary and Joseph and baby Jesus in the manger, the Three Wise Men hovering in shadows.

Whew. No wonder Miss Gloria always looked so overwhelmed.

"Esme?" Miss Gloria's voice floated out to us. "Is that the home health nurse?"

"Yes ma'am." Esme curtsied as Miss Gloria stepped into the foyer. As when I'd seen her before, she was wearing a dirt-brown ensemble.

"Oh." Miss Gloria stared at me, her eyes widening. "It's you."

"Home Services sent me," I explained, holding up my medical bag.

"That's all, Esme." She dismissed the maid without looking at her. "I didn't realize you were a nurse," she continued after Esme departed.

It occurred to me that my presence was making her uncomfortable. What if I happened to tell Reverend Ray Don she'd been next door consorting with Aunt Tessa?

"Yes. I've been an RN for nine years. I have a BSN from Texas Christian University."

"Really? A religious college?"

"Graduated top ten percent of my class," I couldn't help adding.

What did she think I was? Spawn of the devil? Actually, I'd gone to TCU for two reasons. One, it was the closest to home and my family. Two, at the time I went they hadn't required statistics like the University of Texas at Arlington where I'd tried twice to pass the course and had gotten a D both times. Never could understand that bell curve and mean, medium and mode stuff.

She raised a hand to her throat. "Er, about the other day when I was preaching the gospel to your Aunt Tessa..."

"Don't worry," I said, pantomiming pulling a zipper closed across my mouth. "My lips are sealed."

I noticed she was wearing the crystal earrings Aunt Tessa had given her and I couldn't help but wonder what sort of problems had driven her to seek my aunt's counsel.

Her smile was strained. "Thank you."

"Where's the patient?" I asked.

"Napping in the sunroom. Follow me."

We walked for what seemed like miles, past more Jesus paintings and elaborate Venetian tapestries that took my breath. Our feet glided from Oriental rugs to Italian marble tile to teakwood floors.

I couldn't help but think about Swiggly's congregation

and I wondered if they had any notion he lived like royalty while they subsisted on social security and cheap cat food. I remembered Maddie and the check she'd written. Two hundred dollars was a fortune to her. To Swiggly it was a gilded toenail clipper.

"Miss Gloria!" We heard the Reverend before we saw him. "I need another blanket, I'm cold."

Miss Gloria shook her head. "He hasn't been able to warm up since that awful intensive care unit. You know, they wouldn't let him wear his pajamas. They made him put on one of those vile faded cotton gowns with the backside cut out and he about froze to death."

I clicked my tongue and made a tsking sound. Ah. Life was so hard when you were accustomed to the finer things and you ran smack-dab into the reality of the every day.

"Ray Don," she said, leading me into a sunny open room with plate glass windows overlooking the Brazos. A variety of exotic plants shared the room with the man stretched out on a Corinthian leather sofa clutching a worn copy of a large-print King James Bible in his lap. "The nurse is here."

"About time!" he exclaimed, turning his head and catching sight of me.

He frowned.

I smiled.

"Don't you live in that run-down farmhouse next door?" he asked.

"That's me," I said, resenting his jab, but too professional to show it. I set my bag down on the brass and glass coffee table with a large African violet in a ceramic pot as a centerpiece.

"You're the one with the heathen family."

My smile tightened around my clenched teeth. "Guilty as charged."

He glared. "Are you really a nurse? I don't want some

nurse's aid meddling with me. I want a registered nurse with a degree."

"Do you want to see my license?"

For a moment, he actually considered it, I could tell by the gleam in his eyes, but then he motioned me forward. "That's not necessary. I believe in trusting a person until they have proven they aren't trustworthy. That's the way Jesus conducted his life."

"Why don't you let me examine you and then you can tell me what sort of problems you've been having." I affected my most professional tone.

"Is that necessary?"

"It's what I'm here for." I took a stethoscope from my bag and plugged it into my ears. "Shirt up."

Swiggly raised his silk pajama top and I was forced to come close enough to lay the bell against his surprisingly hairy chest. Lub-dub, lub-dub. Silently, I counted the beats.

"Heart sounds good."

"How can it sound good?" he asked. "I had a heart attack."

"No irregular beats."

"That's because I'm on a truckload of medication and if you think swallowing those horse pills is fun then you've never tried it."

"You're right." I smiled benevolently. "I've been blessed with good health."

"Thank God for that, missy. Things can change," Swiggly said darkly.

"I'm aware. So tell me more about your heart attack, Reverend Swiggly. How did it occur?" I folded up my stethoscope and stuck it in the pocket of my lab jacket. My gaze skimmed his body. I assessed his color, his skin turgor and his respiratory rate. Everything checked out.

"What are you quizzing me for? I already gave them that

information at the hospital. Isn't it in your files?" Swiggly groused.

"I need to make my own records."

"Bullshit."

"Pardon me?" I'd bet my favorite pair of running sneakers that *bullshit* was not part of Jesus' working vocabulary.

"Bureaucratic bullshit." Swiggly snorted.

"You've got me there, sir, but you're in the system and I've got to ask these questions. You don't have to answer them but then I will have to document the fact that you were uncooperative and who would ever believe the esteemed Reverend Ray Don Swiggly would resist answering a few little medical questions."

Swiggly glared as if he would prefer to gut me like a fish.

I picked up his file, then sat down in the wicker chair next to him, pulled a pen from my pocket and glanced over the two page faxed admission form we'd received from the hospital. "Let's see, it says here you suffered chest pains on Tuesday evening, is that correct?"

"That's right."

"Did anything precipitate the pain?"

"What do you mean?"

I clicked my Bic. "What preceded the chest pains? Did you receive bad news? Were you mowing the lawn, lifting something heavy?"

He straightened up on the couch, ran his hands through his silver pompadour. "Young lady, I'll have you know a man of my stature does not engage in manual labor."

Well, he certainly slammed me in my place. I'm the one who mows the lawn at my house. I'm assuming that meant I had yet to achieve stature on the scale of the honorable Reverend Swiggly.

"What about upsetting news?"

"Nothing upsets me. I have Jesus beside me."

"Fair enough." I closed the file, stuck the Bic behind my ear. "Why don't you tell me about your current problems."

Swiggly launched into a mind-numbing soliloquy about the degeneration of the health care system, the lack of respect among young people, how his heart medication constipated him.

You name it, he bitched about it. He seemed to be under the impression that I was a family therapist or something. An hour later, after my eyes had glazed over and my butt had gone to sleep, Swiggly finally ran down.

"You've got some legitimate complaints," I said in a brownnosed attempt to placate him.

"And you're going to address them?"

"I can get the doctor to order you something for the constipation."

"No more horse pills!"

Lord, I thought, they really don't pay me enough to put up with his whining. "No horse pills. We'll get you a liquid."

Or an enema.

Swiggly mumbled something I couldn't hear and I chose to ignore him. I picked up my things and headed for the door, forty minutes late for my next appointment.

"When will you be back?" Swiggly asked.

"Monday."

"That's not soon enough," he complained. "I want daily visits. I can pay."

I forced myself not to roll my eyes. "I'll talk to the home health director."

"See that you do. I'll be expecting you tomorrow."

"I'm off tomorrow. You'll be seeing someone else."

"I want you."

When did we get to be such buds?

"I'm afraid that's impossible, sir."

"I can pay," he repeated.

I swept my gaze over the ornate draperies, the expensive carpeting. He was used to pushing people around, accustomed to waving money at obstacles in order to get his way. But I didn't like being railroaded.

"I'm sure that you can but everyone needs a day off, Reverend Swiggly."

"You don't understand. I don't want a bunch of strangers traipsing in and out of here. It's you or nobody."

"Then you'll have to wait until Monday, won't you?" He was treading on my last nerve with army boots.

Swiggly snapped his Bible shut. "Jesus wouldn't leave me stranded."

"Then why don't you give him a call?" I winked then scurried from the room.

CHAPTER NINE

TIM'S FUNERAL WAS HELD on Saturday afternoon at Saint Patrick's Episcopal Church on Curzon. I was supposed to work three-to-eleven at the hospital, but I switched shifts with Glenda Harrington so I could attend the services.

My whole family insisted on turning out for the event, including Denny, who remembered that Tim had helped him design a Dalmatian costume, the year Denny had won first prize at Pecan Harbor's Volunteer Fire Department annual Halloween party.

Mama had baked an apple pie to take by Tim's parents' house following the services and Aunt Tessa planned to offer them a free afterlife reading if they were interested.

Sissy was unusually subdued, trading in her leather pants and spike studs for a real dress and sensible shoes. The dress was left over from her high school days but at least it was appropriate for the occasion.

I sent a silent prayer to the heavens that my sister had the good sense to tone down her attire. The Kehauls were going through enough turmoil losing a son through such an embarrassing accident without having an Elvira look-alike parading down the church aisles.

"You look nice," I told Sissy as we squeezed into the Honda.

"Don't start with me." She glared.

"What did I say?"

"You wish I always dressed like Queen of the Nerds."

"Well, yes."

"Don't speak another word or I'm in the house and into a gold lamé miniskirt and halter top like that." Sissy snapped her fingers.

"Girls," Mama said, in one of her rare parenting moods. "Stop arguing or we'll be late."

We obeyed.

The aroma of apples, butter and cinnamon permeated the car. The scent was enticing, but I recalled the last pie Mama had made and I hoped she hadn't mistaken salt for sugar again.

Mama sat in the front seat next to me, the foil-wrapped apple pie clutched in her lap. She looked so earnest, as if that pie would wipe away all sorrow. Denny, Sissy and Aunt Tessa were crowded into the backseat. I peered into the rearview mirror and noticed Denny had placed a hand on his mother's knee. But Sissy was preoccupied, staring silently out the window. Aunt Tessa meditated, her lips moving as she softly chanted.

Sadness lumped in my throat. Not just sadness for Tim, but for us, too, so remote from each other even though we were crammed side by side.

How many times had I wished for a normal family? A thousand? ten thousand? a hundred thousand? When I was a teenager I'd been ashamed of my family, but I'd outgrown that. I was sorry that we didn't know each other better. They were all I had and I loved them with an intensity that often frightened me, in spite of the fact we rarely understood one another.

I shifted into first gear and scaled the hill to the main road and a flash of memory flitted through my mind—Tim leaping in front of Conahegg's police car. I caught my breath and sank my top teeth into my bottom lip. Had Conahegg's hitting Tim been a harbinger of bad things to come? Had it only been a week ago?

As a nurse, I often witnessed the fragility of life played out before me in an endless cycle. A patient dies unexpectedly, a child gets cancer. You're here one minute and gone the next, and those remaining behind don't have a clue how to go about closing the gap you left in their lives.

I would miss Tim, I realized.

We arrived at the church at two-forty-five, fifteen minutes before the services were due to commence. We spotted Mr. and Mrs. Kehaul sitting in the front pew and made our way over to offer condolences.

Tim's folks were ordinary, middle-class working people. His mother, Anne Marie, who had once been pretty but had faded to a shade of her former beauty, worked at the DMV. She was dressed in a simple black dress with pearl buttons and a sensible pair of SAS shoes. She clutched a pink handkerchief in one hand, a small black purse in the other and her eyes were red from constant crying.

His father, an insurance adjuster, wore an ill-fitting suit and kept his jaw tightly clenched. He shifted in his seat as if he had a bad case of hemorrhoids. His chin was set like an anvil and he had sad, hound dog eyes.

The Kehauls had been terribly upset when Tim had told them he was gay. They'd tried their best to accept it and although they hadn't really cut him off from their affections, they had asked him to leave their home. His parents' discomfort with his lifestyle disturbed Tim a great deal. He'd been the one to isolate himself from them. Sissy told me she didn't think they had even spoken to each other in months.

Mama went over and held out her hand to Mrs. Kehaul. Anne Marie burst into a fresh round of tears. Her husband patted her awkwardly on the back.

My stomach lurched. I felt bad. Really bad. I wanted to reach out and console them, do something to ease their sorrow. But I had no such power and I knew it. When Denny said he had to pee, I was relieved to shunt him off to the restroom.

"I'm sorry Tim's dead," Denny said. "Did you know some of the kids at school said he was gay?"

"That's true. He was."

"How come he was gay, Aunt Ally?"

I ruffled his hair. "How come you ask so many questions?"

He grinned at me. "Because I have a curious mind."

"No doubt."

I led him through the rectory, not sure where I was going. I'd never been in the church but I figured there had to be bathrooms around here somewhere.

Like most houses of worship the place had the smell of old hymnals and wax candles. The rectory was plain and not aging gracefully. There were water stains on the ceiling and corresponding stains on the carpet.

"Here we are," I said, spying a door marked Gentlemen. "I'll wait right by the door. If there's anyone in there and they try to approach you..."

"I know, I know, Aunt Ally. Stranger danger. But don't worry, we're in church."

So? I wanted to add, but why shatter the boy's illusions. "You scream if you need me."

He gave me a gap-toothed grin and disappeared behind the door.

I clasped my hands behind my back and paced the length of the narrow hallway.

This had to be where they held Sunday school classes. Crayola drawings of Jesus decorated a bulletin board. A calendar of upcoming events hung from one wall. Potluck supper on Wednesday. Ida Mae Baker was bringing her famous

King Ranch Chicken and Lucy Keller had signed up for green beans almondine. There'd be homemade ice cream following the meal. Contact Janice Black if you could spare an extra ice-cream freezer.

Somewhere down the hall and around the corner, a door creaked, then the sound of murmured voices.

I had no intention of eavesdropping. Honest, I didn't. But something drew me toward the noise. I turned the corner and stopped. Several yards away, at the end of a second hallway, a door stood slightly ajar and a light shone through the crack. Cocking my head to one side, I strained to listen.

"I'm serious, Hughes, you better not be pulling a fast one on me," said a rough male voice.

"I'm not, swear to God."

It was Rocky, who clearly missed the irony in his statement. There was no mistaking his whiny tone. Why was Rocky at Tim's funeral? More specifically, why was he in the church rectory and not in the chapel with the others? Who was he with? What were they talking about?

Pressing my back against the wall, I inched closer.

"It's a sure thing," Rocky said. "A can't miss. I'm gonna be rich."

Hmm. Sissy had told me the same thing the night she'd come slinking into the house with Rocky's hickeys adorning her neck.

What was he up to?

"Aunt Ally?" Denny touched my hand and I jumped a good foot.

Exhaling sharply, I clutched my chest. "You scared me to death." I could feel my heart beneath my fingers and it was rat-a-tat-tatting like a machine gun.

"I'm sorry," Denny apologized. "I was wondering what you were doing."

I cast a glance at the partially open door, then pressed my palm to Denny's back. "Nothing, sweetie. Come on, let's get out of here."

As fast as I could, I ushered him toward the chapel, fighting the urge to turn my head and look behind me. When we reached the exit, I could resist no more. I sneaked a peek over my shoulder and saw one of the sheriff's deputies who had been in our garage on the night Sissy had shot Rocky.

He stood with his feet apart in a wide cop stance, his hands on his hips. His eyes met mine. His look was hard.

I remembered his name. Jefferson. He rested his hand on his pistol and nodded slowly in my direction.

My mind swirled at the silent threat. I knew what he had said—keep your big mouth shut.

Denny and I slipped into a pew beside Mama and Aunt Tessa as the service started. I couldn't stop wondering what Rocky and Jefferson were up to. I was intrigued, nervous and a little bit scared. I fingered the strap of my shoulder purse and squirmed in my seat.

The church was packed and I couldn't locate Sissy. Either Tim had a lot of friends or most of Cloverleaf had turned out simply for the curiosity factor.

Somber organ music played. A white casket rested at the front of the church. Numerous flower sprays surrounded the coffin and spilled over onto the floor.

Father Turner took his place at the pulpit. He was a slight man, not more than five-eight or five-nine but good-looking in an unobtrusive way. Dark hair, dark eyes, medium complexion. He possessed the lean rangy look of a long-distance runner. He was young, probably not much older than I and he had a slow, deliberate way of speaking as if carefully weighing each word before letting it drop from his mouth.

The priest spoke of Tim's love for his parents, his family,

his friends. He didn't say anything about Tim's *special* love for men but that was to be expected. We're talking Cloverleaf, not San Francisco.

In the middle of the priest's speech, the back door opened. I turned my head along with most of the congregation to see the late arrivals.

Rockerfeller Hughes entered on crutches, careful not to place any weight on his bandaged foot.

To his left sauntered his wife, Darlene, who was dressed in leather pants two sizes too small and a tie-dyed T-shirt. To his right, hovered Sissy. They were giggling, whispering and nudging each other like teenagers. Instantly, I realized that they were stoned.

Facing forward, I closed my eyes and prayed for strength.

Something crashed.

I opened my eyes and looked back again.

Rocky was sprawled on his back in the middle of the aisle. Darlene and Sissy had their hands clamped over their mouths, struggling not to laugh. Rocky waved his crutch at everyone.

"Sorry," he slurred, grinning like a fool. Not only stoned, but drunk, as well. "I didn't mean to interrupt. Just had a tinsy accident. Go on with the service. We're listenin'."

Father Turner cleared his throat and looked uncertain almost whether to proceed or not. The Kehauls' faces paled, their lips tightening with the strain. At that moment I was very ashamed of my sister. I reached over and gave Denny's hand a reassuring pat.

Sissy and Darlene helped Rocky off the floor and pressed themselves into a crowded pew.

"What's he doing here?" Aunt Tessa leaned over Denny to whisper in my ear. "I thought Rocky and Tim despised each other."

"They did," I whispered back.

"And why is Sissy with him? Didn't they break up?"

I shrugged. There was no explaining my sister.

"Ally," Mama said, getting in on the whispering. "I was thinking of doing a set of monks for my next ceramics project but then I really dislike brown and that's what monks seem to wear. Maybe I'll sculpt innovative monks who believe color is good for the soul. They chose colorful robes—pink and purple and yellow. What do you think?"

"Tim would have liked the idea," I said, trying to remind her where we were and why we were here.

A pensive expression crossed Mama's face. "Why, you're right. Tim would have liked my Rainbow Monks. I think I'll do them as a tribute to him."

"That's nice."

After Father Turner finished, a few others got up to eulogize Tim. His first grade teacher, Mrs. Gault, who spoke of his wonderful finger paintings. His uncle who said he remembered how much Tim had liked to go skinny-dipping in the river. Tim's younger brother, Michael, broke down and started crying halfway through his speech and couldn't finish.

Then Father Turner made a major mistake. He asked if anyone in the congregation wanted to relate their personal memories of Tim.

"I do!" Rocky's hand shot up like a lit rocket.

No. Please God, no. Strike him deaf, dumb and blind. Freeze his tongue to the roof of his mouth.

I could smell trouble as foul as the liquor on Rocky's breath. Apparently, however, Father Turner was not given to my low opinion of Mr. Hughes.

"All right, my son." The priest motioned him toward the altar. "Come on up."

Rocky staggered to his feet, thrust the crutches under his

armpits and limped to the front of the church. I cringed and knotted my fingers into fists.

What was he going to say?

Father Turner stood aside and Rocky maneuvered himself to the pulpit. "Hey," he said and the microphone squawked, causing half the congregation to clamp their hands over their ears.

Aunt Tessa rested her chin on my shoulder and mumbled, "Do you think Tim is turning over in that coffin?"

"You're the psychic, you tell me."

"He is." Aunt Tessa nodded, completely serious.

"I wanna say," Rocky continued, struggling to balance on the crutches, "that although me and Timmy boy had our differences, I recently came to realize what an interesting sex life he had."

A gasp went up from the crowd.

I sank my face into my hands.

"That's right." Rocky nodded. "But his death has brought me a greater appreciation of my own life. And I can't wait to party."

Rocky's band and sundry other riffraff friends who'd gathered in the back of the church started cackling and making rude noises.

I raised my head, my gut twisting in pain for the humiliation the Kehauls were undoubtedly feeling. Then I glanced across the church and saw *him* standing in the shadows of a thick wooden support column.

Sheriff Samuel J. Conahegg.

Our eyes met.

My treacherous heart leaped.

He nodded his head slightly in acknowledgment, the vaguest of smiles curving his lips.

For one interminable second, I stopped breathing. Damn. I'd been trying for days to get him off my mind and just when I was succeeding at blocking him out, here he was.

He wore his uniform. Gun at the hip and radio in his back pocket. He had his arms crossed over his chest and a circumspect expression on his face.

A shiver passed through me.

"Uh, thank you," Father Turner was saying. Having realized his mistake, he was trying to hustle Rocky off the podium.

"Dudes," Rocky said, grabbing the microphone. "I mean it. Party at Sissy Green's place on the river. Everybody come."

I shot to my feet and shouted, "No!" before I even knew what I had intended. "There will be no party at our house." I threw a particularly harsh glare at the crowd in the back and I was aware that every eye in the place was on me. "A young man has died, people. Have some respect."

A hush fell over the church.

I sat back down.

Father Turner managed to wrestle the microphone away from Rocky. The frazzled priest set about trying to smooth things over, giving details about the interment, and asking the pallbearers to report to the front of the church.

Grinning at the mess he'd stirred up, Rocky started back down the aisle. He flipped me the bird as he went by.

"My goodness, Ally," Mama asked, "what was that about?"

Then Sissy was standing beside me. "I can't believe you embarrassed me like that. I told Rocky he could throw a wake for Tim at our house."

"You had no right to do that." I was so angry my hands shook.

"It's my house, too."

"No, it's not. Daddy left it to me and you don't even pay rent. I will not allow you to tarnish Tim's memory."

"Fine." Sissy tossed her head. "If that's the way you want it, then Denny and I will be moving by the end of the month."

That wasn't what I wanted. But part of me whispered, *Let her go, it's been a long time coming.*

"I'm tired of you trying to run my life." Sissy glared.

The murmuring crowd milled around us. More than anything in the world I wanted out of that church and away from my sister before I gave in to temptation and smacked her across the mouth.

Sissy grabbed Denny by the hand and, dragging him behind her, flounced away.

Denny sent me a desperate look that said, Help!

"Wait." I started after her but a hand on my shoulder stopped me.

CHAPTER TEN

"HELLO THERE."

I looked up to see Conahegg. What terrific timing.

"What do you want?"

Conahegg suppressed a grin. "With that attitude I can see why you're still single."

"I've had a rough morning. Have you got something to say?" Don't ask me why I was cranky with him, maybe it was because blood was strumming through my veins like an erupting volcano at the weight of his hand on my shoulder. Maybe it was because I felt helplessly out of control in the face of my hormonal reaction to him. Or maybe it was simply because I wanted to kiss him more than anything in the world and I wasn't going to have the chance.

"She talks tough," Mama said, extending her palm to Conahegg. "But it's an act. She's really soft as duck down."

Conahegg's gray eyes glittered at me. "I'll have to keep that in mind. It's nice to see you again, Mrs. Green." He took Mama's hand and had the effrontery to kiss it.

Show-off.

Mama giggled.

Wonderful. There was only one thing that could have made the funeral worse. If Reverend Ray Don Swiggly had been officiating it. *That* would have placed the cherry on the dung cake.

"What are you doing here?" I snapped at Conahegg. I

needed someone to take my frustrations out on and he was closest. Not to mention that he was the very source of my sexual frustrations.

"Paying my respects."

I eyed him suspiciously, not sure whether I believed him or not. That had been his deputy I'd heard talking to Rocky in the rectory. Something was going on. I recalled what Maddie Farnsworth had said about trouble in the sheriff's department and wondered what it meant. Could Rocky and Jefferson be in cahoots on a drug deal?

"Let's go," I said to Mama and Aunt Tessa.

"You're not really throwing Sissy and Denny out of the house, are you?" Aunt Tessa asked.

I shook my head.

"Sheriff Conahegg," my mother asked in her most sugary Southern accent. "We have a delicious apple pie in the car. Would you care to go on a dessert picnic with us at Cleveland Park?"

What on earth? That pie was supposed to be for the Kehauls. And what in the heck was my mother doing inviting Conahegg on a picnic?

"Homemade apple pie?" Conahegg hitched a finger in his belt loop.

I caught his eye and emphatically shook my head. "Don't you have work to do?"

He fixed his flint gaze on me and said, "I set my own hours." Then to Mama, he replied, "Why sure, Mrs. Green, I'd love to have pie with you in the park."

"You're gonna regret it," I muttered low enough so only he could hear. "She has a tendency to use salt instead of sugar in her recipes."

"I'll take my chances," Conahegg whispered back.

"What are you planning on using for plates and forks and

napkins?" I asked Mama the minute we got into the car. "And what on earth possessed you to invite the sheriff for pie?"

"He's good-looking, polite and he likes you."

"He does not!" I denied but my face heated.

"Well, he would if you tried a little harder to be nice to him. When was the last time you went on a date, daughter?"

"Don't start with me."

"Why not? I think Sam would make a wonderful son-in-law."

"No way. Not ever. Uh-uh. Forget it."

"Why not?"

"Oh for starters he's arrogant, high-handed, opinionated and totally bent on getting his own way."

"Methinks the lady doth protest too much," Mama quoted.

"At the risk of changing the subject, what are we going to use for utensils?" My pulse was jumping like a squid in a pond full of piranha at the thought of having dessert with Conahegg.

"Ally—" Mama clicked her tongue "—do you know what your problem is?"

"No, but I'm sure you're about to tell me."

"You have no romance in your soul."

"Come again?"

Mama rummaged in the glove compartment. "Ta-da!" she said, pulling out a box of straws.

I rolled my eyes. "What are we going to do with those?"

"Use them as forks, silly." Mama shook her head. "And we can eat right out of the pie pan."

"I'm stopping by 7-Eleven," I announced. I needed more than plastic forks and paper plates—although I didn't often drink, a six-pack was looking really good right now.

I pulled into the 7-Eleven parking lot. Conahegg parked beside me and cranked down his window. I did the same.

"Detour?" he asked.

"Beer run," I replied.

"Funny. I never pegged you for a drinker."

"Normally, I'm not." I got out of the car, very aware of his gaze on my butt as I sashayed into the store.

Okay, so I put a little more roll into my hips than usual. Might as well show him what he was never going to have.

I got my purchases, sans the beer, having decided I needed my wits about me if I was going to have pie with Conahegg, returned to the car then drove over to Cleveland Park.

There's a picnic area, tennis and basketball courts, swings and slides for kids to play on. I thought of Denny and got a twinge of conscience. I wished I hadn't let Sissy take him off with her.

"Let's get that picnic table in the shade," Mama said, trailing off toward a stone table under an aging elm, the pie nestled in the crook of her arm.

Conahegg got out of the car and grabbed my elbow before I could follow my mother and Aunt Tessa. "I like your hair," he said.

"Really."

"It looks sexy."

I raised a hand to pat my new hairdo, flattered that he'd noticed but determined not to be swept off my feet by his attention. I had no idea where I stood with him. None whatsoever. Did he even like me? Sometimes it seemed yes, other times no.

"I want to tell you something," he said.

"Oh?" I lifted an eyebrow.

"I'm proud of what you did back there in the church, standing up for yourself against your sister and her boyfriend."

"No big deal."

"For you it was." He smiled. How did he know so darned much about me? "You don't like to hurt the people you love so you usually let them roll right over you."

"And what makes you think that?"

"My mother used to be the same way," he said. "A people pleaser to the detriment of her own wants and needs. You won't know true freedom, Ally, until you learn to stand up for yourself."

"Thanks for your unsolicited opinion." I wrenched my elbow from his grip. Damn, one minute he was nice, the next he was telling me how to run my life.

What was wrong with me? Why was I so attracted to him? I liked guys who, well…needed me and I had the distinct impression Conahegg had never needed anyone.

"Ally, bring the plates," my mother called.

We sat around the picnic table eating Mama's apple pie. Surprisingly, it turned out to be very good. Conahegg had three helpings. I eyed him and wondered how he managed to keep his rock-hard figure even with regular workouts at the gym.

"Excellent pie, Mrs. Green." Conahegg patted his belly.

"Thank you, Sam." My mother blushed prettily. "And please, call me, Amelia."

"All right, then, Amelia."

Why was Conahegg trying to win brownie points with my mom? To impress me? Ha. Little did he know I was already impressed, much to my own chagrin.

"I've got to be getting back to work," he said. "Ally, why don't you walk me to my car."

"What for?"

"I'd like to speak with you a moment."

Oh my gosh, he's going to ask me out.

I was both thrilled and terrified. Then I remembered the last time I'd thought he was going to ask me out. Instead he told me I had mozzarella cheese on my chin. Quickly, I swiped a palm across my face to make sure I wasn't wearing pie crust.

"Go on." Aunt Tessa gave me a push.

Reluctantly, I followed Conahegg to his automobile. I was nervous about being alone with him and not sure why.

Don't ask me out, don't ask me out, don't ask me out, I mentally chanted but by the time we reached his car it had somehow turned into—do ask me out, do ask me out, do ask me out.

He stopped, slipped on his Ray-Ban shades and leaned against the hood. He put one foot over the other, crossed his arms at his chest and peered at me through his mirrored aviator sunglasses. At least I think he was peering at me. I couldn't really see his eyes.

"Yeah," I said, feeling a little confrontational and anxious to hide my real feelings from him. "What is it?"

"Are you always so testy?"

"Only when I'm being grilled by a cop." By a good-looking cop who makes me think naughty sexual thoughts. Damn! I felt powerless and I hate feeling powerless.

"I'm not grilling you."

"If I were a halibut I'd be blackened to a crisp."

He grinned. "Good one."

"So what's the deal?" I shifted my weight.

"Would you happen to know where Rocky buys his marijuana?"

I stared at him. "No. I'm not privy to Rocky's secret inner life, thank God."

"But your sister is."

"Well, she doesn't usually say things like—'Hey Ally, Rocky and I are going over to his dealer's house, want us to pick you up a couple bags of Colombian Gold?'—if that's what you're asking."

Conahegg ran a hand through his hair. "I'm handling this badly."

"Oh, I get it," I said, remembering what Maddie

Farnsworth had told me. "You think one of your deputies is dealing from the evidence room."

He arched an eyebrow in surprise. "How did you hear about that?"

"I know you've been away for a long time, Sheriff, but Cloverleaf is still a very small town."

"You're right and I don't want to fight with you."

"Are we fighting?"

"Seems like we're always at cross-purposes." His mouth tipped upward. "That was never my intention."

What was his intention? I gulped.

"Listen, Ally, as far as you know, did Tim do drugs?"

"No. His vices ran along other lines." I forced my mind to stay on the business at hand.

"That's what I thought. We didn't find any kind of drug paraphernalia in his trailer."

I wagged my finger in the air. "Do you think Tim's death is somehow connected to the problems in your department?"

"Not at all," Conahegg said smoothly, but it made me wonder.

I thought of the deputy I had overheard talking to Rocky in the church. I almost said something to Conahegg about it, but I had no proof of anything so I kept my mouth shut.

"If you don't mind, could you put out some feelers about Rocky's drug connection? Maybe ask your sister a few subtle questions."

"All right."

"If you find out anything, let me know." He fished a business card from his shirt pocket and handed it to me. "My home number is on the back. Feel free to call me any time of the day or night."

Palming his card, I casually flipped my hand over, saw a number scrawled in pencil. I got a strange feeling, as if my lungs weren't filling properly. Any time of the day or night? Meaning?

Conahegg's expression was deadpan. I couldn't read a darn thing in his face. "I'd appreciate any help you could give me."

"Okay." I didn't know what else to say.

He unfurled his arms and got in the car. He didn't smile or wave. He simply backed out and left me standing there, uncertain what to do next.

SISSY TORE INTO the driveway about ten o'clock that night, opened the car door and let Denny out, then took off again without coming inside.

I met my nephew on the porch. He had a disgusted expression on his face. I slung an arm around his shoulder. "How you doing, tough guy?"

He shrugged.

"Don't want to talk about it?" I gently ruffled his hair.

"Me and Mom had a fight."

"What about?" I tried to keep my voice light. I didn't want the kid to think I was quizzing him about Sissy's whereabouts.

"That stupid Rocky dude."

"Where did you guys go?"

"To look at some house to rent. Mom said we were going to move in there with Rocky, but I told her I didn't want to." He paused a moment. "It was a real nice house, though. Had a swimming pool in the backyard and a basketball court."

"Where was the house located?"

"Over by the high school."

In Mira Vista Estates? Most of those homes boasted price tags of over two hundred thousand dollars. There was no way Sissy could afford to rent a place in that area of town. Another fine example of my sister's illogical thought processes.

"Then what did you do?" I asked, ushering him inside and locking the door behind us.

"Then we got a pizza and went over to Rocky's place." Denny made a face. "What a roach motel. That's when me and Mom got into the fight."

"Oh." I waited, hoping he would go on without my having to prompt him.

"They went in the back to watch some video on the television in Rocky's bedroom. They left me stuck in that yucky living room with nothing to do."

"I'm sorry, Denny." We went into the kitchen and I poured him a glass of milk. He sat at the bar, his legs kicking against the bar stool.

What had Sissy and Rocky really been up to in that bedroom? Smoking pot? Watching porn movies? I shuddered. Surely, not even Sissy would do such irresponsible things with her son in the very next room.

What was I going to do about my sister?

"Then a little while later Mom came into the living room and she was crying. I asked what was wrong but she wouldn't tell me." Denny's face darkened. "I thought that stupid Rocky had been mean to her or something, so I started yellin' at him."

"Did he hurt you, Denny?"

"No. He told Mom to get me out of there. So she brought me home. She said I have to be nice to Rocky, that he might be my new Daddy. I told her no way in hell and she slapped me." Tears collected in the corners of Denny's eyes but he fiercely swiped them away.

No, Sissy, no. My sister was in deep trouble and I didn't know the full extent of it.

I sent Denny to bed, then I went into Sissy's bedroom. A lot of her clothes were missing and so was a suitcase. She must have come back after Tim's funeral and packed while Mama and Aunt Tessa and I were picnicking with Conahegg.

In her address book I found Rocky's phone number and called his trailer. It rang and rang and rang.

Damn. They were probably out somewhere getting drunk.

I threw the receiver back on the hook and then, not knowing what else to do, I called Conahegg.

CHAPTER ELEVEN

"HELLO."

At the sound of his husky voice that held the same smooth bite as expensive brandy, I almost hung up.

"Hello?" he said again, demanding that I answer.

"Um...hi." I sank onto the edge of Sissy's bed, and twisted the phone cord around my index finger until it turned dusky.

"Allegheny?"

I was inordinately pleased that he'd recognized my voice with so little to go on.

"Yes. Can you talk?" I untwisted my finger and shook my hand to get the blood circulating.

"Hang on a minute. I've got a potpie in the oven."

I heard him settle the phone against what sounded like a countertop. He was talking to me from the kitchen, I deduced. Poor thing. Reduced to eating tasteless frozen dinners from a box. If I were there I'd make him my special chicken potpie with homemade crust and a tossed salad on the side.

"Okay," he said, "I'm back."

"You're eating awfully late." I could imagine him standing in the kitchen. His hair was damp from a shower and sticking up in spiky clumps. Was he in his underwear? I wondered. Or maybe even naked? My heart beat faster.

"Yeah, well, I left work late, then I had to cook and debone the chicken before putting the pie together."

"You made it yourself? From scratch?" So much for my domestic fantasy of feeding Sheriff Burly He-Man. Still, I was impressed that he had made his own chicken potpie. My daydream shifted a little. In my mind's eye he remained naked, but now he wore an apron that read: KISS THE COOK.

"I cheated a little," he admitted. "I used Pillsbury ready-made crust. And I bought the vegetables already cut up."

Ah! He wasn't perfect after all.

"So, what can I do for you?" he asked.

Besides raise my core body temperature and drive me wild with desire? "I need to talk to you."

"Fire when ready."

I heard a chair scrape against a tile floor. I closed my eyes, licked my lips. He was pulling out the kitchen chair, sitting down. The KISS THE COOK apron fell strategically across his bare lap barely covering his large…

"Ally? You still there?"

"Huh?" I felt dazed. Like someone jerked from a deep sleep.

"You okay? You sound…funny."

Try horny, fella.

"Fine, just fine," I muttered, struggling to keep my mind on the topic at hand and off Conahegg's imaginary anatomy. I kicked off my shoes, scooted to the middle of Sissy's bed and tucked my legs beneath me.

"Where are you at?" he asked.

"I'm home."

"Where at home?"

"In bed."

"Ah." His voice cracked.

Startled, I realized Conahegg might be having a few late-night fantasies of his own. The thought revved me up like a finely tuned car engine. Goose bumps spread across my arms.

"What are you wearing?"

Oh my gosh! Obviously he'd misinterpreted the meaning of my call. Time to jump in and tell him about Sissy, to nip the wayward conversation in the bud.

"Or are you wearing anything at all?"

My cheeks flamed. I glanced down at my faded, comfy, frumpy pj's with the top button missing and the grape jelly stain on the collar. I could tell the truth and bring our little tête-à-tête to a screeching halt or I could play along and see where it might lead.

"A negligee," I lied and heard a gulp from the other end of the line. I unfurled my legs, lay back against the pillow.

"What color?"

I could see him. His sweaty hand clasping the receiver, the KISS THE COOK apron making a tent big enough for a family of circus dwarfs to camp beneath.

"Scarlet," I said, rubbing my palm along my feverish neck. "With black lace trim."

He hissed in his breath as if he'd been scalded.

"Black garters and thigh-high stockings," I embellished.

He growled.

"Crimson stiletto heels."

"Stop!" he commanded in his cop voice.

My hand, which had somehow crept from my neck to my belly, froze in place.

Silence hung like a marble curtain.

Then, we both spoke at once, in a rush.

"I didn't mean..."

"I'm sorry..."

Conahegg laughed. A rueful, rough noise that sent fresh shivers clamoring down my spine.

"Listen," he said.

I pricked up my ears. "Yes?"

"I'm glad you called. There's something I wanted to say to you."

"Oh?" The word came out in a whispery Marilyn Monroe whoosh.

"I owe you an apology."

"What for?"

"For my behavior just now and for the other day. At the gym."

"What do you mean?"

"You greeted me cheerfully and I barely even acknowledged your presence."

"You were busy. I shouldn't have interrupted the weight training."

"No," he said. "That wasn't it."

"What was it?"

"You. Ally, you looked so damned hot in those skintight bicycle shorts and that skimpy little sport bra it was all I could do to keep from…"

"Yes?"

"Never mind."

"No, go ahead." I fanned myself with my naughty hand. It had been a very long time since a man I was interested in had talked to me in such a frankly sexual manner. The sensations jolting through me were at once both extremely arousing and quite terrifying. I could lose myself in a man like Conahegg. That idea frightened me. Suddenly, I realized why I'd always been attracted to passive, brooding artistic types. Those guys I could control. They were safe.

Conahegg was not.

"I'm not going to pretend I don't feel something for you, because I do."

"You do?" I parroted.

"Yes. But I'm not the kind of guy who beats around the bush. This is a bad time for me. Both professionally and personally. I know you like me, too, and I don't want to lead you on. I really can't get involved in anything serious. But if you're not opposed to something casual…"

"Excuse me?" He was offering me a fling. A wild, hot affair. He didn't want to meld with me mind, body and soul. He wanted a quick roll in the hay. I should have been relieved. Instead, I was incensed. "Who do you think you are, you arrogant—"

"That's why you called, wasn't it?" He sounded bewildered. "You were the one who mentioned crimson stilettos."

Guilty as charged. And regretting it more with each passing second. What to do? Try to get the conversation back on a proper footing and tell him about Sissy? Or simply hang up and pretend the whole thing never happened.

"Your ego, Sheriff Conahegg, is bigger than the state of Texas." I sniffed. "What on earth makes you think I'd have an affair with you?"

"Lust?" he said, his tone hopeful.

"Think again, smart guy."

"Well, if you didn't call to chat with me, what did you call for?"

"I need to tell you what Sissy's been up to. I think Rocky's got her involved in something shady." I swallowed. What I had to say next was really tough for me. "I need your help."

"You? You're asking for help?"

"Don't rub it in," I snapped.

"Sorry. Please, go on. Tell me about your sister."

If I hadn't been so concerned for Sissy's welfare, I might have told him to forget it. But I thought of the night she'd gotten beat up in the parking lot. I gulped down my pride and related to him everything Denny had told me.

"Would you like me to go talk to Hughes? See if I can shake him up? Tell him to stay away from Sissy?"

"That'd be great."

"Consider it done. Oh, and, Ally."

"Uh-huh?"

"I'm really sorry I'm not in a position to pursue a relationship with you."

"I never said I wanted one."

"I know. But another time, another place, I think maybe we could have had something great."

SISSY DIDN'T COME HOME all weekend, nor Monday, either. Conahegg called me on Sunday afternoon to say Rocky hadn't been home when he'd dropped by to see him. We didn't talk about the *other* thing on both our minds and I hung up really quickly before he decided to bring it up.

Tuesday, I had to do a home health visit on Rocky and there was no way around it. I dreaded the showdown, but it was long overdue. Driving down the same road to Andover Bend that I'd traveled the previous week, I experienced a weird sense of déjà vu.

When I reached Rocky's trailer, I parked on the bare dirt yard, took a deep breath and peered over at Tim's place. The shoddy trailer looked sad and forlorn. I shook my head over Tim's wasted life and girded my loins for the battle before me.

Rocky's rickety steps creaked under my weight. The screen door hung half off its hinges. I pushed it aside and pounded on the aluminum front door. I prayed Sistine wasn't in there with him, even though I desperately wanted to find her. As much as we fight, I love my sister. More than anything in the world I'd love to see her happy and settled. Although Sissy seemed to believe otherwise.

I waited.

And waited.

"Criminey, not again," I muttered. "The louse is probably

either stoned or drunk or both and passed out like a brick." Resolutely, I turned the knob and the door opened.

"Rocky," I shouted, unable to shake the feeling that I'd been through the scenario before. "It's Ally. Is Sistine in there with you?" I certainly didn't want to catch them doing the horizontal bop.

I stepped into the foyer. If you can call it that. It was a twelve-inch circle of parquet that blended into filthy brown carpeting.

Yuck. I saw what Denny meant by calling the place a roach motel. Actually, roach motel was a compliment.

The room was almost totally dark save for the light bleeding in from the opened door. Blankets had been draped over the windows in place of curtains. I had fleeting thoughts of vampires and shuddered.

A guitar lay in the middle of the floor, alongside a high-tech video camera on a tripod. I wondered where Rocky had gotten such expensive equipment and what he'd been doing with it.

Another shiver rippled down my spine as I considered a disgusting possibility. Had Sissy and Rocky been making their own dirty movies?

"Anybody home?" I was surprised to hear my voice quiver.

Nada.

In that instant Tim's naked, hanging body flashed into my mind's eye.

"Rocky!" I inched through the living room and pulled a blanket from one window to let in more light. Dust flew everywhere. I sneezed.

Still no response.

The urge to leave was strong. But I had to discover where my sister had gone. Maybe at least I could find a clue to Sissy's whereabouts.

I took a deep breath and regretted it. The place smelled to high heaven of rotten garbage. An indolent blowfly buzzed around the ceiling.

Unwillingly, I moved deeper into the trailer house, skirting the maze of filth. A couch with the stuffing coming out of it, apparently doubled as a storage closet. There were stacks of clothes and girlie magazines and worn-out sneakers strewn over the cushion. Across from the couch rested a television set and beside it, a broken-down La-Z-Boy recliner as encumbered by debris as the couch.

Obviously, Rocky wasn't lurking in the living room. Unless he was hiding under those dirty clothes. I could see the kitchen from where I stood and he wasn't in there, either.

"Rockerfeller Hughes," I raised my voice but I was beginning to suspect Rocky wasn't home even though his battered pickup truck, the bed littered with A&W root beer cans and whiskey bottles, was parked outside.

I kicked aside more aluminum cans and pizza boxes littering the floor. I wrinkled my nose against the stench. Cripes, why in the world had Sissy brought Denny here? What was she thinking? Did she ever stop to ask herself what she was doing in a place like this with a guy like Rocky?

Sissy was pretty and she could have any man she wanted—well, if she took out the nose ring and the tongue stud. How come she was always attracted to bad boys?

I peeked down the hallway.

Not another closed bedroom door.

"Rocky!" I fairly screamed, praying he'd come staggering out of that bedroom. Hair sticking straight up, scratching his crotch, peering at me with bleary, bloodshot eyes.

But he didn't.

There wasn't a sound. Not a peep. Not a whisper. Not even a belch.

"No," I whimpered. "I'm not going to look inside that bedroom." But even as I was denying my intentions, I was creeping for that door.

I kept thinking about those awful teenage slasher movies where the too-stupid-to-live heroine blithely goes into the spooky dark basement to look for her friends while the entire audience is screaming for her to get the hell out of the house.

But a curiosity I couldn't deny compelled me. What lay beyond the door?

When I got closer, I saw the door stood slightly ajar.

"Rocky?" I whispered but I wasn't expecting an answer.

I nudged the door with my foot. It swung silently open.

There was someone or something sitting on the floor beside the headboard.

Gulping, I flipped on the light.

It wasn't as dramatic as finding Tim's body. Honestly, at first I thought Rocky really was deep in a drunken stupor and had rolled off the bed. He had the sheet over his face and he was naked with one hand resting in his lap.

"Hey," I said, my voice wobbling a little. "Wake up."

He didn't move.

"Rocky?"

The apprehension was back, along with a huge knot in my chest. I moved toward the bed and as I got a better look I realized his body was stiff.

Rigor mortis.

Oh, boy.

I leaned over and lifted the sheet from his face, felt the same shocky kick I'd felt when I'd discovered Tim's body.

I let out a soft cry and backpedaled, running smack into the wall, my hand over my mouth.

Rockerfeller Hughes's face was black. His tongue lolling obscenely. His eyes bulging.

Then I saw it. The belt. One end looped around the bed post. The other end around his neck.

"Here we go again," I whispered and sank to the floor.

"WE'VE GOT TO STOP meeting like this," Conahegg said.

"Har, har. Ever thought about becoming a stand-up comedian?"

"You look pale."

I didn't want or need his concern. Especially when I could tell that he was restraining himself from reaching over and touching my cheek. I wasn't getting involved with a commitment phobic man. Nub-uh, not me. "Stumbling across two bodies in less than a week can do that to a girl."

"Do you always get testy when you're upset?"

"Always," I assured him.

"That's nice to know. For future reference."

I wanted to say "What future?" but I didn't. The less said about our aborted phone sex on Saturday night the better.

We were sitting in his patrol car with the engine idling, while his deputies went through the house. He had the air conditioner going full blast, the vents turned on me.

"Do you want some water?" Conahegg asked. "I've got some on ice."

I nodded. How had he known my throat felt like parchment paper? He was anticipating my needs much too well. I wished he'd stop being so solicitous, but I was too thirsty to stand on principles.

He got out and rummaged around in the trunk then brought an Igloo cooler, the kind they transport organs in, back inside with him.

Opening the box, he pulled a bottle of water from the ice, wiped the outside with a handkerchief, twisted off the top and passed it over to me.

"Thanks." I took a long swallow, concentrated on drinking the icy water, purposely ignoring Conahegg's gaze on my face.

"Ally, things don't have to be awkward between us because of our phone conversation."

Conahegg was one to take the bull by the horns, never mind that you might get gored.

"Let's not go there." I stared out the window at the dried yellow grass.

"All right."

More silence. I polished off the water.

"Do you know where your sister is?" he asked.

I shook my head. "Haven't seen her since she dropped Denny off after Tim's funeral." *Since Saturday night.* "Why?"

"Just curious," he said, but I saw the muscle in his jaw jump. That twitch gave him away. He wasn't being completely honest with me. What was he hiding?

"So," I ventured, setting the empty water bottle between us. "What do you think is going on here? Isn't autoerotic asphyxiation relatively rare? And we've got two guys who lived across the street from each other dead within a week. Doesn't that seem a little suspicious to you?"

Conahegg shrugged, his face still unreadable. He might have been happy, despondent, joyous, lustful or mad. I couldn't tell.

It bothered me how quickly he could shut himself down. A trick he learned in the Marines no doubt, and the skill obviously served him well in his job as sheriff. But I couldn't help wondering how he managed to suppress his feelings like a highly trained actor switching roles.

Me, even when I tried to cut off my emotions, the best I could muster was to make my feelings small like the old-time television sets that faded to a white dot. A dot that lingered for hours on the screen after the power was off.

What happened to his emotions? Did they become such a muddy amalgamation in the back of his brain that he never authentically felt anything? I found the thought disconcerting.

"I figure Rocky heard about Tim's erotic adventure and decided to experiment for himself. With the same disastrous results," Conahegg said. "But it's a supposition."

"You're a guy, tell me, how common is it to try and hang yourself while flogging the dolphin?"

A smile flitted briefly across his lips and I felt inordinately pleased I'd provoked the response in him.

"Flogging the dolphin? Colorful language."

"Figure of speech."

He studied me a moment. The smile gone. "Supposedly the orgasms you reach when your air supply is cut off are tremendous."

"Really?"

His eyes met mine. I couldn't believe I was discussing orgasms with him. "But I wouldn't know firsthand."

"No pun intended?" Suddenly the car was very hot despite the frosty air-conditioning shooting through the vents.

Damn that halfway smile of his. He used it like a razor-sharp knife to slice through my heart. But I didn't trust the smile. Not for a minute. "Pun intended."

"Oh."

"Why don't you go on home? You can drop by the office later and give me a full statement. I'll be working late tonight, so whatever time is convenient for you."

"Okay." I nodded, thankful for the reprieve. Home sounded very welcoming.

"Can you drive yourself? I could have a deputy take you home."

"I'm all right," I said, but was I?

When I got to the house, however, I was surprised, but extremely relieved to see Sissy's car in the driveway. Then my stomach lurched. Might as well get this over with.

I found her in the kitchen giving Aunt Tessa a perm.

"Hey," I said, dropping my purse in a chair and trying to act nonchalant. I wanted to hug Sissy and shake her at the same time.

"Sissy came home." Aunt Tessa grinned, stating the obvious.

Sissy blatantly ignored me, still pissed off about what happened at Tim's funeral I was guessing. I was tempted to lecture her for abandoning Denny for three days but I held my tongue. I didn't want her to run off again.

"I've got more bad news," I said.

"I knew it." Aunt Tessa nodded. "I found a black widow spider in my shoe this morning. That's always a bad omen."

"Actually, it means we need to call the exterminator," I said.

"Don't belittle her intuition," Sissy snapped. "You think you're so much better than the rest of us."

"I do not."

"Hmmph."

"Sissy, you better put that perm solution down and have a seat."

For an instant real fear flashed in her eyes as if somehow she knew what I was going to tell her, then it was immediately replaced by her usual defiance. "Don't tell me what to do."

"I don't want you to screw up Aunt Tessa's hair. Sit down."

"You think…" Sissy started.

But Aunt Tessa must have seen something in my face. She held up a hand. "Sit down and shut up, Sissy."

Amazingly, my sister obeyed.

"Okay. What's the big news?"

I took a deep breath. I couldn't believe I was having to tell her two of her boyfriends had died in one week. It certainly wasn't any easier the second time around. I tried to take her hand in mine but she pulled back.

"Just tell me."

"Rocky's dead."

Her face went totally blank then she said, "I don't believe you."

"It's true."

Her bottom lip began to quiver, then her whole body shook. I went to her and wrapped my arms around her shoulders. "I'm so sorry."

"No, you're not." She pushed me away. "You hated him."

"I hated what he did to you, yes. But I never wanted to see him dead. In fact, I sort of felt sorry for him when you shot him in the toe."

She laid her head on the table and sobbed.

I paced, not knowing what to say or how to soothe her. My heart ached for what she was going through. But Sissy never turned to me for comfort. Not since we were kids.

Aunt Tessa was sitting at the table, a plastic apron tied around her neck, her hair rolled in tight curls. "How did it happen?"

"Same as Tim."

"You mean…" Aunt Tessa placed a hand at her throat and pantomimed choking.

"I'm afraid so."

"No!" Sissy howled and lifted her head. Her nose was running. I reached in my pocket for a Kleenex and handed it to her but she ignored it and ran her forearm under her nose. Heaven forbid she would even take a tissue from me.

I nodded. "Autoerotic asphyxiation."

She shook her head violently. "No. That's impossible."

"I found his body, Sissy. He had one end of the rope tied around the bedpost and the other around his neck. He was naked."

"Rocky could not have hung himself," Sissy ground out through gritted teeth.

"But he did."

"God, you always have to be right, don't you."

"No, Sissy…"

"You're dead wrong." She was screaming. Her eyes flashed wild.

"I was there. I know what I saw."

"All right then Miss Smart-ass. Do you remember that scar on Rocky's neck?"

I recalled the faded thin red scars that marked his larynx. "Yes."

"And he always wore his shirts unbuttoned or with the neck cut out?"

"Uh-huh."

"When he was a kid a horse ran him under a clothesline and almost decapitated him. He was in the hospital for a month and he developed a terrible fear of having anything around his neck. He doesn't even like to be hugged. Once, when we were at a luau party and some woman tried to put a lei around his neck Rocky came completely unglued."

"What?"

"Yeah. Would someone with that kind of fear experiment with autoerotic asphyxiation? I think not," Sissy crowed.

Stunned, I stared at her.

"That's right. Contrary to popular opinion, you *don't* know everything."

Now that she reminded me I remembered times Sissy had started to hug Rocky around the neck but he'd twisted her arms away. I'd thought it was because he didn't like showing her affection.

"He didn't hang himself," Sissy insisted.

I was confused. Nothing made sense. I fumbled for a chair and sat down. Aunt Tessa and I exchanged glances. She shook her head.

If Rocky hadn't accidentally taken his own life playing at autoerotic asphyxiation, how had he really died?

"Sissy," I whispered. "If Rocky didn't accidentally kill himself, what does this mean?"

Sissy stared me in the face. "I don't know."

"Could he have been murdered?"

She started to shake anew.

"Did someone make it look like autoerotic asphyxiation so everyone would think it was an accident?" Conahegg had assumed exactly that. "Someone who didn't know Rocky was terrified of having anything placed around his neck."

My sister whimpered and drew her knees to her chest.

"Sissy, is Dooley Marchand involved?"

"N…no," she denied. "Rocky had made arrangements to pay Dooley."

"How was he planning on doing that?"

She hugged herself and avoided my eye. I reached out, took her chin in my hand and forced her to look at me. "Sissy, what was Rocky involved in?"

"I don't know."

"Please, don't lie to me."

"I'm not lying. It's just that…" She bit her bottom lip.

"It's just what?"

"Nothing."

"Oh, no. You're not getting off that easy."

Sissy jumped to her feet. "Back off, Ally. You don't know what you're dealing with?"

"Do you?" I asked.

But she'd already run from the kitchen, slamming the back door closed in my face.

In the past, I would have let her go, smug in the knowledge that I was in control, that she needed me and would eventually come crawling back. But lately I'd been forced to take a hard look at myself and my part in allowing Sissy's irresponsible behavior to continue. It wasn't pretty.

I couldn't leave things unresolved. Sissy had been running from her problems for too long. Conahegg was right. It was time I stopped making excuses for her. Time we both faced up to our faults.

Resolutely pulling open the back door, I followed her.

CHAPTER TWELVE

"SISSY," I CALLED. "Wait. Please, let's talk."

My sister was stalking toward the dock. "Let me alone."

I hurried to catch up with her. "I can't. It's too important. You've got to tell me what's going on. I know you're in some kind of trouble…."

She plopped down in a lawn chair and glowered at me darkly. "You don't know anything."

"What's Rocky got you tangled up in? You can tell me."

"Ha!"

I sat in another chair beside her. "I'm here to help."

"Since when? My whole life you've been bossing me around. Nothing I do ever pleases you."

"It's only because I care that I'm so hard on you." I reached out to stroke her arm but she gave me a withering look and I backed off.

She stared out at the river, not looking at me or speaking.

"You're right," I said, unable to endure the silence. "You're right. I am bossy."

"And overbearing."

"Not all the time."

A faint smile curled her lips adorned with black lipstick. I itched to pull a tissue from my pocket and wipe it away. "You have your good moments," she conceded grudgingly.

"Thank you."

"But you've got to stop trying to fix everything for me."

"Do I do that?"

"Constantly. I mean I know I'm a screwup. But at least they're my mistakes. I own them."

"I don't get you."

"I know," she said and, a single tear slid down her cheek. "That's the whole problem. You've never understood me."

What could I say? She was right.

"Why do you pick such rotten guys, Sissy? Why do you let men treat you so badly?"

She shrugged and turned her head. "I don't know."

"Don't you?"

"I guess," she whispered in a small voice, "it's because I feel like I don't deserve better."

"That's ridiculous." I snorted.

"Don't belittle my feelings. That's something else you do."

I clamped my mouth shut. I was getting an unsavory view of myself.

After a moment I asked, "Why do you feel you don't deserve to be treated well? Why do you go out of your way to act wild? To invite trouble?"

"I'm one of those crazy Greens," she mumbled. "Don't you know that?"

I took her chin in my palm and forced her to look at me. "You are *not* crazy."

Tears glistened in her eyes. "Oh yeah, tell that to the guys who tried to rape me when I was fifteen. They said a crazy girl like me needed to be taught a lesson. If a car hadn't driven by when it did..."

Her words detonated on the quiet river. A bomb. An explosion.

"W...what did you say?" I stared at her, my heart breaking.

"You heard me." Her jaw clenched hard against my palm.

"Why didn't you tell me?" I whispered. Guilt stacked like firewood in my mind, knocking over my preconceived notions about my little sister.

She barked out a harsh laugh. "Why? So I could hear 'I told you so'?"

"I would never have said that. Oh, Sissy, do you really think so little of me?"

She jerked her head from my grasp. "I'd gone to a Metallica concert. You told me not to go. I went with three guys I barely knew. We were drinking and smoking pot. I had on a short skirt and a low-cut blouse. I figured you'd think it was my fault."

"Never, Sissy. Never would I think that." The remorse was tearing me apart. My sister had needed me but she'd been too afraid of my condemnation to come to me with the most serious thing in her life.

"Really?" She was shaking, sobbing.

I gathered her in my arms and held her tight. "I'm so sorry, baby. So very, very sorry."

Her tears were wet against my shoulder. She seemed so small, so vulnerable.

We sat for the longest time, holding each other. Finally, Sissy pulled back. I handed her a Kleenex from my pocket and she wiped at her face, the mascara smearing, giving her raccoon eyes.

"That's a heavy secret to have carried for so long."

"Well," she said. "I did tell Tim. Except for the being gay part, he was a great boyfriend."

"I still can't believe you didn't tell me when it happened."

"I was ashamed to tell you, too. You're Miss Perfect. You never do stupid things or get involved with the wrong people."

"What? Are you nuts? Of course I do. Remember Casey Yearby? My first boyfriend," I said, trying to make her feel better.

Sissy swiped a straggling tear away. "Oh, yeah. I forgot about him. Your tortured poet. He sat on the front porch, drank blackberry wine and recited odes to death. Didn't he become an undertaker?"

"Last I heard."

"I guess that career choice was inevitable."

"Or what about Thomas Lutten? The art historian. I dated him for a year."

"What a wimp," Sissy laughed. "I swear if he said 'Yes, Ally, whatever you want' once, he said it a million times. Whatever happened to him?"

"He married a prison guard from Gatesville."

"Now that's a match made in dysfunctional Heaven."

We grinned at each other and I felt closer to my sister than I had in a very long time.

"But Casey and Thomas weren't really bad guys. They were spineless. You need a strong man, Ally. Someone you can't push around."

"Maybe you're right," I said and thought of Conahegg.

"That kind of head-to-head relationship would keep you on your toes."

"The fur would fly," I agreed, still thinking of Conahegg.

"But, oh, the sex would be fantastic!"

Yeah, that's what I was afraid of.

"Listen, Sissy," I said, switching the topic off me and back to her. "You've got to talk to me. Tell me what was going on between you and Rocky. Was it drugs? We can get you into a rehab center. Is it money?"

"You can't fix the problem, Ally. That's a hard thing for you to realize, I know, but I have to handle things on my own."

"Are you sure? I can—"

"Shh," she interrupted. "All I need for you to do is keep Denny for a few days."

"Done. Where are you going?"

"I can't tell you. At least not yet."

"Don't be so melodramatic. Tell me."

"I thought we were trying to mend our relationship."

"We are but…"

"Then you have to let me go."

She was right again. "All right. But if you get into trouble, please call. I'm here for you."

"I know, Ally. And that's always been my crutch."

LATER THAT EVENING, after Sissy had waved and driven away on God knows what mission, I went into Cloverleaf to finish giving my statement to Conahegg.

I couldn't stop thinking about my conversation with Sissy. If I was going to have a man in my life, he'd have to be a strong one. But that didn't mean it had to be Conahegg.

"I'm here to see the sheriff," I told the gum-popping, fire-engine redhead seated behind the glass partition separating the visitors from the rest of the building. I recognized her from high school, although she had been a few grades behind me. Mindy Sue Linkletter.

"Name?" Mindy Sue was doodling something on a yellow legal pad. She simultaneously blew a bubble, popped it and quickly sucked the gum back into her wide pink mouth. It was official. The woman could write and chew gum at the same time.

"Allegheny Green."

Her head came up and her pouty lips tilted in a smirk. "Are you any kin to the Greens that live over on Brazos River Road?"

"Yes."

"Your aunt, she's the kook who supposedly channels some dead cavewoman."

"That's right." I felt the old anger and humiliation welling up inside me. For the duration of my entire childhood I'd been forced to put up with the Mindy Sues of the world. I couldn't walk through the school corridors without hearing whispers and jeers.

"Your mom, she's weird, too. Makes castles and trolls and dresses up like it's sixteen century England?"

Seventeenth century to be exact but I wasn't about to correct Mindy Sue's history. Wouldn't want her to make use of it and end up a finalist on *Jeopardy.*

"That would be my mother." I clenched my fists and mentally told myself slapping Mindy Sue wasn't worth spending a night in jail, but it was mighty tempting.

"And your sister, she's kinda trashy, isn't she? Hangs out with the redneck rock and roll musician, Rockerfeller Hughes?" Mindy Sue chattered, "Boy, talk about a loser. And before that, she went out with that gay dude, Tim Kehaul. Guess she didn't know how to keep a man happy since both those guys were found dead whipping the weasel."

"Should you be discussing ongoing investigations with the general public?" I asked her, proud that I had managed to keep my anger on a leash. As a child, I had failed in that endeavor many times. Once, I had even gotten a black eye when at age ten, I'd tussled with a boy twice my size because he had called my family crazy.

"Uh…" That took her aback.

"When I have my talk with Sheriff Conahegg, I think I'll mention to him he might want to do something about confidentiality leaks in his department."

She paled visibly. "Er…please, don't say anything to the sheriff. I was only joking. I didn't mean anything by it. Your family gives local color to Cloverleaf." She was talking fast, and sweat actually broke out on her forehead. Obviously, the woman was terrified of Conahegg.

"Well...I don't know. It's really not very nice of you to put people down."

"I wasn't putting you down. God, I swear on a stack of Bibles I was only joking." Mindy Sue gulped and she must have swallowed her gum because she dissolved into a minor coughing fit.

I could understand her reaction. Conahegg was an imposing man and I had no doubt he would probably fire her if he knew how she'd spoken to me.

"Please," she whispered after the coughing subsided. "Don't say anything to the sheriff."

"Well..." I let her suffer.

"He is really strict. I need this job. I'm a single mom. I've got two kids to support." Mindy Sue squirmed like a worm on a three-pronged fishing hook.

"Tell you what, you keep your mouth shut about my family and I'll keep my mouth shut about what a total blabbermouth you are."

"Oh, right. Sure. Thanks. Thanks a lot."

"By the way, are you going to tell Conahegg I'm here? He's expecting me."

"Just a sec." She held up one dragon-red faux fingernail and punched in some numbers on the telephone intercom. "Sheriff Conahegg?" Her voice had gone from brassy bitch to timid mouse. "There's a Miss Allegheny Green here to see you."

She replaced the receiver and gestured toward the benches out front. "Have a seat, he'll be with you in a moment."

"All right."

"Oh and thanks again. I really appreciate you keeping quiet."

I took a seat and thumbed through a decade-old copy of *Field and Stream.* I was anxious about seeing Conahegg again. If only I could stop picturing him naked.

"May I help you, Miss Green?"

I jerked around to find Conahegg standing before me, a blank expression on his face. He acted as if he didn't even know me.

"Uh...I'm here to give my statement." I stared into flint-gray eyes. He didn't even blink. "Like you told me to."

"Yes. Good of you to come down."

He sounded formal, official. All cop. What was going on? Where was that flirtatious teasing? Had I done something to offend him?

Stop obsessing Ally.

But dammit. Why couldn't I take my eyes off those firm, hard lips. Why did I care whether he was friendly or aloof? No skin off my teeth. Right?

"Let's go into my office."

Oh yeah. As if I needed to be in a closed room with Conahegg. Don't ask me why I had the hots for him. I honestly couldn't tell you. I never considered myself a particularly sexual woman. I'm all for holding hands and sharing meaningful glances but I've found the actual sex act isn't all it's cracked up to be. At least not with the men of my past experience. Something told me, however, that sex with Conahegg would be quite different.

"Have a seat." He ushered me inside his office.

Why did I feel like a kindergartner sent to face the school principal?

"Would you like something to drink?"

"No thanks. But it's nice of you to ask." I smiled engagingly, hoping to elicit a similar response. I was going nuts here. There was definitely a cool breeze blowing off him and I was desperate to find out why.

Conahegg didn't smile. His chin took on a bulldog set. His feet were placed firmly on the floor, his spine planted straight against the back of the chair, palms splayed flat across the top of the desk.

"Are you mad at me?" I asked.

"No."

"Then why are you acting so weird?"

He cleared his throat, met my gaze like a head-on collision. "May I be frank with you?"

My stomach churned. "By all means."

"It's recently been brought to my attention by concerned citizens that my physical attraction to you is unprofessional."

"Excuse me?" I blinked.

"After careful consideration, I realize that perhaps our er…friendship…has been clouding my judgment in regards to the ongoing investigations."

"I don't believe this."

"It's not my intention to upset you," he said mildly.

The paradox was I'd spent my whole life kowtowing to Cloverleaf's gossipmongers, trying desperately to redeem my family's name. I strove to be a good girl, do the right thing, to fit in. Normally, I would be the first to drop any liaison that might get my name strung on the local grapevine, but I couldn't believe that Conahegg was letting the nosy neighbors tell him what to do.

I leaned across his desk. "Why are you letting them scare you? There's nothing going on between us, Conahegg."

"Isn't there?" He raised an eyebrow.

"No! We've never even kissed."

"It's not from lack of desire on my part," he said. "And therein lies the problem."

He wanted to kiss me? My heart thumped.

"I've got something important to tell you," I blurted out, unable to deal with his revelation. "Something about Rockerfeller Hughes."

"All right." He seemed relieved that I'd change the trajectory of the conversation.

"Rocky didn't die of autoerotic asphyxiation."

"No?"

"No." I shook my head. "He didn't."

He toyed with a paper clip. It was the first restless thing I'd ever seen him do. My focus narrowed on those thick long fingers with short clipped fingernails to the point where I could see nothing else. My gaze followed his hand and I wondered at the hot rush of blood that surged through my own fingers.

The silence stretched. I could hear the clock on the wall tick off the seconds.

"So," I said finally, unable to stand the silence for a moment longer. "What do you think about that?"

"You're suggesting murder?"

I clenched the chair arms in my sweaty palms and nodded. "Yeah."

"Based on what?"

"Rocky has a severe phobia about putting anything around his neck." I related to Conahegg what Sissy had told me about Rocky's childhood accident with the clothesline. "So you see, he simply wouldn't have tied a belt to his throat."

"Where did you hear this?"

"My sister."

"Your sister is not a reliable source of information. She was involved with the deceased. She has a history of drug use. Why isn't she here telling me the story herself? How do I know she's not lying?"

"Why would she do that?"

"You tell me?"

What was he getting at? I frowned. "I don't think she's making up Rocky's phobia."

"Maybe murder sounds better to her than autoerotic asphyxiation. Maybe she doesn't want to accept the fact he was engaged in masturbation."

"Everyone masturbates," I snapped and immediately regretted opening up *that* can of worms. The last image I wanted imprinted on Conahegg's brain was the picture of me involved in a little self-gratification. I spoke swiftly, "But masturbating and hanging yourself while you're doing it are two different things. Suppose for a minute my sister told the truth."

"All right, for the sake of argument let's say Hughes had a fear of having anything placed around his neck." Conahegg indulged me.

"Then he had to be unconscious when the belt was placed there."

"What do you want me to say, Ally? That Rockerfeller Hughes was murdered and someone tried to make it look like autoerotic asphyxiation."

"Bingo." I pointed a finger at him.

"We'll wait for the autopsy before drawing those kinds of conclusions," he said.

"That could take a week or longer."

"With the current backlog, that's correct."

"But if someone did kill Rocky, and believe me there were people lining up to do the job, the murderer will be long gone before you get up off your duff and do something about it."

I couldn't believe his complacency, his utter lack of concern that a murderer might be roaming free in Cloverleaf. Then it dawned on me. He was being pressured to wrap the investigation up with as little fanfare as possible, probably by the very same bunch that told him to quit hanging around me.

"Aren't you being a bit melodramatic?" Conahegg's lips twitched as if he was struggling not to laugh right in my face.

"You're not taking me seriously."

His shrug was as good as admitting the truth. He thought

I was off my nut. So much for our friendship. So much for our budding romance. Who wanted a fling with a guy who thought you were a joke? My feelings were hurt.

"When we get the report back, we'll see who's right and who's wrong," I said.

"For the sake of argument, tell me, who do you think would kill Rocky?"

I held up a finger. "Dooley Marchand."

"Motive?"

"Unpaid debt."

"That would be stupid on Dooley's part. If Rocky's dead then he'll never get his money."

"Nobody ever said Dooley was a brainiac."

"What else you got?" Conahegg cocked his head to one side and gave me the once-over.

"How about the person or persons who was dealing drugs to Rocky?"

"Again, what's the motive?"

"I don't know. You're the professional. You tell me."

"What about your sister?"

"What about her?" I frowned.

"She has a motive for killing Rocky."

I made a noise of indignation. "What motive?"

"The same reason she shot him in the foot. Jealousy."

"Jealousy?"

"He was going to leave her to go back to his wife. They'd already rented a house together."

I had not known that. "Well, then maybe Darlene killed him for being with Sissy."

"And maybe Rocky hanged himself while jerking off."

"You've a hard head, you know that?" I rose from my chair.

"So I've been told. May I suggest you mind your own business."

"Why? So you can please the mayor and the wealthy bigwigs in this town. Well, news flash, Sheriff. You can't tell me what to do. Last time I checked it was still a free country."

"I don't want to pick a fight with you, Ally."

"Too late, you already did." I strode to the door.

"Wait," he said. "I never did finish taking your statement."

"And you can wait until hell freezes over." I stalked over the threshold. How dare he dismiss me as inconsequential. How dare he use the town as an excuse not to deepen our relationship.

Seething, I drove home, swearing never to have anything more to do with the arrogant Sheriff Samuel J. Conahegg.

SISSY WAS STILL GONE when I got home. Mama told me to be patient and that things would work out. I didn't want to think about any of it anymore. I wanted to collapse into my bed and sleep for a century.

The next day, I took some ribbing at the office about being the angel of death. Then I saw Reverend Swiggly again. That today he was so warm and welcoming I wondered if maybe he had multiple personality disorder. Esme made me some chocolate chip cookies, while Miss Gloria lurked in the background.

On Thursday Darlene held a funeral for Rocky at Vincent's Funeral Home on Miranda Street, but I didn't go. Neither apparently did Sissy. Rhonda dropped by to check it out. She told me Rocky's band members had shown up along with Darlene. And Conahegg was there. She said he looked really sexy and she flirted with him a little but he didn't ask after me.

Good. I didn't care if I ever saw him again. How on earth had I ever found him attractive? I'd been too long without a man. That was the only explanation. Rhonda was right. I needed to start dating again. Anything to keep my mind off Conahegg.

I was worried about Sissy and that helped me not think

about Conahegg some. I had no idea where she'd gone or when she'd be home. She was a big girl. As long as she didn't drag Denny along with her, I had no choice but to back off. In fact, it was something of a relief to cut her free, to see if she could indeed stand on her own two feet. But letting go didn't come easy for me.

Friday night, I checked my work schedule for the weekend at the hospital, and I was surprised to find I had the entire weekend off. I frowned. That never happened.

"Aunt Ally?"

I looked up and saw Denny standing in the doorway. "Hi, honey."

"You didn't forget that we're going camping tomorrow, did you?"

Inwardly I groaned. I'd completely forgotten. "Course not," I fibbed.

"We need to get the camping equipment out of the garage," he reminded me.

"So we do."

I put on my slippers and bathrobe and we walked outside. Life had been so crazy lately I hadn't been inside the garage since the night Sissy shot Rocky. Apparently, neither had anyone else. The place was a total mess with Rocky's blood still staining the cement.

I got a strange feeling in the pit of my stomach. *Had* someone murdered him as Sissy believed? Or was Conahegg right and I was tilting at windmills?

Brushing aside self-doubt and sentimentality, I retrieved the camping supplies, then sent Denny off to bed dreaming of his treasured trip.

CHAPTER THIRTEEN

SIX O'CLOCK IN THE MORNING came too early. Denny bounced into my room and leaped on the end of the bed. "Get up, get up, sleepyhead. Time to go camping."

"Give me five more minutes, please," I begged and pulled my pillow over my head.

"Aunt Ally, come on." He tickled my feet.

"Hey, cut that out."

"Please get up."

Sighing, I threw back the covers. "If I only had a tenth of your energy," I grumbled. "I could be a superhero of unparalleled strength."

Denny giggled. A sound that did my heart good.

After Denny swallowed a bowl of Froot Loops and I downed two cups of black coffee, I dressed in blue jeans shorts, a Cowtown Marathon T-shirt left from my running days and hiking boots. I didn't bother with makeup. What was the point? I would be spending the weekend on the river with ten eight-year-olds.

We stuffed the trunk with camping gear and strapped our orange fiberglass canoe to the top of the Honda. Fifteen minutes later, we pulled into the rendezvous spot at the public boat ramp already crowded with excited campers and their families.

Kids whooped and hollered and ran around in circles while bemused parents tried to hug them goodbye.

"Here." I handed Denny a red-and-yellow life jacket.

"Aw, already?" he whined.

"You know the rules."

"No life jacket, no getting near the water."

"Good boy."

Making a face, he wriggled into the bulky flotation device.

"Where are the other chaperones?" I asked as we unloaded our backpacks and a cooler of food.

"It's just you," he said. "And the troop leader."

"Really?"

"Uh-huh, nobody else volunteered."

Great. "Is your troop leader here?" I scanned the crowd. "Do you see him?"

"He's over there." Denny pointed.

And for the first time I saw the black sports utility vehicle. I must really have been distracted not to have noticed it when we drove up. It was parked to one side and surrounded by canoes and camping gear. A man was leaning over, digging life jackets from the backseat.

He straightened.

And looked my way.

My heart stuttered. No. It couldn't be.

"Uh, Denny," I said, tugging on my nephew's sleeve. "Is that your new troop leader?"

He squinted and a big smile broke across his face. "Yep. That's Sam."

Sam.

As in Conahegg.

"I HAD NO IDEA YOU WERE Denny's troop leader," I told Conahegg after the parents had scrammed, leaving us with their precious darlings.

"I know," Conahegg said, looking much finer in a pair of

khaki shorts and hiking shoes than he had any right to look. Especially after the way he'd treated me when last we laid eyes on each other. He began loading sleeping bags and tents into the three canoes we were taking with us. "Or you wouldn't have volunteered."

"That's not true," I protested.

"You don't have to lie to me." He grinned. Why was he wasting it on me? "I took over as troop leader last month."

"Do you think the two of us can handle ten eight-year-olds?" Worriedly, I nibbled on my bottom lip.

"I'm an ex-MP, you're a nurse, I think we've got the bases covered."

"Yeah, but neither one of us are parents." I glanced over my shoulders at the kids roughhousing on the dock.

"You're a parent." Conahegg lugged an ice chest over to my canoe. "You don't have to give birth to assume the role." He nodded at Denny. "He's a good kid and I know it's mostly your doing. You should be proud of yourself."

"Er, thank you." I wasn't going to allow myself to be pleased. I didn't trust him. Was he buttering me up for some reason?

He took a map of the river from his pocket. "Here's our destination."

"I don't need a map. I was born on this river. I know every nook and cranny. Tell me where we're going and I'll get you there." I couldn't help bragging.

"Sanchez Creek. We're looking for the underwater caves."

"The kids'll love that."

"You ever been inside the caves?" Conahegg arched a brow.

I hated to admit I hadn't after my I'm-a-dyed-in-the-wool-river-girl speech, but I knew where they were located, so I nodded.

"Okay, troop." Conahegg clapped his hands. "Listen up." He gave them a safety lecture, then positioned us in the boats.

We launched from the dock at the same time. Conahegg had me lead the way while he brought up the rear, the canoe without adults sandwiched between us. I wondered if the kids in the middle canoe would have the stamina to row without an adult but the wind was to our back and before long they were skimming along like water spiders.

I took a deep breath of fresh morning air and felt the tension leave my body. I had many fond memories of canoeing and fishing with my father on the Brazos. Sissy hadn't been interested in the water, a fact I could never fathom. I loved it. The peace, the quiet, the isolation. Whenever I felt overloaded, burned out or down in the dumps, I would come out on the water and see life from a new perspective.

The weather was spectacular. We had that to be grateful for. Not as hot as normal for July due to a nice breeze blowing from the north.

At lunch, we picnicked on Campbell Island. Eating sandwiches and fruit and potato chips. Sam and I sat on the beach and allowed the boys to romp in the water for an hour before loading them up and heading on.

Conahegg and I didn't speak much. We didn't have to. There was an unwritten truce between us. That's another nice thing about the river. There's no hurry, no expectations, no facades. He had ceased being hardheaded, uncompromising Sheriff Conahegg and I'd ceased being dead-body-finding Nurse Green. We were Sam and Ally out for a weekend canoe trip with our ten kids.

I have to admit. I kinda liked it.

For the first time in a long time I felt young and carefree.

We arrived at Sanchez Creek by midafternoon. It's a narrow but deep strip of water that forks off from the main body of the Brazos. It's surrounded by ranch land. Overgrown trees with ancient roots and long dangling branches reach out into the water as if to grab you. The banks of the creek were almost ten feet tall and straight up, adding to the spookiness. If you fell out of the canoe and had to swim to shore, your chances of pulling yourself up to dry land were almost impossible.

The kids got quieter the farther we went up the creek. Leaves littered the surface of the water and cattails grew in wild profusion. Along the banks we saw snakes' and turtles' heads pop up on occasion to eye us with idle curiosity.

We passed two fishermen in a johnboat. They smiled and waved and when prodded by the boys, held up their string of fish. Because of its twenty foot depths, there was good fishing in Sanchez Creek. I'd even caught my first crappie here.

The wind shifted and we caught the unmistakable stench of something rotten and when we paddled around the corner we discovered the source of the odor.

A dead, bloated Hereford cow lay half in the water, her baleful eyes gazing sightlessly at the sky, one back leg turned at an odd angle. It was clear she had trundled down the cliff in search of water and had broken her hind leg in the fall.

"Oooh gross," Denny's best friend, Braxton exclaimed.

"Yuck!" said another boy.

"That's disgusting." The chubby kid in my canoe who was always looking for an excuse not to paddle, slapped a hand over his pug nose.

"Settle down," Conahegg said, his voice firm but soothing. "It's just a dead cow. Hold your breath until we get past."

I couldn't look at the cow even though we had to float right past her. I'd seen enough of death in the last few days. I didn't need any extra.

We kept paddling until the sun slipped low on the horizon. Another island lay ahead. Smaller than Campbell Island and without the beach. I docked first. Denny stepped out and tied us up to a tree.

"Good work," Conahegg complimented us as we secured the canoes up tight for the night. I felt inordinately proud but quickly shook it off. What was wrong with me? I didn't need his approval.

"Not so bad yourself," I quipped, then hurried off.

"Okay, boys. Let's pitch our tents and start a fire."

We set to work and by the time the sun disappeared we were sitting cross-legged in front of our tents, roasting first wieners for hot dogs and then marshmallows over an open fire.

Frogs croaked, crickets chirped and in the distance, cattle lowed. Thirty minutes later, the kids trundled off to bed without any prodding. Poor things were exhausted. Before he went into our tent, Denny came over to sit beside me for a moment.

"Aunt Ally?"

"Uh-huh." I placed an arm around my nephew.

"Thank you, for coming along. I'm having a great time."

"Me, too." I smiled and realized it was the truth. Despite Conahegg or maybe even because of him, the day had been wonderful.

"Mom sure missed out on a fun trip, didn't she?"

"Yes she did, Denny, and I'm sure she wishes she were here."

"You really think so?" He looked skeptical.

"Sure," I lied.

"Good night."

"Sleep tight. Don't let the bedbugs bite."

He leaned over and kissed my cheek. "I love you," he whispered softly in my ear. I squeezed his hand, a lump in my throat.

"Love you, too."

After the boys had bedded down, that only left me and Conahegg to enjoy the night.

Conahegg prodded the fire, rearranging the logs and then casually dropped down next to me. I pretended my blood didn't suddenly run hot.

"You're quite a trooper," Conahegg said.

"Pardon me?"

"Most women aren't that fond of sleeping on the ground, cooking over an open flame, sitting in the woods in the dark. Battling mosquitoes and fire ants."

"Oh no?"

He shrugged and smiled. "Well, at least none of the women I've ever dated."

"Maybe you've been dating the wrong women."

"Maybe." He picked up a nearby stick and began doodling in the sand with it, but not before I saw a faint smile flit over his lips.

The fire crackled and snapped.

I heard him exhale deeply. The sound stirred something primordial and very womanly in me.

"Listen," I said, trying to find something else to talk about besides what kind of women Conahegg thought he ought to be dating. "Are you still convinced Rocky's death was accidental suicide?"

Conahegg glanced over his shoulder at the row of tents behind us. "Shhh."

I lowered my voice in deference to the kids. "Seriously, Conahegg, don't you have doubts?"

He paused a moment before answering me. "There's room for that when the autopsy report comes back. Until then I'm going to refrain from speculation."

"Must be nice to be able to control your curiosity."

"The Marines teach control."

Control in every aspect of life? I wondered briefly, my mind veering straight for the gutter.

"So what about you, Ally Green?"

"What about me?"

"How did you come to be mother of your entire family?"

"Born with a guilt chip in my brain, I guess. I fear if I don't take care of them, they'll fall apart."

"Have you ever given them an ultimatum?"

"You shouldn't go around issuing ultimatums to people unless you are prepared to act on them."

"You haven't reached your saturation point." Conahegg nodded.

"What does that mean?" I cast a sideways glance at him. There was a wistful note in his tone, a faraway look in his eyes that told me he was thinking about something in his own life.

"Time comes, Ally, you've got to make your own way and they've got to make theirs."

"Is that right?"

"That's right." There was that smile again. A quick flash, then it was gone.

I admit, I was flattered by his attention. My family never listens to me. Talking to Mama is like talking to a wall; Aunt Tessa is somewhat better but not much; Sissy does the opposite of whatever I suggest.

Now, here was Conahegg, all ears and understanding. It made me feel weird and comfortable at the same time.

"What about Sistine?" he asked.

"What about her?"

"She's giving you a few gray hairs." He reached over and lightly touched my temples where I do have a couple of gray hairs that I'm usually pretty ruthless about plucking. His warm fingers almost seared my skin. Terrific. I had to get an observant guy who even notices my hair. "Tell me about Sissy."

Damned if I didn't spill my guts to him. I told him about Sissy and her boyfriends. About how upset she'd been with Tim when he'd dumped her for a male lover. How her temper had caused her to shoot Rocky when she'd found out about Darlene. I even told him about what happened to Sissy at the Metallica concert.

"My sister never got over our father's death," I whispered, brought my knees to my chest and hugged myself. "When he died it was as if she lost her moral compass. And I recently found out that she'd almost gotten raped." I shuddered. "It must have been awful for her."

"She needs counseling, Ally," Sam said.

"I know. But how do I make her go?"

He swung his gaze toward the tent and nodded his head. "She's got a pretty terrific son. Do you think she would do it for him?"

"I don't know." I didn't want to talk about Sissy's shortcomings anymore. It made me feel like a failure. I leaned over and retrieved a marshmallow from the bag and thrust it onto a skewer.

I burned the marshmallow to a crisp, blew on it to cool it, then popped it in my mouth. The burnt skin crunched against my teeth, then the gooey middle stuck to them. I was in hog heaven. It had been far too long since I'd roasted marshmallows and sat before a crackling fire. I missed camping more than I realized.

"You want me to show you the real way to roast a marshmallow?" Conahegg asked.

"No thanks." I torched another one. "I like them this way."

"That's only because you've never had Marshmallows Conahegg."

"Marshmallows Conahegg?"

He took the skewer from my hand. "Sit back and watch the master at work."

All right. It was nice to have him take charge although a part of me wanted to wrest the skewer away from him and tell him to go roast his own marshmallows. I don't know what it was about him that caused so many conflicting emotions inside me, but whenever he was near, I rarely knew my own mind.

He crouched by the fire, his attention thoroughly focused on the job at hand.

My gaze strayed from his hand up his arms, to his shoulders, then down to his muscular behind and fabulous legs. In those shorts he looked hotter than the hard-body UPS guy who delivered our supplies at work. The nurses fought to sign for his packages.

I thought about kissing him. Would he be a good kisser? How was his technique? Was he one of those grab-you-and-go-at-it types? Or was he as controlled in his lovemaking as he was in every other aspect of his life? Would my knees go weak with desire? Or would his lips be a mild diversion and nothing else?

I was dying to answer those questions, but fear and common sense held me back. I couldn't kiss him. Not here. Not with the kids a few feet away. Not when I was still uncertain of his feelings for me.

Would there ever be a right time for us?

"Here we go." He brought me the most perfect marshmallow ever cooked. Nicely tanned on the outside with a few bubbles but no burned spots.

I reached for it.

"No, no." He took his fingers and gently tugged the marshmallow from the skewer. "Open up."

I parted my lips.

And then his fingers were touching my mouth. Rough manly fingers that felt too damned good against my skin and filled my head with dangerous thoughts. I snared the marshmallow between my teeth.

The marshmallow tasted exquisite. I was embarrassed by the automatic, low, sexy sound I made at the delicious flavor.

I inhaled sharply and accidentally swallowed the thing whole. It lodged in my throat.

I coughed lightly, hand over my mouth, trying to be ladylike at first.

"Ally?" Conahegg loomed above me, concern and firelight sculpting shadows across the hollows of his cheeks. "Are you all right?"

I splayed a palm over my chest and tried to nod reassuringly, my neck muscles working furiously to push the marshmallow along. I must have looked like a sand crane trying to gulp down a too-big fish.

"Are you choking?" he demanded, dropping to his knees behind me.

I tried to speak but couldn't. I raised one finger indicating he should give me a moment.

Desperately, I tried to suck in air but that only seemed to wedge the marshmallow tighter. My head was starting to ache. I could feel the veins at my temples bulging. I made a noise like, "kakakakak."

"You are choking."

Then before I could signal that it might be a good time to institute the Heimlich maneuver, Conahegg's big hands were around my waist, his fist knotted against my diaphragm.

He gave a short, explosive thrust and the marshmallow flew from my throat and landed in the fire with a hissing sound.

I inhaled deeply and wiped saliva from my chin. So much for romance.

"Thanks," I croaked.

"No more Marshmallows Conahegg for you," he said in a shaky voice.

After that, there was nothing to do but call it a night.

CHAPTER FOURTEEN

THE BOYS, CHATTERING like tree monkeys, awoke before dawn. All they talked about was finding the secret underwater caves. I groaned and rolled over onto my side, my back stiff from the ground, my midsection tender from Conahegg's impromptu administration of the Heimlich maneuver the night before.

My, Sheriff, what strong arms you have.

I was confused about my relationship with Conahegg. I wanted him and yet I didn't. I yearned for his kisses but yet the thought of making love to such a masculine guy scared me witless.

Bottom line?

I was terrified.

Afraid to trust him. Afraid to trust myself. Afraid to let loose. Afraid of getting hurt.

Ah. There was the rub.

I'd had boyfriends before. After a fashion. I'd been kissed. I'd had sex.

But I'd never had real intimacy. I'd never snuggled next to a man confident that he was mine, that I didn't have to worry. I'd never spilled my darkest secrets to a man, confiding to him things people didn't even tell shrinks. I'd never whispered those three powerful words—I love you—to a man.

Part of it was because of my family. How could I get intimate with a man when my family always came first? But I'd started thinking that maybe part of the fault lay with me. Had I been using my family as an excuse, a buffer against my fears of intimacy? Maybe I needed them as much as they needed me.

The thought was revolutionary.

Most importantly, what was I so afraid would happen if I fell in love and why?

"Ally? You up?" Conahegg stuck his head in my tent, a good-morning grin on his face.

My heart caught.

"Who could sleep with that noise?"

"Those boys are wound up tighter than fresh boot camp recruits on their first leave."

I groaned again. "It's too early in the morning for Marine analogies."

The smile deepened to include his eyes. "Rise and shine."

I lifted a hand to my tousled hair. I must look like hell. "Aye, Aye, sir." I gave him a mock salute and crawled from my sleeping bag.

I hated not having a shower but I did sponge bathe with bottled water, a washcloth and one of those complimentary bars of soap you pick up in hotels. Neither the boys nor Conahegg bothered with even a spit bath. They were wild river men, they didn't need no stinkin' soap and proceeded to tell me so repeatedly. They didn't have to say anything. I could smell them.

The boys stripped off their shirts and went around like extras on the set of *Lord of the Flies.* Luckily, Conahegg kept his shirt on. Undoubtedly, he didn't want me choking on a breakfast sausage.

"Okay, troops," Conahegg said when the sun had risen to a respectable zenith and the young heathens had gulped down the eggs and bacon he'd cooked. "Time to pack up the canoes. It's off to the caves."

A cheer went up and they set to work, busy as ants, folding tents, stuffing backpacks, carting ice chests. Try getting ten boys that excited about arithmetic or cleaning their rooms.

The morning sun shimmered brilliantly on the water's surface as we cast off and I was surprised to discover that I was as excited as the kids. All my life I'd heard tales about these underwater caves. Supposedly, you entered the caves from the river but once inside you could climb out of the water and onto the rocks.

Sanchez Creek meandered through the ranch land and narrowed so much at one point that we were forced to get out and carry the canoes. Conahegg had us singing Marine songs as we marched and I realized I was having a good time.

We put back into the water a quarter of a mile later. Conahegg took the lead canoe and I had the pleasure of watching him row. His lean muscles glistened from sweat and sunscreen. His swim trunks rode his slim waist. He looked powerful as a cheetah and twice as deadly.

Once he turned his head to look back at me, and caught my eye. The pure sexual energy in his stare almost caused me to drop my oar. What did he think of me? Did he imagine me naked, in his bed? Just as I fantasized about him?

Heat swamped my body. I clung to my paddle and rowed so fast we bumped into the canoe of boys in front of us.

For another hour we were at it, then, we heard a faint rushing noise. We paddled around the bend to investigate and emerged from the creek into a wide crystal-clear pool. I hadn't been here in a very long time.

"Cool," the kids exclaimed. "A waterfall."

It wasn't a waterfall as in rain forest waterfall. Rather it was a small cliff where part of the river diverted and trickled over an outcropping of jagged rocks, forming the pool.

"Everyone listen to me," Conahegg said. "We're going ashore."

"Here?" I turned and looked at him.

He held up the map. "I thought you said you knew where the caves were."

"Well sure, of course I do," I lied through my teeth. Couldn't have Conahegg thinking I made claims I couldn't substantiate. "But it's been a long time. The terrain has changed."

From the look on his face, I knew he knew I was lying but he had the good grace to let it go.

"Canoes to the bank." He motioned with a finger.

We beached the canoes and got out. Conahegg gave the boys another wilderness lecture. He even took a hunting knife from his backpack and showed them how to turn a stick into a spear for hunting or fishing. They were mesmerized by his survival training stories and hung on every word.

Truthfully, he was fascinating. As he talked, it was easy to imagine him in the spit and polish military. Shoulders back, chin out, flint eyes straight ahead. Doing his duty, putting his life on the line for his country. I wondered what rank he had achieved. Let's face it, I was practically drooling.

I watched him with the boys, and I found myself wondering why, at age thirty-five, he wasn't married with a passel of kids of his own. I mean, many women would find him attractive if you went in for those macho, hard-ass, soldier-boy types. And he seemed to love teaching these kids and they lapped up his attention like kittens at milk.

"Okay, men, are we ready to search for the caves?" he asked.

In answer, they beat on their chests with fists and grunted manfully.

"First you must listen to me very carefully. We're going to be taking off our life jackets because you can't dive with them on. Is everyone a strong swimmer?"

Ten heads bobbed in unison and ten life jackets went flying through the air. Conahegg took off his shirt and I had no words to describe the beauty of his ripply chest. Suffice it to say, I was not disappointed.

He rigged his hunting knife and a waterproof flashlight to his belt. "All right. You guys stay right beside me. Ally?"

"Uh-huh?"

"You coming?"

Eleven pairs of eyes rested on me. Was I going to be a wuss and stay on the shore or was I going to be part of the gang?

"Why sure," I said with more bravado than I felt. I shimmied out of my shorts and T-shirt, stripping down to the one-piece bathing suit I wore beneath.

I raised my head to find Conahegg's gaze riveted on my butt and legs. Finally, those long hours on the StairMaster were paying off.

He realized I caught him in the act of ogling my body but he didn't look away in embarrassment. He held my stare. Sunlight dappled a surreal pattern across the water, across our skins. It seemed we were the only two people alive. Never mind those pesky kids. In that moment I knew exactly what was on his mind and it didn't have anything to do with underwater caves or Junior Adventurers or advanced survival techniques.

More like advanced sexual techniques.

He was a bold man with bold appetites.

Yikes!

"Ready," I said, snapping his attention back to the moment.

He narrowed his eyes, swallowed so hard I could see his jaw clench with the effort of reining himself in.

Hey, what can I say? I was flattered.

After peeling his gaze from me, Conahegg herded us to the water's edge and gave us instructions on where to dive. The caves, according to his map, were hidden beneath the waterfall.

I was panting, overwhelmed by what had passed between

us. If we had been alone, I'm certain we would have had sex right there in the grass. The urge was that damned strong.

But I forced myself to ignore my stoked libido. If he could behave so could I.

We jumped in, Conahegg leading the way. The pool, warmed by the noonday sun, welcomed us in its embrace. We dog-paddled for a bit, then Conahegg had us get into a circle and tread water.

"Stay here with Ally for a moment," he told the boys. "I'm going to check things out first."

We waited. The kids splashed each other. I floated on my back, enjoying the day and indulging in very naughty daydreams about me and Conahegg.

In a couple of minutes, Conahegg returned. "It's here." He beamed. "Come with me."

And we did. Taking deep lungfuls of air, then diving under the water, one after the other, following the leader. We went down, down, pushing past the rocky overhang.

Then we leveled out and angled to the right. Just when my lungs were starting to ache, Conahegg veered upward and we popped like corks into the deepest darkness I have ever experienced. The sound of twelve people gasping resounded in the confines.

And then a shaft of light.

Conahegg played his flashlight along the walls of the cave. "Here's a place where we can get up," he said, guiding us to a large flat rock that lay half submerged, half out of the water on the cave floor.

The kids pulled themselves up and I obsessively counted heads. Eight. Nine. Ten. I relaxed.

It was at least a dozen degrees cooler inside the cave than it had been outside. My hair was glued to my face and I had to drag it from my eyes with a palm.

We huddled on the cave floor, acclimating ourselves to our new environment. Conahegg continued to play the flashlight beam over the ceiling.

"Bats," he said, pointing out the sleeping creatures to the kids.

Denny's friend, Braxton, squealed in fear but Conahegg quickly reassured him that he was safe from them.

"How did they get in here?" I asked. "The bats don't swim underwater."

"There's got to be an outside entrance, Aunt Ally," Denny supplied and I felt proud of my smart nephew.

"That's right," Conahegg replied. "Probably a small hole farther inside the cave."

"Can we explore?" one of the boys asked.

"No," Conahegg's voice was firm but kind. "It's too dangerous without the proper equipment."

Suddenly, I found myself thinking additional recalcitrant thoughts. Like what if it were Conahegg and I alone in the cave with an air mattress and a glass of wine? His body and mine entwined in the inky darkness, our inhibitions liberated by vino.

Knock if off, Ally. There are children present.

"Okay, troops, time to head back."

It amazed me how they followed his command so completely. If their parents could see their sons, they wouldn't believe the change.

Conahegg killed his flashlight. "On the count of three," he said. We took a deep breath of the dank, musty air and dived into the water.

Seconds later, we broke through back into the pool, the kids grinning, filled with the excitement of adventure. I counted heads. Six. Seven. Eight. Nine.

I counted again. Still only nine.

Apparently Conahegg was counting, too. His eyes met mine. "Who's missing?" he asked.

"Denny." I meant for my voice to sound calm, but it came out reed thin.

"Get the other kids ashore. I'll find him."

My heart was beating so hard my blood thundered through my ears. My brain spun horrifying images. I had to reach into the depths of myself and dredge up my nursing training to remain in control.

"Out of the water, boys," I shouted, slapping my palms together. "Move it, move it."

The gaiety of the moment instantly vanished. Faces solemn, the boys swam ashore, their gazes cast over their shoulder at the waterfall.

Dear Lord, I prayed, *please let Denny be all right.*

"Get your life jackets on," I said, to keep them busy. I paced the banks and wrung my hands, I felt so utterly helpless.

Then, when I thought I'd never see either of them again, Conahegg broke through the water's surface, Denny clutched in his arms.

Conahegg's bare chest expanded like billows as he sucked in air. He swam for the shore, Denny cradled in the crook of his elbow.

My nephew's face was far too pale and I could not see his chest rising and falling.

Dear God, please.

Conahegg reached the bank and passed Denny to me. I gathered him in my arms, then laid him out flat on the ground. He wasn't breathing but he had a heartbeat. I started mouth-to-mouth resuscitation.

I felt as if I were standing outside my body, watching myself work on Denny. It was an eerie sensation, as if I had disconnected from the physical plane. I wondered if this was how Aunt Tessa felt when she channeled Ung.

In a matter of a few seconds Denny coughed up water and

his eyes flew open. He inhaled sharply, then began to cry, his small nostrils flaring.

I hugged him to me and rocked him gently. The other boys, solemn little soldiers, stood silently around us. Conahegg lay on the ground, his body shaking from the effort of Denny's rescue.

"What happened down there?" I croaked after a very long moment.

"His foot got tangled in some weeds," Conahegg gasped. "He couldn't get loose on his own." He paused. "Luckily I had my knife and cut him free."

"Yeah, but you lost that cool knife down there," Denny murmured. "You oughta go back for it, Sam."

"Water's too murky," Sam replied. "Besides, we need to get you home."

I laughed nervously. "Who cares about an old knife? The only thing that matters is that you're safe."

I clenched my jaw. I could see the awful scene on the projector of my mind. The vicious slimy green weed wrapping around Denny's ankle, pulling him down. Minutes before we'd been happy and laughing.

And I'd been having lustful thoughts about Conahegg. How could I have been so lackadaisical, so irresponsible? I knew how tenuous life was. Not only from my nursing experiences but from finding two dead bodies in the last two weeks. I'd recklessly dropped my guard and look what happened.

"You're blaming yourself. Don't," Conahegg said, as if he could read my every thought. Did I give myself away so easily? He pulled himself to his feet and came over to me and Denny, drops of water running down his body. "I'm the senior officer in charge. I assume full responsibility."

I shook my head. "It's not your fault, either. It was an accident. It could have happened to anyone."

"No. I shouldn't have taken the boys into the cave. I don't know what I was thinking. It was too dangerous."

"You were trying to teach them something. And I think they learned a valuable lesson. Right boys?" I found myself soothing Conahegg who ran an agitated hand through his wet hair. It stuck out in spikes at odd angles and made him look endearingly unguarded.

The kids nodded.

"Yeah," Braxton said, "never go swimming alone."

"And take your knife when you go inside an underwater cave," volunteered another boy.

"Make sure you know CPR," expounded a scrawny kid named Jake, who'd barely spoken two words on the entire trip.

"See," I said, exonerating Conahegg. "No harm done."

Denny was all right. In fact, he'd already broken free from my embrace and was swiping at his tears with the back of his arm. His friends circled around him, murmuring softly.

But I could tell from the look on Conahegg's face that he had not forgiven himself.

I had to do something to make us both feel better. I reached over, wrapped my arms around his waist and gave him a tight hug.

At first he didn't respond and when I began to worry that I'd made a mistake in touching him, he put his hand to my back.

We stood for a brief moment, taking comfort in our contact. He was so solid, so invincible. It was hard to believe he could feel as vulnerable as everyone else.

In that moment I stopped thinking of Conahegg as superhuman and started thinking of him as a real man with insecurities like the rest of us.

My change of perspective made me like him even more.

"Come on," I said, stepping back. "It's time we went home."

CHAPTER FIFTEEN

DENNY AND I DECIDED it was probably best not to worry Mama and Aunt Tessa with the details of what had transpired at the caves. It turned out to be a good decision. We arrived home at five-thirty Sunday afternoon to find Mama and Aunt Tessa in a tizzy.

No sooner had we pulled into the driveway than Aunt Tessa ran out to greet us, her face pulled taut with concern. She was fingering her crystal necklace and talking so fast we could scarcely understand her.

"Wait, slow down," I said, getting out of the car. I felt headachy and water logged and I had sunburn on my shoulders and the tip of my nose. I had been so rattled by Denny's accident, that I'd forgotten to reapply my sunscreen. "What's the matter?"

"Your mother was so upset she took a Valium and went to bed."

I held Aunt Tessa's hand. "Calm down. Deep breaths." Over my shoulder, I winked at Denny. "Do you feel like unloading the car?"

"Sure," he said bravely but his skin remained pale beneath his freckles.

"People have been here," Aunt Tessa said. "Really nasty people."

I led her inside the house and gently pushed her onto the sofa, then I knelt at her feet.

Denny trudged in behind us, hauling his backpack. I told him to go to his room and rest until supper. After his adventure-packed weekend, he didn't even argue. His feet made heavy thudding sounds on the stairs.

When I was satisfied he was out of earshot, I returned my attention to Aunt Tessa. "What people?"

"They were friends of Rocky's." The sound of my mother's voice drew my focus to the doorway. She wore a white flannel nightgown and her hair was loose around her shoulders.

"Here." I held out my hand to her and settled her on the couch next to Aunt Tessa. I sat on the coffee table facing them. "All right, what happened?"

"Late last night, about one o'clock in the morning, a strange man came looking for Sissy." Mama's bottom lip trembled.

"He wasn't very nice," Aunt Tessa added.

"He was awful," Mama corrected, lifting her hand to her face. "He cursed at us and worse."

"Worse?" I swallowed hard.

"He said if he didn't get his money our house might burn down," Aunt Tessa said.

"What money?"

"He said Sissy had money that belonged to him. Do you know what's he talking about, Ally?" Mama looked so worried, I wanted to take her into my arms and hold her tight against my chest. Who was the creep that had threatened my family? I fisted my hands. What had Sissy brought upon us?

"Did he say what his name was?" I asked.

Mama frowned. "I don't remember, I was so scared. He had an ugly scar running from his eyebrow to his cheek and the coldest eyes I've ever seen."

"He had an odd name," Aunt Tessa supplied. "Something like Dugan Marcher."

"Dooley Marchand?"

Aunt Tessa snapped her fingers. "That's it!"

Oh, boy. I let out my breath.

"He said he was a friend of Rocky's," Mama said. "I told him we didn't know anything about it but then he…he…" Tears sprang to my mother's eyes.

"What did he do?" I was afraid to ask but unable to resist.

"He broke the Rainbow Monks I made for Tim's memorial." Mama dissolved into full-fledged sobs. Aunt Tessa reached in her pocket for a clean tissue and passed it over to Mama. "Busted every one of them into little bitty pieces."

"I'm calling Conahegg." I started to my feet, but Aunt Tessa put out a hand.

"Wait. There's more."

"More?" Jeez, I didn't want to hear any more. I didn't know if Rocky had been murdered or not, but something very weird was going on. Something I feared my younger sister was involved in right up to her pretty neck. Where had she gone? Was she safe? Or was she lying unconscious in a ditch somewhere?

"A woman claiming to be Rocky's wife came by the house."

"Darlene?"

"Chain-smoking, bleached blonde?"

"That's her. What did she want?"

"Well," Aunt Tessa continued. "She claimed she wanted a past life reading."

"Did you give her one?"

"Yes. I even gave her a pair of crystal earrings. I went into a trance and Ung took over but while I was out, the nosy woman gets up and leaves the reading."

"I found her going through Sissy's room," Mama chimed in. "When I asked her what she was doing, she wanted to know what Sissy had done with Rocky's money."

Where had Rocky acquired the money everyone was so anxious to get their hands on? And where was it now? I had a sneaking suspicion the money was in the same place as my sister. Wherever that might be.

"And—" Aunt Tessa sniffed "—she left without paying me for the reading or the earrings."

"Have you heard from Sissy?" I asked.

"No," Mama said. "Where do you think she's gone?"

I shook my head. "I don't know. But I'm calling the sheriff." I got my purse out of the car, dug around for the business card Conahegg had given me, then called him at home. After four rings, the answering machine picked up.

"Conahegg," his automated voice said. "Leave your message."

"Um…Sheriff…"

I heard a click when he picked up. "Ally?"

"Uh-huh."

"What's wrong?"

"It's Sissy," I told him. "She's in worse trouble than I thought."

MY ANGER OVER Dooley Marchand and Darlene Hughes terrorizing my family combined with my concern for Sissy's welfare, rendered me into a frazzled ball of nerves. Restless as a pregnant mom three weeks past her due date, I paced the kitchen until Mama and Aunt Tessa banished me outside where I paced the dock and repeatedly glanced at my watch.

Where was Conahegg?

The sun was strolling down the horizon in a burst of splendid color when his patrol car finally pulled into the driveway.

"We could have been dismembered by a serial killer in the time you took to get here," I greeted him when he stepped from the Crown Vic.

He didn't apologize. "You're upset," he said.

"Damn right I'm upset."

"Calm down, Ally." He reached out and took my elbow. "I'm here."

I wanted to snap, whoop-dee-doo, but his presence did have a soothing effect on me and I wasn't sure I liked admitting that. Gently, he nudged me toward the dock.

"Let's sit down and watch the sunset."

I balked. I didn't want to sit down. I wanted arrests. I wanted heads to roll. I wanted justice. I wanted Conahegg to stop looking at me as if indulging a wayward child.

How could he be so composed, so complacent? My family had been threatened. My sister was in grave trouble.

"I don't want to sit down, I want you to do something."

"Not until we've talked. No problem is ever solved by going off half-cocked. You're still shaken from what happened to Denny. You've had a pretty rough couple of weeks. Now sit, Allegheny, and watch the damned sunset."

He guided me into the redwood love seat then eased down beside me. One minute he was stern, the next minute tender. Maybe it was what I needed.

I sat stiff as a department store mannequin and then to my horror, I burst into tears.

Conahegg slid his arm around me. "There, there. Let it out. You'll feel better. You've been holding it in for too long."

His masculine scent curled inside my nostrils. I could feel the crispness of his shirtsleeve against my cheek. Turning, I buried myself against his chest and sobbed.

Slowly, he drew me into his lap, held me the way my father used to. For the first time since my father's death I had someone to turn to. Someone to share my burdens with. That made me cry even harder. Weeping for the fourteen-year-old girl who'd assumed so much responsibility at such a tender age.

Conahegg knew none of this about me and yet he seemed to understand. I surrendered myself to his protectiveness. My actions were completely out of character. I was supposed to be the strong one. The comforter. But somewhere along the line I'd run out of energy. I couldn't fight the temptation to let him take care of me any longer. I wanted it. I needed it. I hated my weakness but there it was.

He stroked my head and held me tightly until the tears played out. From his back pocket he produced a clean handkerchief and dabbed at my eyes. "Feel better?"

I nodded, although what I really felt was foolish. How had I let myself get so worked up? So what if I'd found two dead bodies in two weeks. So what if my sister was being chased by loan sharks and parolee ex-wives? So what if my nephew had almost drowned? I was Allegheny Green, caretaker extraordinaire. I did not break down.

"Stop thinking," Conahegg commanded. "I can look into your eyes and see your mind whirling a mile a minute. Try and relax, Ally. Feel the breeze on your skin. Let go. Just for a little while. Soon enough you can slip back into *Zena Warrior Princess* mode."

I took a deep breath, caught a fresh whiff of his scent.

God, he smelled so good. Manly and clean. Sweet and very sexy. Idly, I stared at a button on his shirt and wondered if he tasted as good as he smelled.

My gaze traveled upward. One button, two button, top button unbuttoned. Tanned muscular neck. Chin you could bounce a quarter off of. Lips. Full and firm.

Slate-gray eyes that caught mine.

I ran my tongue along the inside of my mouth, imagined I was running it along his lips.

What was I thinking? I couldn't kiss Conahegg.

Why not? chimed the little voice at the back of my head.

Why not indeed? Because he posed the very real potential of breaking my heart?

He brushed my hair back from my face with one hand, and slipped the other hand to the nape of my neck where he massaged my muscles with his thumb and index finger.

I sighed—almost purred, actually—and relaxed against his forearm. I felt as if I were melting into him.

Mmm, melting like chocolate. Warm and smooth and shivery.

Wait a minute, Ally, my conscience kicked in. What are you doing? Get away from him. Go find Sissy.

Like a splash of cold water in the face, I came back to reality. I tried to shift away from Conahegg but he held me tightly on his lap.

"Th...thanks," I mumbled and ducked my head. "I guess I needed a good cry. You were nice to indulge me."

He took a finger, tipped my chin up, forced me to look into his face. He smiled tolerantly, as if he knew a great secret. As if he knew something very important that I should know but didn't.

His expression annoyed me. What gave him the right to be so smug? To be so damned good-looking? I felt far too hot and uncomfortable clutched in his arms on my dock.

I turned my head and tried to push myself away but Conahegg didn't seem to realize I wanted free. He kept staring into my eyes and smiling like a silly lunatic. A bizarre sensation, something akin to panic or fear, swept through me.

"I'm okay," I said, hoping to assure him that if he let me go I wouldn't unravel at his feet. "Thanks for being here when I needed a shoulder to cry on."

I wanted him to realize that I would have broken down to anyone who'd been willing to pose as a watershed for my tears, that his presence had merely been coincidental.

That my letting loose on him wasn't personal. In fact, a sponge could have done his job. Sit silently and absorb moisture.

But he must not have understood because he kept one hand over my lap, the other still quietly massaging my neck.

I *had* to get away from him. I was too big, too old to be sitting in a virtual stranger's lap. Never mind that we'd gone to the same high school. We'd never moved in the same circles, never really known each other.

His nearness was playing havoc with my common sense. I was aware of many things about him that I hadn't noticed when I'd been preoccupied bawling my head off. Like, he was so *big*...and hard. All muscle and sinew. I felt strange to be held by someone so overwhelmingly strong. Strange and a little frightening.

And kind of sexy.

"You can let go of me." Enough beating around the bush.

"I know," he said placidly, not moving an inch.

I waited. For what, I wasn't sure. I peeked surreptitiously at his face. Maybe he was joking. Ha, ha. But he wasn't smiling.

In fact, he looked a little ominous, the descending twilight bathing his angular features in deep shadows. He stared at me, his eyes dark and hypnotic. He didn't move. Didn't twitch an inch.

What control! What discipline! I admired him more than words could say. And yet I was a little scared of him, too, but I wasn't about to let him know that.

I stared back, desperate to prove I was as strong as he.

A stillness settled over the evening. Complete silence. No fish splashing in the river beyond. No crickets chirping. No dogs barking. No lawn mowers firing up in the distance.

Mere minutes ago I felt safe in Conahegg's sheltering arms, now I felt anything but.

Conahegg shifted slightly against the seat and I nearly leaped out of my skin at the tension. What was he going to do?

He pressed his thumb to my lips and still, he said nothing. But his eyes said everything.

Uh-oh. Trouble. Warning, warning, danger, danger.

To my utter confusion and amazement I felt such a powerful rush of sexual attraction for him that it almost propelled me backward out of his arms and into the river. I jerked. He held on tight.

"Ally," he said in a perilously soft voice. "I'm hanging on to you until we get things out in the open so stop trying to get away."

Oh my God. Time for the showdown. Time to face the inevitable. Time to stand up and admit that I had a thing for Conahegg.

But I wasn't that brave. I wasn't ready to face my attraction to the town sheriff. Not yet. I decided to play dumb.

"Er..." I stammered. "Get what out in the open?" Yet even as I spoke, I was distracted by his maleness. His straight white teeth, the cleft in his chin, his ears which were a tad too big.

"You know."

"I don't."

"Let's talk about chemistry, shall we?"

"Oh, I was lousy at that in nursing school. Barely passed."

"You underestimate yourself, Ally."

"No really," I chattered. "I struggled to understand that ionic bonding stuff and the only half-filled shells I was interested in had ricotta cheese and marinara sauce."

He ran his thumb along my chin. It was a roughed, callused thumb that raised the hairs on the back of my neck.

"Stop playing dumb, it doesn't suit you."

"How do you know what suits me? You don't even know me."

"I know you far more than you think."

"Oh yeah?"

"Yeah. For instance I know you're scared to death."

"I wouldn't say 'to death,'" I grumbled.

"But you're scared."

"Oh, all right," I admitted. "I'm scared."

"And why is that?"

"Because I want you to kiss me."

"Very good, Ally. Because I want to kiss you, too."

Red alert!

My stomach lurched as it does when I ride the Shock Wave at Six Flags. Conahegg and I were staggering toward unknown territory, crossing over into uncharted waters. If I had any sense I would demand he let me go. But I was in short supply of common sense at the moment. It had been used up. Sucked dry from years of thinking and doing for everyone in my family. I was empty. Waiting, no yearning, to be refilled.

We hovered in space like hummingbirds at a feeder, our mouths almost touching, moving infinitesimally closer.

Finally, when I didn't think I could stand the tension one second longer and my vocal cords were stretched to the screaming point, Conahegg bent his head, pressed his lips to mine and kissed me.

I kissed him back because—hey go ahead and shoot me—I wanted to kiss him.

Talk about your rockets red glare, talk about your bombs bursting in air. It was absolutely the most perfect kiss on the face of the earth.

Why, I moaned inwardly, couldn't it have been lousy? Why couldn't he have been one of those sloppy mouth breathers? Why couldn't he have been a face licker? But oh, no. Conahegg had to be faultless.

Should have known.

Just my luck I get the best kisser this side of the Mason-Dixon. He was more delicious than Godiva chocolates. He had an exquisite mouth and the firmest skin. He tasted sweet and hot and full of sin.

I was aware of nothing but him. He was a man. A real man. Not some pasty-faced wimp like Casey Yearby. Not a whiny Mama's boy like Thomas Lutten. He was all male and if the bulge under my thighs was any indication, he thought I was all woman.

That's when the fear set in as I realized what I'd stirred up. Could I handle a man like Conahegg? I was used to being in control. I liked being in charge. With Conahegg it would be a constant scrap to keep a foothold. Was I ready?

In a word?

No.

I was trembling. Because I liked kissing him so much. Because I was so powerfully attracted to him. Because I was so terrified of losing myself in the strength of his personality.

But damn me, I wanted to have sex with him. No-holds-barred, wild, rough animal sex right there on the dock, so anyone who happened to stroll by could see. I didn't care.

Perhaps that's what scared me most.

I'd lost all sense of what was important and that was from a single mind-numbing kiss.

He must have detected my change in attitude because Conahegg pulled back. He was breathing heavily, his pupils dilated. His hair, despite its short length, was mussed. He looked very different from his normal, composed self. My heart strummed when I realized I'd caused his transformation from self-contained sheriff, to sex-crazed wild man.

"I've been wanting to do that from the moment I saw you," he rasped.

I fluttered my eyelashes, trying to make light of his pronouncement. "Aw shucks, Sheriff, I bet you say that to all your material witnesses."

"I'm serious, Ally."

"Look, Conahegg," I said, my voice shaky.

"Sam."

I ignored his offer to call him by his first name. "We can't do this again."

"Why not?"

"Because…" I couldn't meet his gaze. "I'm not available."

"You mean you have a male friend."

"No. It means there's no room in my life for a male friend."

"Why not?"

I waved my hand at the house. "You know my family. I work two jobs. When do I have time for a dalliance?"

"Is that what you think I want? A dalliance."

I could not, would not look him in the eyes. "It doesn't matter what you want."

"Ally?"

We both leaped about a foot at Mama's voice, me scooting from Conahegg's lap at record speed. Somehow she'd sneaked up on us. I busily patted my mussed hair.

"Evening, Mrs. Green," Conahegg greeted her.

"Hi, Mama," I said sheepishly.

"Allegheny Allison Green, what's happened to your manners? Aren't you going to invite your guest inside for tea?"

CHAPTER SIXTEEN

CONAHEGG SPENT the next half hour sipping herbal tea and listening to Mama and Aunt Tessa tell him about their unwanted visitors. Me, I slunk off into the corner to deal with my jumbled emotions and only occasionally reached up to finger my lips.

I could still taste Conahegg.

He finally left after assuring us he'd have his men look out for Sissy and that'd he'd personally pay a visit to Dooley Marchand and Darlene Hughes.

I felt a little better, but not much. That night I barely slept, between sizzling fantasies of Conahegg, nightmare images of Denny drowning and Sissy running from an angry, troll-doll-smashing man.

The unease I'd been feeling since finding Rocky's body grew into full-blown anxiety. If I didn't do something constructive soon, I was going to scream. That and the fact I needed something to keep my mind off Conahegg and what had happened on my dock.

Finally, at dawn, I threw back the covers and got up before the alarm went off. I skipped breakfast and arrived at the home health care office before anyone else. I spent that time combing through Tim's and Rocky's charts. I wasn't sure what I was looking for and I didn't find anything of value.

At eight, I left the office for Swiggly's house.

The good reverend was in a surprisingly upbeat mood.

When I arrived, he was finishing up a morning swim with his personal physical therapist, a strapping, buff, lifeguard type he introduced to me as Gunther.

Gunther—who with his blond hair, blue eyes and straight white teeth could have passed for one of those California beach musclemen—carried Swiggly from the pool. He sat him at the patio table and vigorously toweled him off while I questioned Swiggly about his health.

Miss Gloria came into the backyard, a bankbook in her hand. She took one look at me and stopped. "Oh," she said, then turned and went back into the house.

"I'm doing pretty good, aren't I?" Swiggly asked. He rang a bell and Esme magically appeared. "Orange juice," he told her. "And toast. Wheat bread."

She bobbed her head and disappeared.

Swiggly looked at me. "You want anything? I can call her back."

"No thanks."

"In fact," Swiggly continued, "thanks to the Power and Glory of our Lord Jesus Christ in heaven, praise God, thank you, Amen. I won't be needing your services any longer, Miss Green."

He did look exceptionally well. His color was good and his eyes bright. He even hummed a few bars of "The Old Rugged Cross."

"Your doctor wants us to see you for another month, Reverend Swiggly."

Swiggly waved a dismissive hand. Gunther plugged in a blow-dryer to an extension cord. "What do doctors know? They think they are God, when it's the Lord Jesus Christ who controls our fate, not the minor machinations of so-called healers."

Oh boy, I could feel a rant coming on.

"Besides…" Swiggly smiled up at the tanned Adonis standing beside him wielding a hairbrush and the blow-dryer. Gunther turned on the hair dryer and began arranging Swiggly's pompadour. "I've got Gunther. He can take care of my health care needs," Swiggly shouted over the noise.

"It's your choice, sir," I shouted right back. "But I'll have to make your doctor aware of your desires."

"I would expect no less from you."

Somehow, that sounded like a put-down. Hell, I didn't care. I had enough problems without having to kowtow to a pompous, egomaniacal holy man.

"Great." I closed his chart and got up. "I wish you a speedy recovery, Reverend Swiggly."

"Why, thank you, my girl."

I left that house feeling very happy to be gone, but as I pulled from the drive I happened to glance up and saw the curtain from the upstairs bedroom drop.

Someone had been watching me.

"ALLY, ARE YOU IN SOME KIND of trouble?" Joyce Kemper asked when I returned to the office.

"No." I frowned, signing off on Swiggly's chart and handing it to the secretary for processing. "Why do you ask?"

"Sheriff Conahegg called here. He wants to see you in his office. ASAP."

"Is that what he said?"

Joyce nodded.

A thrill shot through me. Conahegg wanted to see me. Apparently, he wasn't taking no for an answer when it came to our relationship. I was both pleased and irritated. How did that man simultaneously evoke such opposing emotions in me?

"I'm sure it's nothing," I said, retrieving my purse from my desk drawer. "You know that the sheriff is Denny's Junior Adventurers troop leader and we took the kids camping on the river over the weekend. It's probably got something to do with that."

Joyce grunted, unconvinced.

But while I was spinning tall tales for Joyce, my pulse was thrumming. For better or worse, I was going to see Conahegg again.

Turning, I fled the office and arrived at the sheriff's department in five minutes flat when the trip should have taken ten.

I didn't even bother to announce my presence to the dispatcher. The front desk looked pretty busy anyway. I strode down the corridor as if I knew what I was doing and knocked on Conahegg's open door.

He was parked behind the desk, busily dispatching a stack of paperwork and looking more delicious than any human being has a right to look. He glanced up, but didn't smile. Was something wrong?

My stomach plummeted and I forgot about sexual attraction. Did he have bad news concerning my sister? I braced myself for the worst.

"Come on in." He raised his chin. "Shut the door behind you."

"Uh-oh, this doesn't sound good." I tried to sound lighthearted, hoping to make him smile.

He didn't smile back. "I'm afraid it's not."

"Did you find Sissy?" I whispered, almost afraid to ask.

Conahegg shook his head.

I plunked down on the seat, clutched my purse to my chest. "What then?"

He cleared his throat. "Bad news."

"Tell me straight," I said, feeling like a character from some bad fifties film noir.

"You were right." Conahegg laced his fingers together and cracked his knuckles. That's when I realized he was nervous, too. What did he have to be jittery about?

"What about?"

"About Rocky."

"What do you mean?"

He pushed several sheets of stapled papers across his desk toward me. "Autopsy report."

My hand shook and my mouth went dry. Okay, I had great intuition. Why then did I suddenly feel so horrible?

I picked up the papers and held them next to my nose because I didn't want to put on my reading glasses in front of Conahegg. I skipped to the section marked: cause of death—asphyxiation.

"I don't understand. I thought you said I was right."

"Keep reading."

And read I did. There were discrepancies in the marks on Rocky's throat. The coroner concluded he had been asphyxiated first and then his neck had been broken. There had also been a lump on the side of his head indicative of blunt trauma, but that wound had not caused his death.

"I still don't get it." I looked at Conahegg. "From reading the report, he suffocated himself, then fell off the bed, breaking his neck and hitting his head."

"The logistics don't add up. No matter how he fell, he wouldn't have hit his head in that spot."

"No?"

"And," Conahegg said. "I got to thinking about what you'd told me concerning Rocky's phobia."

"You did?"

"I talked to Darlene and some of his friends. They confirmed what you'd said. He was terrified of having anything around his neck."

"So you believe it was murder and someone tried to cover it up as autoerotic asphyxiation?"

"Yes."

"But who?"

He took a deep breath and when he didn't meet my eyes I began to worry. Conahegg is a straightforward guy. He's not into avoidance.

"We found fingerprints on the belt used to hang Rocky," he said.

I clamped my hands into fists, dreading what he was about to say next. The pitying expression Conahegg gave me was the one you reserve for families of the deceased. A shiver blasted through me.

"No," I whimpered.

"The fingerprints belong to your sister."

I shook my head. "It's a mistake."

"There's been no mistake."

"The lab screwed up. It happens."

"I'm afraid not."

"Sissy's innocent."

"I'm afraid your sister looks guilty as sin, Ally," he said softly. Pity flashed on his face but only for a second. "She had the means and no alibi."

"But why? What's her motive?"

"Anger. Money. You told me yourself she had bad experiences with men. She had already shot Rocky once for lying to her about his wife."

"You're wrong. My sister isn't capable of doing something like that."

Could Sissy have killed Rocky?

It was unthinkable, unimaginable and yet she *had* shot him in the foot. My sister did have many secrets, as I'd recently discovered, that she held close to the vest.

"You told me yourself she wasn't happy with Tim Kehaul after he left her for another lover. Is that the action of a rational woman?"

"Sissy isn't crazy."

"Men have taken advantage of your sister for her entire life. She has ample motivation for murder."

"Next thing you know, you'll be telling me that Sissy killed Tim."

"There is that possibility."

"What? Are you telling me Tim didn't die from autoerotic asphyxiation, either?"

"No. That's exactly what Tim died from as far as we can ascertain. What I am telling you is that it might not have been an accident. What if Sissy went to see Tim and pleaded with him to be her lover again? What if she convinced him to play kinky sex games with her? What if, right when she has him where she wants him, she kicks the stool out from under him and doesn't cut him down? The way Tim died is more indicative of having a partner. Most autoerotic victims sit in a chair or lie on the bed, not climb up on a step stool."

I slapped my hands over my ears. "No. I won't listen to your ridiculous theory."

"What if Sissy decides to make Rocky's death look the same as Tim's? But she can't kill him that way. He has a phobia about having anything around his neck. So she goes to his trailer, gets him drunk and stoned." Conahegg waved at the report. "If you'll notice he had not only alcohol and marijuana in his bloodstream but Valium, as well."

I thought of my mother's Valium prescription. Could Sissy have stolen a few pills and done exactly as Conahegg suggested?

Impossible.

"When Rocky's out like a light, Sissy smothers him with a pillow. Except, he rouses and tries to fight her. She grabs the nearest thing that's handy. I figure it's the bedside lamp, there's a chip knocked out of the base. She beans him on the noggin. When he stops struggling, she finishes the job. She ties one end of the belt around his neck and knots the other end around the bedpost and then she kicks him off the bed, breaking his neck."

I caught my breath. It sounded so plausible. Yet if I knew anything, I knew my sister was not a killer.

But then why had she run away? I remembered the night she told me about the near rape. How desperate she'd seemed.

"There are any number of people who could have killed Rocky. Why have you zeroed in on my sister?"

"She's the most promising suspect. And there are those fingerprints."

"But she was his girlfriend. Is it so unrealistic that her fingerprints would be in his bedroom?"

"On the belt?"

I felt my stomach go empty and the color drain from my face only to be immediately replaced by searing anger.

"You bastard," I said, springing to my feet. "You're using everything I told you in confidence on that camping trip against my sister." I couldn't believe Conahegg was betraying me. The man I lusted after. The man I'd kissed.

"That's not true," Conahegg said.

"Bullshit! You're using it to build a case against Sissy."

"Be reasonable. It's my job to search for suspects."

"You didn't even believe me when I first told you there was something suspicious about Rocky's death."

"I believe you now."

"This is crazy." I shook my head.

"You're upset, that's perfectly understandable."

I leaned across his desk and jammed my finger under his arrogant nose. "Don't you dare try to placate me with platitudes."

"I wish you would calm down."

"And I wish you'd never come back home to Cloverleaf."

He said nothing for a moment. My anger thrust hard against the inside of my chest making it difficult to breathe, impossible to think rationally.

I had confided in him and he had broken my trust. I should have known better. He was a cop for heaven's sake. What had I been thinking?

"How do you know it wasn't me?" I asked.

"What?"

"Maybe I killed Rocky."

"You didn't." He shook his head.

"How can you be so sure? I disliked him."

"You have no motive."

"He was mistreating my sister, stealing things from my house."

"You never told me that."

"I told you too damned much."

"Look, I know what you're doing, but it's not going to work. Sissy's fingerprints are on that belt, not yours. And she's missing. You're here. For once in your life stop taking the blame for other people. Stop trying to cover up for your family. When are you going to realize that you're not responsible for what they do."

"You don't understand. You don't have a family who depends on you."

"I understand more than you think I do," he countered.

I didn't know what he was talking about and frankly, I didn't care.

"Sistine is my sister," I murmured, suddenly the anger was gone and only sadness remained in its place.

"Ally, you're entitled to your feelings, but I called you over here to let you know face-to-face. I have issued a warrant for Sissy's arrest. For murder in the first degree."

CHAPTER SEVENTEEN

IF CONAHEGG was convinced my sister was guilty, clearly I had no choice. I had to find out the truth about what happened to Rockerfeller Hughes on my own. I would not allow my sister to spend her life in prison because some good-looking misguided sheriff had gotten the notion in his thick skull that Sissy was a killer.

Honestly, I felt a little betrayed by Conahegg. I mean, I know it's his job and if the evidence points to Sissy, then he had to consider her a suspect. But after kissing him, I'd secretly hoped deep down inside that maybe we'd get together. His prevailing attitude ended any chance of advancing our relationship.

Ah well. It wasn't as if I wasn't used to being manless.

I had to forget Conahegg. More pressing matters required my attention. Like where and how to start my investigation? Just call me Gumshoe Ally.

Should I start with Darlene Hughes? I wasn't a private detective; I had no idea how to find her.

After spending a near-sleepless night wrestling with the questions, I called in sick to work the following morning. Since I had never taken sick leave in the seven years I'd been employed by Joyce, she didn't give me a hard time.

"What are you up to, Ally?" Aunt Tessa asked me. Apparently, she'd been standing in the doorway listening to me lie badly to Joyce. My aunt was dressed in a silky blue caftan, feathered matching mules and enough crystal jewelry to choke the whole of Sedona, Arizona.

I hadn't yet broken the news to her and Mama about the charges Conahegg had leveled against Sissy. I'd been trying to protect them, but I realized I was going to have to tell them the truth and even ask for their help. Someone would have to look after Denny while I was gadding about town in search of suspects.

"Bring Mama in here," I said. "I've got something to tell you both."

"More bad news." Aunt Tessa nodded. "I knew it." She trotted out to the pottery shed and retrieved Mama, who was covered in flecks of paint.

"What is it, dear?" she asked.

I told them about Sissy and the murder charge. Mama stared at me for the longest moment. I ran to stand beside her in case she was going to faint. But she shocked me by squaring her shoulders and looking me straight in the eye.

"Sissy didn't kill Rocky."

"I know that."

"You've got to prove it to Sheriff Conahegg."

"I know that, too."

Then my mother said something I rarely heard her say, "Let me help."

"What?"

"I'll try to find Sissy."

"But how?"

"I'll visit her friends, stop by the beauty shop."

"Really?" My mouth had dropped to the floor.

"Your sister needs me."

A recent voice in the back of my head sniggered, "You needed her for years," but I let it go. Mama had risen to the occasion and I couldn't be more proud.

"I'll take Denny to spend some time with his friend, Braxton," Mama continued, "so we won't have to worry about him."

Stunned, I simply nodded. "Thanks, Mama."

She smiled faintly. "You're welcome."

Then it dawned on me. Conahegg was right. Mama needed to be needed. All these years I'd been taking care of her because I thought she was so fragile and helpless. I'd had it all wrong. Was Mama's dependency mostly my fault? If I hadn't been so strong, so capable, would she have risen to the occasion long ago? It was a real eye-opener.

"I'll change clothes," Mama said. "And call Braxton's mother to see if it's okay if Denny spends the night."

I nodded and eased down at the kitchen table still amazed at the transformation in my mother.

Aunt Tessa sat beside me and placed her long lacquered fingernails on my arm. I noticed the paint had chipped. She needed Sissy to come home and give her a fresh manicure. That thought made me feel sad. A lump formed in my throat.

"I had a vision," she whispered. "You're walking into danger."

No shit, Sherlock. "Aunt Tessa…"

"You need protection. Let me come with you."

"You don't even know where I'm going," I said, wanting to protect her.

"To see Darlene Hughes."

I stared. "How did you know that?"

"You'll take me with you?"

"No."

"Please. I can be a big help."

"It's not a good idea."

"I know where she lives," Aunt Tessa enticed me.

"You do?"

"Uh-huh."

"And you're not going to tell me if I don't take you along." I sighed.

"That's right." She gave me a rakish smile.

I thought of Mama again. I met Aunt Tessa's gaze and I have to admit it was nice to know I wasn't shouldering the burden alone. "Let's go."

Aunt Tessa directed me to the grungiest part of Cloverleaf, not too far from the sheriff's department. We had to pass it on the way but unlike other occasions, I had no desire to stop in and see Sam Conahegg.

We parked outside a small frame house with peeling paint and a litter of broken kids' toys in the front yard. Did Rocky have children? I shuddered at the thought.

I knocked several times before the front door opened to reveal Darlene, her eyes caked with sleep, a Marlboro dangling from her bottom lip, a pair of mismatched socks on her size ten feet.

"Oh." She yawned and scratched a breast clothed in a stained and faded T-shirt proclaiming: Stardust Casino, Loosest slots in Vegas. "It's you two."

"May we come in?"

"What for?" she asked, keeping the ripped screen door closed between us.

"We want to talk to you about Rocky."

"There's nothing to say."

"We know where the money is," Aunt Tessa said.

I looked at her.

Aunt Tessa shrugged.

Darlene threw the door wide. "Come on in. Don't mind the mess."

We stepped over beer cans, more broken toys, empty pizza boxes. She swung an arm at the couch, knocking off a pile of debris. "Have a seat," she said, then plopped her backside into a purple Naugahyde Barcalounger.

Tentatively, Aunt Tessa and I settled on the edge of the couch.

"You found out where Rocky hid that money?" she asked, fishing a lighter from the breast pocket of her T-shirt and setting fire to the end of her cigarette.

"What we want to know," I said, "is where the money came from."

"Beats me," Darlene said and blew a cloud of smoke in our direction. Aunt Tessa coughed delicately. "But I wantcha both to know that's my money. Rocky was still married to me when he died and Texas is a community property state. He was my husband," she said. "And I loved him."

"Darlene," a man's voice bellowed from the back of the house. "Who the hell was at the door?"

"Nobody. Go back to sleep."

I looked at my watch. It was ten o'clock in the morning. "Loved Rocky a lot, did you?" I couldn't resist asking.

"Oh, you mean Hank? Don't worry about him. He's just my boyfriend."

Lovely.

"Listen, Darlene—" I leaned forward, ad-libbing as I went along "—let me be straight with you. My sister Sistine has the money and it seems she's left town. We can't give it to you until we find her. But in order to find Sistine, we need to know where the money came from."

"I just got out of prison, lady. I hadn't seen Rocky in thirteen months till you caught us kissing in his hospital room."

"But surely he told you what he was up to. How he expected to get money."

"Actually," Darlene said, gnawing at a cuticle, "he tried to borrow three thousand dollars off me." She swept a hand at her surroundings. "Does it look like I got that kinda dough?"

No, it did not.

"You're holding out on us, Darlene."

"What makes you think I'd tell you anything, anyway?" she asked.

Greed.

"You'd like to see justice done."

"What are you talking about?" Darlene narrowed her eyes at me.

"Rocky didn't kill himself while choking the chicken."

"No?"

"He was murdered."

If I expected her to be surprised, I was wrong. Darlene didn't bat an eyelash. She picked a fleck of tobacco off her tongue and flicked it onto the floor. "Is that right?"

"According to the coroner's report."

"Well, what do you know."

"Where were you on the night Rocky died?" I asked, not really knowing what I was doing but finding myself swept away by an unexpected excitement.

"You're not going to pin this one on me, sister. I was at an all-night AA meeting. With plenty of witnesses. Here. I'll give you my sponsor's phone number." She reached over, tore a hunk from an envelope lying on the lamp table next to her and wrote down the information for me.

Damn. There went a suspect. Of course, I'd have to check out her story. I had a feeling Darlene wasn't opposed to lying if it served her purposes.

"Are you certain you have no idea what Rocky was involved in?"

"Nope."

"Liar!"

Aunt Tessa, who had remained silent through the interrogation spoke. Except it wasn't Aunt Tessa but Ung. My aunt, glaring like the wrath of God, pointed at Darlene with a three-inch-long fingernail.

"Hey," Darlene said. "She's doing that thing she did the other day at your house."

"She's channeling her spirit guide," I explained.

"I know all. I see all. You lie," said Ung.

"Make her stop," Darlene whined and hugged herself.

"I can't. She's not an attack dog."

"Those who lie rot in hell with the damned!" Ung's voice was deep and gravelly as a rusted chain. She got to her feet and moved toward Darlene in jerky, Frankenstein's monster movements.

I was worried she was going to catch the heel of her mules on the rubble-riddled floor. But she seemed to step effortlessly over the crap as if in a perfectly choreographed ballet.

"Worms will eat the flesh from your skull. Maggots will feed on your brains," Ung intoned.

Sometimes Ung comes on pretty strong.

Darlene lifted her hands in front of her face. "Okay, okay, I'll tell you the truth, just get her out of here."

I stood and placed a restraining hand on Aunt Tessa's arm. "Spill it."

"I think Rocky was blackmailing someone."

"Who?" I demanded.

"I don't know for sure. Maybe Dooley Marchand. Maybe one of the sheriff's deputies."

"Liar!" Ung screeched.

Darlene cowered. "I'm not lying. Honest."

"I believe you," I said. "Thanks for the info."

"Hey," Darlene said as I took Aunt Tessa's hand and guided her toward the door.

"Yes?"

"When do I get my money?"

"SO," AUNT TESSA SAID, fluffing her hair with one hand. "Did I do good or what?"

"You were faking Ung?"

"Uh-huh." She giggled.

I slanted her a glance. "Do you always fake Ung?"

"Why, Allegheny Green, I don't believe you asked me that." Aunt Tessa sniffed and stared out the window. "I am a true and honest psychic."

"Okay, I apologize."

"And you wouldn't have gotten that much from Darlene without me."

"That's probably true. Thank you."

I looked at my aunt. Had I been ignoring a resource right under my nose? "Aunt Tessa, do you really think Ung could help us find Sissy?"

"Of course."

"Do you think you might be able to contact Ung?"

"I can try."

Ung could be fickle, showing up when she wanted to, ignoring requests when she wasn't in the mood.

I hesitated, not knowing how to ask this next question. "Do you think you can contact Rocky?"

"You mean from the grave?"

No, from eating peanut butter and banana sandwiches with Elvis at Graceland. "Can you do it?"

"I thought you didn't believe in afterlife readings."

"Hey," I said, "it's better than nothing."

When we got home, Mama gave us a report. She'd gotten Denny organized and taken him over to his friend's house. Then she'd gone by the beauty shop but no one there had seen Sissy in a while. She'd tried a few of Sissy's friends but no one claimed to know where she was.

Aunt Tessa told Mama about the séance and she insisted on being included. We entered Aunt Tessa's parlor and drew the curtains. Mama lit the special candles Aunt Tessa used for enticing spirits. The strong scent filled the room and made me want to sneeze. Aunt Tessa seated herself in a plump straight-backed armchair like a queen on her throne.

Mama and I sat around the antique lacquered table that Aunt Tessa and her second husband, Robert—an eccentric inventor who'd been struck by lightning while trying to perfect his aluminum water skis—had picked up in Hong Kong back in the early seventies. The three of us clasped hands and Aunt Tessa began preparations for her trance.

Aunt Tessa closed her eyes, took several deep cleansing breaths and started her ritual incantation.

She chanted for a few minutes, then abruptly, she sat up straight and her eyes flew open. Her grip on my hand tightened.

"He is here," Aunt Tessa said in Ung's voice, staring at someone I could not see.

"Who's here?" I asked.

"Man with name of rock." Being twenty-five-thousand-years-old limited Ung's vocabulary.

"Rocky?"

Aunt Tessa nodded.

I couldn't help it. I craned my neck and looked around the room. Nothing. No strange breeze blowing out the candles, no prickly sensation on the back of my neck, no ghostly whispers.

"Can we talk to him?" I ventured.

"Speak," Ung invited.

"Uh, Rocky, Ally Green here. You wouldn't happen to know where Sissy is?"

Silence.

I squirmed in my seat.

"Sanctuary!" Ung shouted. "Sanctuary!"

Great. Now, she was calling up Quasimodo. "Are you saying Sissy is in a sanctuary?"

"Safe place." Ung grunted.

Okay. That was good.

"Ask Rocky who killed him?" I leaned over and murmured to Aunt Tessa. It would be nifty if Rocky's ghost told us who'd strangled him. It would cut through a lot of red tape. Unfortunately, it would be pretty hard to substantiate in a court of law. I could just see Aunt Tessa-Ung on the witness stand.

"Man," Ung said.

"A man killed him?"

"Man with gun."

"A gun?"

"Man with star."

A man with a gun and a star? I frowned. "Like a policeman?"

"Powder," Ung said.

"Powder?" I was thoroughly confused and discouraged to boot. The séance was getting us nowhere and I was feeling dumber by the minute for even suggesting it.

"Drugs."

Hell, wasn't that exactly like Rocky? Even in the afterlife he was looking to get high.

"Tell him thanks for the trouble," I said, pushing back my chair.

"Wait."

I froze in midscoot. "Yes."

"Bad man."

"Okay, okay, I get it." I snorted impatiently. "Bad man with gun and star and drugs." Then as soon as I spoke the words, something Maddie Farnsworth had told me clicked into my head.

Conahegg had problems in his department. Someone was stealing drugs from the evidence room and selling it on the side. A deputy. Like the one I'd overheard talking to Rocky in the church rectory at Tim's funeral.

As Oprah Winfrey is fond of saying, it was a lightbulb moment.

Could Conahegg's deputy, Jefferson Townsend, be the one who killed Rocky?

I LEFT MAMA TO MINISTER to Aunt Tessa who slumped like a dishrag in her chair. Normally, I would have been the one to lead her to bed, bathe her face with a washcloth, make her tea and stay with her until her strength returned. But I was burning with the need to follow any lead and I was relieved to realize I could rely on Mama to take care of Aunt Tessa while I was gone. Feeling lighter than I had in years, I reviewed my theory.

Maybe Jefferson had been dealing to Rocky from the evidence room and Rocky knew where he was getting the drugs. Then Rocky, pressured to come up with the money to pay off Dooley Marchand, told Jefferson he'd better give him three thousand dollars or he'd go to the sheriff. Jefferson, not having the money, killed Rocky to protect his secret and got the idea from Tim's death to make it look like autoerotic asphyxiation so no one would suspect the murder was drug related.

What I needed was something more substantial than a testimony from beyond the grave. I needed proof to tie Jefferson to Rocky.

But what was Sissy's role and how had her fingerprints gotten on Rocky's belt?

I pushed those nagging questions aside and took off to Jefferson's place.

I hadn't gotten very far down 51 when I spotted a car pulled over on the shoulder of the road. I slowed. It was a powder-blue Cadillac El Dorado. I stopped alongside the vehicle.

Gloria Swiggly was in the driver's seat, her head slumped over the steering wheel. For one awful moment, I thought she was dead. Then she raised her head and stared at me. Her eyes were red rimmed. Any fool could see she'd been crying. The way I figured it, living with Reverend Ray Don was enough to make anyone burst into tears on a regular basis.

I rolled down my passenger side window and leaned as far over as my seat belt would allow.

Seeing that she wasn't going to get out of having a conversation with me, Gloria lowered her window, too.

"Are you all right?" I asked.

She blinked as if she didn't recognize me.

"It's me. Ally Green. Your husband's nurse."

"Oh yes," she forced a smile. "Nice to see you again. How are you?"

"I'm fine. But I'm worried about you. Are you having car trouble?" I motioned at the Cadillac.

"No, no," she chirped brightly. "Just pulled over for a little prayer and meditation. One can't pray too much you know."

"I suppose not."

She started the engine. "Bye, bye." She wriggled her fingers.

"Bye," I said and pulled aside to let her go past, wondering if the woman was on Prozac or whether she needed to be.

CHAPTER EIGHTEEN

SHERIFF'S DEPUTY Jefferson Townsend lived in a small apartment complex in the middle of town. No one answered my knock. For a moment I had the freaky sensation that behind that front door lay another body attached to a rope, but I resolutely shook off the feeling.

I knocked again.

"He ain't home, lady."

I looked down to see a little girl about six years old sticking her tongue out through the hole where her front tooth used to be.

"He's not?"

She wagged her head. "He just left."

"Oh. Well, I'm a friend of his and I dropped by to say hi. Do you know when he'll be back?"

She shook her head. "No, but if you wanna go inside and wait for him, he keeps a key under the rug." She peeled back the welcome mat and handed me the key.

"How do you know?"

"He's my Momma's boyfriend."

I stood looking first at the key in my palm and the six-year-old leaning against the railing. Let myself in or not? What about the kid?

"Are you his girlfriend, too?" she asked.

"No." I shook my head.

"My Momma's got more boyfriends than him." She jerked a thumb at Jefferson's apartment.

"That's nice."

"None of 'em is as nice as my daddy, though."

I wished the kid would scram. If I was going to break into Jefferson's apartment I didn't want a pint-size accomplice along for the ride.

The kid, however, had other plans. She plucked the key from my hand, inserted it in the lock and pushed the door open. "Come on in." She beckoned.

And so I did.

"What's you name?" she asked.

"Ally."

"Mine's Katie," she said. "My daddy calls me Katie-did."

"Like the bug."

"Uh-huh."

We stepped into the living room and my eyes widened. Every available space was crammed floor to ceiling with unopened boxes of electronic equipment—cell phones and computer components, DVD players and surround sound systems, satellite dishes and video cameras. Expensive cameras like the one I'd seen in Rocky's trailer.

I gulped. Jefferson was lifting more than marijuana from the evidence room. It looked as if he'd hijacked a Radio Shack delivery truck. Maybe I really was on the right track.

Katie hopped up onto a box that housed a big screen television, whipped a Game Boy from her pocket and began playing Pokémon.

Stunned, I wandered around the apartment, not really sure what I was searching for.

I went through his bedroom, found rolling papers and roach clips and small brown vials of white powder. Jefferson's blatant drug use was stupefying. Conahegg had far more problems in his department than I realized. No wonder it was easier for him to accuse my sister of Rocky's murder than search for the real killer.

Sinking to my knees, I lifted up the bedcovers and peered under the bed. More electronic equipment and a huge baggy of greenish-brown leaves I feared was not tobacco. I thought of the kid in the living room. I needed to get her out of here.

And then I heard the words every girl was loathe to hear when she was in the midst of breaking and entering a drug dealer's apartment.

"Sheriff's Department. Get to your feet, put your hands against the wall and spread your legs."

"WOULD YOU LIKE to tell me what in the hell you were doing in Jefferson Townsend's apartment?" Conahegg leveled me a dark stare.

I'd never seen him so mad. One vein at his temple was distended. His fists were clenched at his side. His speech was slow and measured as if it took every ounce of control he possessed not to yell.

"Trying to find something to connect Jefferson to Rocky." I wondered why his contained anger excited me, and brought fresh sexual fantasies surging into my mind.

"That was a very stupid thing to do."

"Somebody had to do something to prove Sissy's innocence."

I avoided his glare by busying myself with slipping a finger under the corner of my blouse to retrieve my errant bra strap which had the irritating tendency to slide down my shoulder at the most inopportune times.

Conahegg was watching me like a lion stalking an antelope. His brows dipped low in a deep frown. "Since when did you become a private investigator?"

"Since you decided my sister was guilty of murder and stopped looking for the real killer."

"I suggest you let me handle this. For your own good."

"Oh, so now you know what's best for me?"

"Believe it or not, I care about what happens to you. If you keep breaking and entering into drug dealer's apartments you're bound to get hurt."

He cared? My heart lurched but I couldn't seem to leave well enough alone. I didn't need for him to assume the role of my daddy.

"I'll take my chances. It's better than sitting around twiddling my thumbs, waiting for you to make a move."

He shoved a hand through his hair. I realized I was in trouble when I saw that his hand was shaking. Uh-oh. He must be really mad.

"You don't give me enough credit."

"Well, I come by my skepticism honestly. I've seen my share of incompetent men."

He leaned forward, teeth bared, both palms splayed across the top of his desk. "Are you calling me incompetent, Ms. Green?"

Lordy! Get the fire hose! My loins were burning.

"Simmer down. I don't think you're incompetent. I think you're an extremely hardheaded man who's accustomed to getting his own way."

Conahegg made a choking noise. "Me! I'm hardheaded? Lady, if I didn't know better I'd swear your head was made of cast iron."

"I'm a little stubborn," I conceded. "Especially when it comes to my family."

"A little stubborn? That's like saying the Grand Canyon is a little wide."

"You gotta calm down, Sheriff. You'll have an ulcer before you're forty."

He mumbled something under his breath that I didn't catch. Probably a good thing.

"So is there a connection between Jefferson and Rocky?" I prodded the conversation back to the issue at hand.

Conahegg heaved a long-suffering sigh and slumped in his chair, the anger dissipated from his face. Apparently, I'd worn him down. I should have been triumphant. Instead I felt slightly disappointed.

"There is a connection between Jefferson and Rocky," he said. "Although God knows why I'm talking to you. Jefferson was stealing drugs from the evidence room and peddling them on the street. Rocky was a regular customer. Jefferson's been up to some bad things but he's got nothing to do with Rocky's murder."

"How do you know Jefferson didn't kill Rocky?"

"Because on the night Rocky was killed, Jefferson was on patrol with his partner."

"Oh." And just like that, my entire theory vanished.

Conahegg shifted in his seat. "Will you for once give me some credit? Go home and take care of your family. Leave the police work to me. Can you do that, Allegheny? Or am I going to have to handcuff you to my desk in order to get some peace and quiet around here?"

CHAPTER NINETEEN

OKAY. JEFFERSON didn't kill Rocky. And Darlene claimed to have an alibi, although I hadn't yet called her AA sponsor to confirm her story. I put that on my mental to-do list.

Which left me with only one suspect. Loan shark and bouncer, Dooley Marchand.

It was early afternoon when I returned home from my set-to with Conahegg. I seriously doubted if I would ever see eye to eye with that man. I'd decided to ignore his strict advice to let him handle the investigation. For one thing, my sister's life was at stake. For another I was having more fun hunting down leads than I had in a very long time.

Aunt Tessa and Denny were fishing on the dock. Aunt Tessa wore a wide-brimmed straw hat and Holly Golightly gloves up to her elbow and a dozen strands of crystal beads. Mama sat under the umbrella at the picnic table painting a ceramic jousting knight.

I greeted them, then went into the house. I called Darlene's sponsor and confirmed that she had indeed been at a marathon AA meeting at the time Rocky had been murdered. Frustrated, I got out the phone book and looked up Dooley Marchand.

I dialed his number and an older woman answered. When I asked for Dooley she said she didn't know where he was but I could catch him at work at Tits-a-Poppin' around eight o'clock that night. I thanked her and hung up.

Since there wasn't much else to do, I took a nap to prepare myself for what lay ahead. Mama surprised me by making open-faced roast beef sandwiches, mashed potatoes and green beans for supper with strawberry parfait for dessert, but I was too nervous about meeting Dooley Marchand to eat much.

Still, the excitement energized me in a way nothing ever had. It dawned on me that I liked the danger. What was happening? I'd never been the type to take unnecessary risks. When had I started to change? What would happen when the murder investigation was over? Could I go back to my ordinary, mundane life?

At eight o'clock I dressed in a black Lycra pantsuit, the only slinky thing I owned, and a pair of two-inch black pumps. At five-nine, I refused to go taller than two-inch heels. Not sure whether I was trying to fit in or call attention to myself, I did the whole war paint thing along with perfume and jewelry.

Too bad Conahegg wasn't here to see me. I twirled before the mirror. I tousled my hair, pursed my lips and winked at myself.

"Hey, there, big boy," I purred to an imaginary Conahegg. I saw him, gray eyes gleaming with lust, steel jaw clenched against his desire, arms crossed over his chest.

I was way past horny.

Shaking my head, I dispelled Conahegg's visages and applied an extra coat of mascara to my lashes. Satisfied that I looked as slutty as I could, I quickly tiptoed past my family in the living room.

I stopped at the garage to retrieve granddaddy's twenty-two pistol from the wall safe and shoved it in my purse before darting out to the car, my heart racing, my palms sweating and my sexuality slammed into overdrive.

I hadn't been this excited since...well since never. I was getting off on the rush of tracking down Dooley Marchand, going against Conahegg's orders, doing something forbidden.

The sun had slipped behind the horizon as I pulled into the parking lot of Tits-a-Poppin'. A gaudy neon sign of a woman taking off her clothes flashed rhythmically. Shirt buttoned, prim expression—lights yellow. Shirt unbuttoned, boobs popping—lights red and green. Santa's perverted wet dream.

I'd never been in a strip club but I had seen Demi Moore in *Striptease,* so I sorta knew what to expect. Except the girls didn't turn out to be as cute as Ms. Moore. Nor was the clientele as high rent as Burt Reynolds in Vaseline and cowboy boots.

On the wall outside the club was a big sign warning gun toters about the legal risks of bringing weapons into a place of business where alcohol was consumed. I swallowed hard and clasped my purse tightly. Should I take the pistol back to the car?

And face Dooley Marchand with no protection?

I'd take my chances.

Feeling like a very wicked woman and thrilling to my bravery, I sashayed up to the door as if I owned the place.

The doorman eyed me suspiciously but didn't stop me. The place was as dark as a movie theater. I had to stand to one side and allow my eyes to adjust to the change in lighting before proceeding.

In the center of the room stood a stage with a runway that ended in heavy velvet drapes, with two smaller stages off to either side. Colored lights strobed. Currently, one girl gyrated in the middle of the center stage, wearing nothing but a sequined silver G-string and six-inch heels that tilted her forward and made her butt stick out.

She was a little flabby and I could see her cellulite from across the room but she had big boobs, although you could tell they weren't real. They jutted out like a hood ornament and the skin over her breasts was stretched to capacity.

Tits-a-Poppin' was not as glamorous as its tag line—a

Gentleman's Cabaret—promised. First, there were no gentlemen in attendance and second, this was no cabaret. Which to my mind brought provocative images of Liza Minnelli and Joel Grey in outlandish costumes with interesting music played by a live band.

Here, "Hot Stuff" blasted from a cheap stereo system and customers vomited uninhibitedly on the cement floor.

Rocky's kind of place.

"What's the matter, lady, you looking for your old man?" A voice that sounded too much like one of those wrestlers rang in my ears.

I raised my eyes. The guy *looked* like a wrestler. Long blond hair, bulging forehead veins, arms thick as car tires. He had a cauliflower ear and an ominous scar running from the right side of his eyebrow to the top of his cheek.

"Uh, no. I'm looking for Dooley Marchand. I understand he works here as a bouncer."

His eyes narrowed, his lips pressed into a thin line. "I'm Dooley. Whatcha want with me? The car payment is in the mail, swear to God."

I stared at him. "Do I look like a repo agent?"

He sized me up. "No. I guess you don't. So who are you?"

"I'm looking into the death of Rockerfeller Hughes."

"You don't look like no cop, either. Let me see your badge."

"Did I say I was a cop?"

"You a P.I.?"

"Wrong again."

"Who *are* you, then?"

"Sistine Green's sister. The police think she killed Rocky and they've issued a warrant for her arrest."

Dooley snorted. "Figures. The stupid dude offed himself. The cops don't know their asses from a hole in the ground."

I was inclined to agree. No offense, Conahegg.

"Rocky owed you money," I said.

"Yep. Three grand."

"And he never paid."

"No, but he called here the day before he died bragging that he was making some kind of big score and that he was going to pay what he owed."

"Did he tell you where he was getting the money?"

Dooley shook his head. "Said it was a secret."

A secret huh? Well that little secret was probably what had gotten him killed.

"So where were you the night Rocky died?"

"Right friggin' here."

Great. Another suspect with an alibi. But that didn't mean he hadn't slipped away from work, killed Rocky and hurried back. Except Andover Bend was on the opposite side of the county and a forty-five minute drive from here. No doubt someone would have noticed if Dooley had been gone for an hour and a half. But I'd ask around and find out.

"You don't know what happened to the money?"

Dooley shook his head. Then his eyes narrowed further and he stuck his hands on his hips, arms akimbo.

"Wait a minute, I'd bet anything your sister's got the loot."

"What makes you say that?"

"She's missing and so is the money."

"How do you know she's missing?"

"Your loony aunt told me."

Ah yes, when he'd shown up to break Mama's troll dolls. I shouldn't forget that he could be a violent man.

"Put two and two together," Dooley said. "Your sis is vapor. Probably in Mexico blowing the loot on bad tequila."

I feared he might be right. Except Sissy had been trying to turn over a new leaf. Or so she'd told me.

"Maybe the cops are right," Dooley continued. "Maybe

your sister did kill Rocky. In which case *she* owes me money. Guess that scare I put into her the other night didn't do much good." He slammed a hammy fist into his open palm.

Anger leaped through me. "It *was* you who beat her."

He shrugged. "I couldn't find Rocky. Sistine was the next best thing."

"You get off on beating women, do you, big man?" I can behave like a real fool at times, especially when I see an injustice. Especially when it's aimed at my family. It's a dangerous flaw of mine.

He took one arm and braced it on the wall over my head. I gulped. He leaned way over until we were nose to nose.

"Yeah," he whispered. "I do get off on beating women. If you don't get me three thousand dollars by Friday, you're gonna be next."

My hand slipped inside my purse and I wrapped my fingers around the twenty-two and, keeping it concealed, pointed it at his crotch.

"I have a gun," I said, opening the flap of my purse real quick so that he could see I wasn't lying. "Step away from me if you value your gonads."

"Huh?" He looked confused.

"Your balls! If you don't want them shot off, move over there." I motioned toward a table. I talked tough but my knees were whamming together so loudly I worried he'd hear and know I was bluffing.

"It's against federal law to bring a firearm into a bar," he said.

"Duh," I snapped, as if committing a felony was a daily occurrence for me. "Tell me something I don't know. Now move it." I jammed my purse into his groin, which was too close to my eye level.

"No," he said.

What now?

"I could break your arm in two pieces." Dooley snapped his fingers. "Like that."

"You must not mind pissing from a tube," I said, desperate to hold on to my bravado. It was the only thing I had going for me. Sweat rolled down my breast and pooled in my cleavage. *Come on, Marchand, sit down so I can get away from here.*

He hesitated, gauging my seriousness.

A drunk appeared from the shadows near the front door and staggered toward us, a misshapen cowboy hat pulled low over his forehead.

At least I thought it was a drunk.

The man stumbled into Marchand.

"Hey," Dooley said, "watch what you're doing."

"Hot Stuff" morphed into "Hot Legs" and the first dancer wandered offstage and another equally bored colleen took her place. No one paid any attention to us.

"You're not threatening a lady, are you?" The drunk asked in a deadly voice. I saw his teeth flash in the darkness as he smiled a predatory smile.

"Shove off." Dooley placed a hand on the man's chest and gave him a push.

But the stranger was lightning quick. He clamped down on Dooley's wrist like a mongoose on a cobra.

The stranger was big but Dooley was bigger. Much bigger. I sucked in my breath. Someone was fighting for my virtue. Well, not my virtue really, since I didn't think Dooley had intended on having his way with me sexually, but rather my reputation.

Dooley cocked back his other hand.

Before he could even release the punch, the stranger flipped Dooley over his shoulder onto the cement floor. There was a loud, ugly thud.

I cringed. That had to hurt.

The next thing I knew the stranger had one knee pressed hard against Dooley's throat.

"Tell the lady you're sorry," the man growled and in that moment I recognized the voice.

Conahegg.

My face turned hot. My body, too.

Dooley said something that sounded like, "Ah tworry." But I couldn't be certain.

My mind whirled. What was Conahegg doing here in street clothes? Was Tits-a-Poppin' his after-hours hangout? He really didn't seem the strip club type, but who knew?

"You won't be contacting Ms. Green or her family under any circumstances." Conahegg put more pressure against Dooley's neck until his veins bulged. He pulled his badge from his pocket and held it in front of Dooley's eyes. "Because if you do, I'll arrest you for stalking. Got that?"

Dooley nodded or tried to.

A few of the patrons had stopped salivating at the stage long enough to cast vaguely curious glances our way.

Conahegg got to his feet. Dooley lay stretched out on the floor moaning.

A big black dude came thundering from the back. His jaw was clenched and he looked ready to fight. "What's going on over here?" He glanced from the downed Dooley to Conahegg to myself.

"Misunderstanding," Conahegg said. "Resolved."

"You knock over my man, it ain't resolved," the black man said, moving toward us in a slow, menacing manner, his fists upraised.

Conahegg flashed his badge again. "Before you open your mouth, I suggest you find out if that girl dancing on the stage is over eighteen. Don't make me shut the place down."

"Oh, uh, right." The guy quickly backed off.

"Come on," Conahegg said, taking my elbow and hauling me from the club.

CHAPTER TWENTY

"WHAT IS THIS," I carped, once we were outside and I had twisted from his bear-trap grip. "I'm not yours to manhandle, Conahegg."

A light rain had begun to fall. The shine from the neon sign flashed a reflection in the water puddles on the asphalt. Red, green, yellow.

He pushed the cowboy hat back on his forehead. "I saved your stubborn hide. Doesn't that afford me some sort of momentary proprietorship?"

"No." I glared at him but my heart went thudda-thudda-thudda.

"Can we at least get in out of the rain?" he asked, opening the passenger side door to his SUV.

"I've got my own car, thanks."

"Get in, Allegheny," he growled.

I thought about telling him to get stuffed but he had such a no-nonsense expression on his face and I was getting wet, so I climbed inside.

Conahegg slid behind the wheel and the dome light came on, illuminating him for a close-up.

Even drenched he looked good. Like Indiana Jones fresh from a field expedition, all manly and macho and full of himself.

"Please, tell me that's not a gun in your purse." Conahegg

groaned and cast a glance at my handbag which lay open on the seat between us.

"It's not a gun," I replied, happy to oblige his fantasy by hastily snapping my purse shut. "Besides, it's not loaded."

Conahegg whipped out his hand, grabbed my chin and forced me to look him square in the eye. "Your behavior isn't funny, Ally. You're in over your head. You don't go after men like Dooley Marchand with an unloaded gun."

His nostrils flared and his pupils constricted. I could smell the scent of his cologne, the tang of his toothpaste. His collar had gotten flipped up in the scuffle with Marchand, the white of it startlingly bright against his tanned neck. Right at that moment I wanted nothing more than to bury my mouth in the hollow of his throat, taste that skin, lose myself in him.

"Okay," I admitted, even though I was loath to confess my weaknesses. "I'm in over my head."

Conahegg let me go and leaned back against the seat. "Do you realize what a pain in the posterior you can be? You scared the daylights out of me."

"What are you doing here?"

"Following you."

"And you called Dooley a stalker?"

"Don't start with me, Ally," he warned.

"Why were you following me?"

The dome light faded to black. Conahegg's SUV was parked facing the Majestic liquor store. We watched the manager lock up for the night.

"I dropped by your house to speak with you and I saw you driving away."

"And you decided to tail me."

"Yes."

"I never spotted you." I couldn't believe I'd been so oblivious to Conahegg tracking me.

"You're not trained."

"Do you think Dooley Marchand could have killed Rocky?" I asked.

"No. He's got an alibi."

"You checked him out?"

"Of course. The day after you found Rocky's body."

I was impressed. Okay, so maybe he hadn't been sitting on his hands as I supposed. "But you still think Sissy did it."

"She's the only one who's skipped town. It doesn't look good, Ally. Sooner or later, you're going to have to face facts."

"Sissy did not kill Rocky." I peered out my window. Our breath formed moisture against the glass. I wiped a circle with my fingers.

"We need to find her. If she didn't kill Rocky, then she probably knows who did and she's afraid."

That had never occurred to me. "Do you think Sissy is in serious danger?"

"Could be. Do you have any idea where she could be?"

"No."

Rain drummed on the roof. I was uncomfortably aware of Conahegg's presence not three feet from my reach. If I stretched out my hand, my fingertips would graze his hard muscled thighs.

"Ally," he said, his voice strangely soft.

I raised my head. "Yes?"

"I want you to promise me you'll stop doing crazy things like this." He waved a hand at the strip club. "You're going to get into serious trouble. Will you leave the law enforcement to me?"

"I can't promise that."

"You mean you won't."

"How can I trust you to look after my best interests," I said.

"You're the sheriff. Your job comes first. With me, it's my family."

"If I had to, I could put you in jail to keep you safe. That pistol in your purse is grounds enough."

"But you won't." I met his eyes. They were hard and soft at the same time.

"No. I won't."

I exhaled, only then realizing I'd been holding my breath.

"Ally, I'm worried about you. I'm afraid the next time you get into a scrape I won't be there to bail you out."

"Don't worry, I can take care of myself."

"Can you?"

"I've been doing it for seventeen years. Myself and everyone else."

"Maybe it's time to let someone else do the caretaking." He reached for me but I shied away.

I didn't want him to touch me. I didn't want to care about him. I didn't want to be at the mercy of runaway emotions.

But it was too late and I knew it.

"By the way—" his eyes raked over me, his tone lightened "—I like the pantsuit."

"What?"

"You look very nice. Much too nice for here. Would you like to go grab a bite to eat?"

"Are you asking me out?" I blinked at the abrupt change of conversation.

"Would you say yes if I were?"

"I thought you said I wasn't ready for a relationship."

"Who's talking about a relationship? I'm proposing a steak at Taggert's Diner."

"I gotta go home."

"Why? Are you afraid to be alone with me?"

He knew I couldn't pass up a challenge.

Damn Conahegg. Damn him for tailing me. Damn him for being so attractive when the last thing I needed was to be entranced by him.

All I wanted was for Sissy to be cleared of murder charges and for my life to return to normal.

And then a little voice in the back of my head spoke up loud and clear.

Liar, it said.

He ran his callused thumb along my wrist. I felt as if I were rushing headlong into an abyss but I couldn't seem to stop myself from charging straight ahead.

"If not dinner," he whispered, "maybe a drink? You need a little fortification after your run-in with Marchand."

"Dinner's fine." Although I was hungrier for beefcake than beefsteak.

Don't ask me what I was thinking, because I wasn't. Not a coherent thought entered my head. I registered everything through a primitive, elemental filter.

Man. Big. Strong. Hands on steering wheel. Scent. Musky. Sexy. Immediate. Taste. Salty. Sweet. Eagerness.

Feel. Leather seats. Fingernails biting into palms.

Sight. Rain. Headlights cutting the darkness. Sound. Windshield wipers. Whoosh, whoosh, whoosh.

Was this how Aunt Tessa's Ung experienced the world? Blunt. Raw. Unadorned.

It felt real. I felt alive. I wanted more.

I wanted Conahegg.

Silence expanded in the vehicle. Filling my ears. Blossoming until it was its own noise.

I sneaked a surreptitious glance at the man beside me.

He turned his head, caught my eye.

The way he looked at me had me feeling as if I'd unleashed a chained beast. His breathing was heavy, his eyes murky.

I gulped, leaned toward the door.

He finally snapped his gaze away, forced to focus on the road and pulled into Taggert's parking lot.

The lights were out. A Closed sign on the door.

We both stared at the empty building.

"Oh," I murmured. "I forgot. Jim Taggert closes the restaurant the third week in July for his family vacation."

"Ah," Conahegg said and nothing else.

The digital clock, numbers glowing green from the dashboard, flicked over. Ten o'clock. Not yet late.

"I've got steaks in my freezer," Conahegg ventured. "If you're still interested in dinner."

Our gazes met and held as if we'd been superglued together.

The ball was in my court. If I went to his place we both knew we'd never get around to those steaks.

"Um, uh."

"Or I could take you back to your car."

It could just be sex, Ally, it doesn't have to mean anything.

Except I'd never had meaningless sex in my life.

So try something new.

Why not? If nothing else it would be a pleasant distraction from murder and mayhem, from dependent family members and a missing sister.

"Can I be honest?" Conahegg broke through my dithering.

Oh God.

I nodded.

"I want to spend the night with you," he said. "I've wanted it from the moment I laid eyes on you, Allegheny Green. The steak was an excuse."

"I know," I whispered, my pulse racing at an impossible gallop.

"My place?" His voice was hoarse as sandpaper.

"Yeah."

"Are you sure?"

In my heart I knew going to Conahegg's house wasn't a good idea. That we were both feeling vulnerable and swept away by passion. I didn't want to hurt him. Hell, I didn't want to hurt me.

I almost told him to forget the whole thing. I was only kidding, ha, ha. But the desire I saw reflected in his eyes was my undoing. No man had ever looked at me in quite that way. As if I was the most beautiful creature on the face of the earth and he couldn't wait to bury himself inside me. Heady stuff for a small-town girl who didn't get out much.

"I'm sure," I said, even though I was anything but.

He threw the SUV into overdrive and stamped on the gas.

We shot from Taggert's parking lot like an emergency ambulance headed for a ten-car pileup.

IT TURNED OUT Conahegg lived in a two-story log cabin with ten-foot beamed ceilings, three miles south of Cloverleaf. I briefly got to meet his German shepherd, Rex, whom he promptly escorted to the garage.

"Come here," he said, shutting the garage door behind him and moving across the living room toward me.

And I went. Meeting him halfway.

Equals.

Hey, I couldn't let him have the upper hand, could I?

He rested one hand at my waist. His eyes glittered in the dim lighting. I felt strange in his room, but comfortable in his arms.

He lowered his head to my lips.

I waited. Ready.

In that moment our mouths came together. Frantic, hungry. We clung to each other, kissed as though we could never get enough.

My groin was on fire. Aching, burning for release.

His fingers were fumbling with my zipper. I tore at the buttons on his pristine white shirt. I heard them snap loose, then hit the floor. The sound and my own wildness fueled my desire. I wanted Conahegg in a way I had never wanted another. He induced the most animalistic response in me.

Man. Woman. Sex.

Simple equation. Nothing complicated about that.

Gasping, I wrenched my mouth from his. "Wait."

He stopped, my zipper half-down, his chest heaving. "Uh," he grunted, his eyes heavy lidded.

"Condoms?" I could barely speak myself.

"Got 'em."

"Bed?" Although I don't know why I asked. I was so hot for him, so wet and ready I would have done him right there on the hardwood floor.

"This way."

He took my hand and led me upstairs to a bedroom with a four-poster king-size bed. The blinds were open and the rain had stopped. A sudden moon shone through the curtainless window, illuminating his body in a shimmery glow.

His shirt gapped open where I'd torn away the buttons. I could see the honed definition of his tanned, muscular chest. My stomach flipped in anticipation.

He guided me to the bed, propped me against the pillows. He removed his clothes while I watched, then slowly he finished undressing me.

I ran my fingertips over his skin. He hissed in his breath at my touch, as if I were a sizzling branding iron—and, indeed, I felt hot enough to mark him.

"I feel like an explorer," I whispered, strumming his body from cheek to chin, shoulder to forearm.

"Delve to your heart's content, Christopher Columbus, as long as I'm afforded the same privilege."

His fingers skimming? His palms kneading my flesh? His tongue tangling with mine?

Hi-yi-yi.

Breathless, I placed kisses along his body and he did the same with mine.

We lay beside each other—feverish, trembling—touching and stroking, our hands gliding over naked skin.

It was a dance, a play, a sonnet.

A fantasy. So unreal and yet so authentic.

We lay shaken, awestruck at the power surging between us, snared helplessly in the sensations and newness of our discovery.

It was awkward at moments. Where do you put your mouth? Ouch, your nose hit mine. But at other times it was blindingly intense, the things we were feeling.

I say *we* because I know I was not alone in my wonderment. I could see the delight in Conahegg's eyes and I reveled in the notion that I was giving him so much pleasure. I found the power exhilarating. I'd never had a man marvel at my sexuality and his marveling made me marvel.

He signaled his desire to me in small sounds, gentle movements and I responded in kind, the fierceness of our earlier passion receding into something incredibly poignant.

Knowing we might never make love again, each breath, each sigh, each soft moan became important and imprinted on my brain.

He was unlike anything I'd ever experienced and everything I'd ever dreamed about. Sexy, funny, tender, hard.

I rode the crest of pleasure, enjoying the foreplay, savoring every sensation. But then, in the end, when Conahegg moved to cover my body with his, my niggling doubts rose to the surface, refusing to be silenced any longer by my raging libido. Sensible Ally could only be banished for so long.

What was I doing here? Making love with the man who wanted to put my sister behind bars. Why was I allowing my hormones to get the better of me when I knew there was little chance for a lasting relationship between the two of us? We were both too stubborn. Both too accustomed to being in control. We'd both been single for a very long time. I was dedicated to my family. Conahegg was dedicated to law enforcement.

Was there room in our lives for more? Could I learn to stop mothering the world? Could Conahegg learn to relinquish command? Could either of us learn to compromise?

I frowned, jerked from the warm cocoon of sex by my nagging conscience. My body stiffened.

"Shh," Conahegg whispered and laid two fingers over my lips.

"But I didn't say anything."

"No, hush your mind. Stop thinking, Ally. Be here in the moment with me. Don't worry about tomorrow. Just feel."

It sounded so good. Just let go.

But it felt a bit like drowning. Overpowered, overwhelmed, washed away by my senses and the intoxication of Conahegg's kisses.

I should be grasping at reality, pulling myself back from sweet oblivion. I wanted to struggle and yet I didn't. I was caught. Snared on the twin prongs of passion and guilt.

It was exquisite and it was horrible.

Was I sure? Come morning would I regret what we had done?

This is Conahegg. The guy who's convinced your sister is a murderer. Is this smart?

"Ally," he said. "Look at me."

He hovered above me, the bulk of his weight supported on his forearms, his legs spread over mine, his hard penis throbbing against my thigh.

Compelled, I stared into his eyes.

And found myself.

We hung there, suspended in time. Looking and looking and looking into each other.

Then Conahegg dragged in a ragged breath, leaned over to reach into the bedside table for a condom.

Before I knew what had happened, I was helping him put it on, feeling him come alive in my hand and quickly discovering that Conahegg was a large man in every way.

He kissed me again. Deeply, almost rough.

I answered in kind, lightly nipping his bottom lip.

"I'm on fire." He groaned. "Got to have you." Then finally, scarily, he whispered, "Mine."

Mine.

As if I belonged to him.

But I was too swamped by emotion and "just feeling" to analyze the meaning of the word or register my feelings regarding it. He'd successfully turned off my mind and turned on my body.

Boy, had he turned on my body.

I had no idea I could simmer like a hot spring. But I ached to boil over. To erupt. To explode. I needed relief. I needed Conahegg inside me. Nothing else would alleviate my desperate ache.

"I'm gonna take you," he warned, his pupils dilated, two magnetic pools sucking me under.

"Take me now," I hollered, like some melodramatic soap opera actress. I threw my arms around his neck, pressed my forehead to his and stared into him until my eyes crossed.

And take me he did.

My sanity shattered as he entered me. I cried out in delight at the shock of him.

He glided, smooth and thick, filling me up. Making me whole.

I was in the moment. Living and breathing every sensation.

I was not thinking about my family or my work or the grocery shopping. I was cognizant of nothing but Conahegg and what we were doing together.

"Ally, Ally, Ally." He chanted my name.

I clung to him, digging my fingernails into his shoulders, urging him onward.

We writhed and burned and throbbed. We grunted and groaned and moaned.

"More," I cried, "more," and clasped his bare buttocks with both hands.

My entreaty incited him to greater heights. He thrust harder, pushing deeper into me.

Heat and wet. Pressure and friction. Faster, faster, faster.

Oh my God.

Is this what it feels like?

I hung on the precipice, willing myself to tumble over. Conahegg gasped. Called my name again. Cupped my face in his palms.

Then I splintered into about a million pieces, falling, spinning, flying into a blinding, black pleasure. Then slowly, softly, I began to drift down, down, down into the warmth of Conahegg's arms, sated, completed, undone.

I grinned into the darkness as I realized what had happened.

For the first time ever, I, Allegheny Allison Green, had experienced a mind-altering, earth-shattering orgasm. And the big man nestled beside me was responsible.

CHAPTER TWENTY-ONE

IT WAS AFTER MIDNIGHT when I awoke with a start. Reality crashing in on me like bouncing down Niagara Falls in a barrel.

I'd made love to Conahegg.

And we'd irrevocably altered the trajectory of our relationship.

Where did we stand? Was I Conahegg's lover? His girlfriend? Or a one-night special? What did I want? Just because we'd had spectacular sex didn't mean we were compatible as a couple. Then there loomed the all-important question. Were we still at loggerheads over Sissy? Or by making love to me did that mean he'd come around to my way of thinking and no longer considered my sister his number-one suspect? Was I simply kidding myself?

Probably. I admired Conahegg because he was a strong person. He didn't waffle, he wasn't indecisive. I even liked that he didn't cave in to my objections. He stood his ground. But his strength could be my sister's downfall and in essence, I'd slept with the enemy.

Conahegg's arms were still wrapped tightly around me, one leg thrown over mine. I was pinned down. Trapped. He was breathing deeply, his chest rising and falling in a slow, steady rhythm.

The selfish part of me wanted to curl into the curve of his body, and fall right back to sleep. But too many years of conditioning and family responsibility kept me from indulging myself.

I had to get home. Mama and Aunt Tessa had no idea where I had gone. They were probably beside themselves with worry.

Then I realized I was stuck. My car remained in the parking lot at Tits-a-Poppin'. How was I going to get home? It wasn't as if Cloverleaf boasted a fleet of yellow-checkered cabs idling at the ready for my sneaking-out-of-one-night-stands getaway.

Groaning, I covered my head with a pillow. What on earth had I been thinking? I'd always harbored a secret superiority to people who allowed themselves to be led around by their sexual appetites. Making mistakes and gumming up their lives for a little nooky. Suddenly, I was one of those people.

I was both ashamed of my transgression and strangely invigorated by it.

Who was I?

Lately, my whole world had shifted, starting with the night Sissy shot Rocky in the foot and culminating in my ending up in bed with the sheriff.

This wasn't the rational behavior of staid, predictable Allegheny Green. The woman who scrutinized the terrain with a microscope before she leaped. The woman who always put her family first no matter what. Last night, that woman had disappeared and an intriguing stranger stood in her place.

Who had I become?

I glanced over at Conahegg. In the moonlight, I could make out his profile. His hard features had softened in repose. He looked almost boyish.

My heart twinged. I had an urge to reach out and run my fingers along his face.

Aw, jeez. I was in deep. I had to get out of here.

I tried to slide from underneath him but his leg weighed a ton. I squirmed. I twisted. I turned. And I marveled at how sore I was in certain places. Still, I couldn't get away from him.

"Conahegg," I whispered.

Nothing.

Dammit. How was I going to escape? I was ready to gnaw my arm off to get away from him. Not because he was coyote ugly, but precisely because he wasn't. He posed a serious danger to both my family and my heart.

"Conahegg," I repeated louder.

In response, he grunted in his sleep and tucked me tighter to his chest.

If I was the romantic type savoring our affair I'd admit it felt pretty great in his arms. But I had no time to luxuriate in the afterglow. What if something had happened and my mother was frantic to find me? What if Sissy had come home?

But he smelled oh-so-sexy and his arms felt too darned good.

"Conahegg!" I tugged at his earlobe. "Wake up."

He snorted and bolted to a sitting position. "Huh? What? What's going on?" His hair was sticking straight up and he rubbed at his eyes with a fist.

"I need a ride home."

"Now?" He yawned and scratched his bare chest. "What time is it?"

"Twelve-thirty."

"At night?"

"Yes." Boy, was he out of it. Did he always conk out so soundly after lovemaking?

"But we just went to bed. Roll over and go back to sleep. Or…" His tone turned suggestive and his hand slid down my waist and over my hip. "We could stoke that flame."

"No. Stop it." I pushed his hand away before I could succumb to his tempting suggestion. "I've got to go home and I need a ride. My car is back at the strip bar." What had I been thinking? Coming to his place without a getaway car?

"You're running out on me?"

"My family doesn't know where I am."

He switched on a reading lamp. We both blinked owlishly at each other. I hauled myself up against the headboard, tugged the sheet to my breasts.

"Give 'em a call." He nodded at the phone on the bedside table.

"I can't simply call. They're not used to me staying out so late."

"And you're how old?" he said sarcastically.

"Hey, don't start with me."

"Why not? You feel free to use me sexually and then run away."

"I did not use you!" I declared hotly. "And I'm not running away."

"Oh no? What do you call it? Fleeing your lover's bed in the middle of the night."

"I'm not fleeing." I notched my chin in the air and willed my cheeks not to flush. "I want to go home."

He snorted. "Chicken. You're scared."

"I'm not. I've got to go to work in the morning. I don't have any clothes here."

"Lame excuse." He crossed his arms over his chest and glared over at me.

"I don't owe you an explanation."

He studied me for such a long moment that I began to fidget. "I have feelings, Ally. In case you don't realize that."

Great, guilt.

"So do I."

"Feelings for your family, yes. But do you have any feelings for me?"

I couldn't look at him. Hell yes, I had feelings for him. Too many. Feelings I didn't understand. Feelings that threatened to complicate my life in ways I wasn't prepared to deal with.

He mumbled something I didn't quite catch. Something that sounded like, "I knew better than to get involved with you. I knew you weren't ready."

"What's that? What did you say?"

"Forget it." He got out of bed, searched the floor—likely for his underwear. Apparel was strewn across the room.

I didn't want to stare at his naked body, but something compelled me. Buns of steel. Washboard abs. The works. And he wanted me. And I was about to throw it away.

"No." I got on my knees in the middle of the bed, the bedcovers still clutched around me. "I want to talk."

"Oh, so now *you* want to talk." He found his BVD briefs, put them on and snapped the elastic band with his thumb.

"What do you mean, I'm not ready?"

His eyes glittered with anger. He scooped a T-shirt from a dresser drawer and jammed it over his head. "Exactly that. You're not ready for a relationship. You're still too wrapped up in your family. You're not ready for your own life."

He was wrong. I was more than ready, but I didn't know how to go about untying the apron strings. "Easy for you to say. No one depends on you."

"You don't think the citizens of Cloverleaf depend on me doing my job?" He jutted out his chin. "But that doesn't mean I owe them my soul."

"It's not the same thing."

"Face facts. You don't want to admit the truth."

"The truth according to Conahegg."

"That's right."

"So okay, oh wise one, enlighten me."

"You tell yourself you're the protector, the caretaker, but

in reality, Ally, you're hiding behind your family's dependence on you."

"I am not!"

"Then why do you play to their weaknesses? Why do you assume responsibility for your sister's actions? Why do you let your aunt and your mother live off you?"

"They can't take care of themselves."

"Because they've never had to. You've always been there to wipe their noses, clean up their messes."

Guilty as charged, but I wasn't about to confess that to him. He already had a Goodyear-blimp-size ego.

"And where did you get your degree in psychology?" I wanted to spring from the bed and retrieve my own clothes but I was feeling shy about exposing myself to him. Never mind that he'd already explored every inch of my body.

"From the school of hard knocks. I know what I'm talking about, Ally. I've been there."

I sank back onto the bed, deflated. "What do you mean?"

"We're just alike, you and me. Or at least we used to be. Before I grew up and learned my lesson."

"Yeah?"

"Yeah." He gave me a half smile, sat down on the edge of the bed beside me. "When I was growing up my mother was like yours. Clingy, dependent. She was terrified to let me go outside and play. I was a sissy. Bullies used to pick on me."

"You?" I studied him. "But you're so strong. So tough. So in control."

He nodded. "That wasn't always the case. My father was an alcoholic and my mother fed his dependency. She bought beer for him, made up excuses when he was too drunk to go to work. She facilitated his drinking and so did I. Eventually, his drinking got so bad he couldn't function. He lost his job.

I was only fifteen years old and I had to take over earning a living. My mother never once confronted him."

"I never realized," I murmured, aching for him. We were a lot alike. "I mean I knew you sacked groceries after school but I had no idea you supported your parents."

"The minute I turned eighteen I joined the Marines. I was looking for the stability only a discipline like that could give me. The Marines molded me into the man I am today."

"How did you find the courage to leave your mother? I mean who was going to take care of her with you gone?"

"I had no choice. I knew if I didn't leave I'd end up like my father. I did the best I could. I sent Mom my paycheck every month."

"How did she survive?"

"My leaving was the best thing that ever happened to her. It gave her courage. She saw that she could escape. That she could change. That she could make something of her life. It took a few years but finally she worked up the guts to leave my father."

"So what happened to her?"

"She started her own business. Met my stepfather, a man who treated her right. They live in Florida. She's a completely different woman. Happy, vivacious. Her only regret is that she didn't leave sooner. She looks younger now than she did ten years ago."

"And your father died drunk."

He nodded. I saw pain in his face. Anguish over the past, the choices he'd made. He was trying to spare me some of that pain.

"Let go of your family, Ally," he said. "Let go and they'll fly and then you'll be free."

"I can't," I whimpered. "Not yet. Sissy still needs me. She's in too deep. If you find her you'll arrest her for murder." I met his gaze. "Won't you?"

"I have to."

"And yet you expect me to sit by and let that happen?"

"You don't have any choice in the matter."

"Yes I do. I can find the real killer."

"Ally…" His voice held a note of warning.

"You're ready to send her to prison for the rest of her life. What else can I do?"

"Let me handle this. It's the only way you'll learn to let go. The only way Sissy will learn to accept responsibility for her own actions."

"I can't," I whispered. "She's my baby sister."

"Do you think I want her to be guilty? Do you think I want to hurt either one of you?" He leaned over, hooked a finger under my chin and forced me to look at him. His eyes held nothing but concern.

"No, but if you cared about me you'd be out looking for the real killer."

"That's not fair, and you know it. I'm doing the best job I know how. The evidence points to your sister. If I don't arrest her when we find her then I'm not doing my job and you wouldn't respect me."

He was right. But I was right, too. My sister had not murdered Rocky. I knew it with every cell in my body. He had his job to do and I had mine. When Sissy's innocence had been proven maybe then I could take a stand, and confront my family. But until then I had to depend on what had served me well for thirty-one years—my ability to take care of those who needed me.

"When you can allow your sister to stand on her own two feet, when you can move your family out of your home, then you'll be ready for a relationship, but until then this isn't going to work out between us."

"I know," I said, appalled to hear tears in my voice. He was indeed correct. I wasn't ready to let go.

"I'm not going anywhere. I'm right here. But I only want you to come to me when you're prepared for an equal partnership. When you're willing to put yourself and your needs ahead of your family. We both deserve that."

I nodded, too afraid that I would burst into tears if I spoke. I felt angry and sad and confused. He'd painted a verbal picture of me from his eyes and it wasn't pretty.

"Come on," he said gently. "Get dressed and I'll take you to your car."

CHAPTER TWENTY-TWO

BACK HOME, I COULDN'T SLEEP. I stared at the ceiling. I counted sheep. At 4:00 a.m. I even broke down and listened to one of Aunt Tessa's meditation tapes but the trickling background music made me visit the bathroom.

The bed was too soft, my pillow too lumpy, the house too darn lonely without Conahegg in it. I'd arrived home to find Aunt Tessa and Mama snoring soundly. I'd forgotten Denny was spending the night with Braxton. I felt a little hurt that no one missed me. Perhaps Conahegg's theory wasn't so far-fetched. Maybe I was dependent on my family's dependency.

I had a sudden urge to cry again and blamed it on PMS. But my melancholia went deeper than hormones and I knew it.

On the one hand Mama and Aunt Tessa and Denny were counting on me to exonerate Sissy, to perform magic like some kind of female David Copperfield. On the other hand Conahegg had warned me away, suggesting that if I didn't keep out of things and let him do his job that I would be jeopardizing any chance of a future with him.

Part of me wanted to rail against his authority and tell him to go butt a stump. Another part of me feared I'd already fallen in love with the big lug.

In truth? I had no idea what I was doing. Neither in the romance department or the crime-solving arena. I had no notion of where to look for Sissy, no clue how to follow leads.

I was a nurse for crying out loud, not a cop. Everything I'd tried had backfired and in the process I'd insulted the only man who could really tell me what I needed to know.

Except he was on the opposite side, determined to prove my sister a murderer.

I had to do something. I couldn't stay in bed five minutes longer. I got up, dressed in shorts, a T-shirt and sneakers, made myself a Dr. Pepper, then went outside.

The rain had stopped but the ground was still moist. In the light from the vapor security lamp, I sat on the dock and stared out at the water listening to the crickets chirp and watching the alligator gar patrol just beneath the river's surface searching for bugs attracted by the light. A light breeze blew and it felt good against my heated skin.

I lay back against the dock's damp wooden planks and stared up at the endless sky awash in a sea of stars. The world was so vast, my problems nothing more than a speck in the whole scheme of things. Yet in my microcosm those problems loomed gigantic.

Mentally pushing all thoughts of Conahegg aside, I rehashed the events that had led me to this point. From Sissy shooting Rocky to my finding first Tim and then Rocky's body, to Sissy's disappearance. Every potential suspect had an alibi. All evidence pointed to my sister. She had the means, the motive, the availability. But I knew in my heart, despite her faults and flaws and erratic behavior that my little sister was not a killer.

I had to be missing something. Some key piece of the puzzle remained hidden. But what?

Determined to unknot my tangled brain, I left my Dr. Pepper sweating on the dock, untied the canoe from its place in the boat slip and got in.

I pushed off into the inky darkness with nothing but stars

to light my way. I had no conscious destination in mind. I was simply allowing the river to soothe and guide me as it had throughout most of my life. I dipped my oar into the water and forged ahead.

Night sounds were magnified out here. Nutria splashed along the banks, bullfrogs thrummed a deep-throated chorus, coyotes howled in the distance. I paddled on, past the housing developments, the rock quarry and signs of people living there. I felt like an early settler awed by the majesty of nature.

Not much more than a hundred years ago Commanche and Kiowa Indians had roamed the territory, made their home on this river. I could feel the spirit of their legacy singing through me as I skimmed over the water, enveloped in the warm, summer night.

I rowed until my arms ached. Past Campbell Island and Sanchez Creek and the pool where the hidden caves were located. On past the spot where Conahegg had saved Denny's life. I recalled that moment, my gratitude for Conahegg, my paralyzing fear. The instant when my feelings toward him had begun to shift and I saw him not only as a determined sheriff but as a kind, caring human being.

A lump formed in my throat. Ah Conahegg, what was I supposed to do about these fresh new feelings I had for you? I continued upriver and when I spotted the lights of Andover Bend I realized where I'd been headed all along.

The river narrowed, grew shallow. I guided the canoe through a tree stump graveyard, turning down one slender slough and then another. I inched past river shacks. Dogs ran along the banks barking at me, more from curiosity and boredom than any real attempt to thwart me from coming ashore. In the darkness, in the unfamiliar terrain, it took me a while to find the pathway that led to Rocky's trailer.

I beached the canoe and got out. My arms trembled from the effort of my early-morning journey. Walking toward his trailer, I saw crime scene tape still blocked the door. I tore it away.

The door was locked but it didn't take much to jimmy it. I used a crowbar from the back of Rocky's truck which still sat in the front yard.

Once inside, I discovered the electricity had been turned off. I went back outside and searched Rocky's truck for a cigarette lighter but instead found a flashlight. The beam was weak, but it would do.

Urged on by an instinct I could not explain, I entered the house. The rank smell remained but the place was tidier. I figured in the process of gathering evidence, the deputies had been forced to clean up.

It was harder than I thought it would be to walk toward that bedroom door again. And spookier with only the flagging flashlight to guide me. Goose bumps spread up my arms and I began to feel like the starring attraction in a slasher film. I wanted to drop the flashlight and run.

But I couldn't. Not only was Sissy's freedom hanging by a thread but my whole family was counting on me to make things right. Finding out the truth behind Rocky's death was to be my last contribution. I would save my sister but after this, they were on their own. I kept hearing Conahegg's words in my head, "You'll never be free until you let them go." I'd denied the truth for too long.

Rocky's bedroom had been stripped clean. The sheets were gone from the bed. The floor had been vacuumed. The miniblinds dusted.

I checked the closet, the drawers, the windowsill. It was slow going with a dim flashlight.

"This is getting you nowhere." I sighed out loud. "What the hell do you think you're playing at, Nancy Drew? Conahegg's crew has been through the room with a fine-tooth comb. You're not going to find anything."

My full bladder complained and I went into the bathroom, promising myself I wouldn't sit on Rocky's grungy toilet seat. I played the flashlight beam into the little room before me and something ground under my heel. I bent to pick it up.

A crystal earring.

Like the kind Aunt Tessa gave out by the dozens.

She'd given a pair to Darlene, I remembered. Had Darlene lost an earring in her husband's trailer? What did it mean? Just because it was here didn't mean she'd dropped it on the night Rocky was strangled. After all, her sponsor had sworn Darlene had been at the AA meeting at the time of Rocky's death. Unless the sponsor was covering for her. But why would she do that? Knowing it probably had nothing to do with Rocky's death, but loath to let go of any clue, I pocketed the earring.

The flashlight chose that moment to give up the ghost and I had to find my way out by touch. Dejected and bereft of ideas, I made it back to my canoe and headed for home.

I ARRIVED AT MY PLACE as the sun was pushing against the eastern horizon. I found Aunt Tessa in the kitchen concocting a breakfast smoothie that consisted of bean sprouts, tofu and goat's milk. She offered to make one for me but I declined.

"Where have you been?" She eyed me suspiciously. My clothes were wet, my hair frizzy, my eyes bleary.

"On a fool's errand." I plunked down at the kitchen table.

"Are you going to work today?"

"Yeah." I sighed, knowing if I didn't hurry I'd be late. "Listen." I pulled the crystal earring from my pocket. "How many of these have you given away in the last couple of weeks?"

Maybe Rocky had more women on the string than Darlene and Sissy. The idea was something I hadn't considered.

"Let me think. I haven't done too many readings lately. Just my regulars and they've already got earrings, and that nosy Darlene who didn't pay me." Aunt Tessa took a big swallow of her smoothie. "Oh, and the preacher's wife. I tell you it sure made my day when she came seeking my help. Sort of a real victory for the New Age movement."

I settled my elbows on the table, then rested my chin in my palms and fought back a yawn. "Why *did* she come to see you?" I asked.

Aunt Tessa tittered. "Well, I don't really know for sure, but I'd guess…" Aunt Tessa glanced around the room as if Miss Gloria was lurking about waiting to catch her spilling her secrets. "She was worried that her husband was fooling around on her."

"Age-old problem." I yawned again.

Aunt Tessa's eyes danced. "Yes, but there might be a bit of a twist."

"Yeah?" I could barely keep my eyes open. "Make me a cup of coffee while I get ready for work, will you? I'd be forever grateful."

"You got it." Aunt Tessa nodded and I slunk off to the shower, feeling more stymied by Rocky's murder than I had before my wasted canoe trip to Andover Bend.

LATER THAT MORNING Rhonda met me at the home health care offices. "Let's go to breakfast," she suggested.

"Can't."

"Come on." She took my elbow and practically threw me out of the office. "I'll bring her back in fifteen minutes," she hollered at Joyce over her shoulder.

We went into the pancake house next door. I ordered black coffee with three packets of sugar. Rhonda got Belgian waffles with strawberries.

"Okay," she said. "Spill it."

"Spill what."

"Don't try and pretend you don't know what I'm talking about."

"I don't."

"Lester saw you at Tits-a-Poppin' last night."

Lester was Rhonda's stepfather. He worked at the brewery in Fort Worth and on the drive home had a tendency to pop into the strip club to see what was popping out.

I never asked what Rhonda's mother, a petite attractive blonde who kept an immaculate house, thought about Lester's hobby but I knew she spent a lot of time baking. Cheesecakes and brownies, chocolate chip cookies and hazelnut bars. When her kids were in school she'd been the dream of the PTA. Now the Baptist church on Asher street, where she went to pray for Lester's soul, was the prime beneficiary of her culinary talents.

"Were you really there?" Rhonda asked. "Or was Lester hallucinating?"

I sighed. Cloverleaf and the gossip mill. "I was there."

Rhonda squealed. "No kidding!"

"It's not as cool a place as you might imagine."

"I imagine a bunch of old guys playing with themselves while women dressed like schoolgirls take their clothes off on stage."

"Yeah," I admitted. "It is pretty much like that."

"Lester's a descriptive storyteller." She leaned back in her chair, and flipped her fingers backward with a come-here gesture. "So give it up. What were *you* doing in a strip club and who was the stranger who fought Dooley Marchand for your honor?"

I rolled my eyes at the gossip mill's description of the incident. "I went to the club to speak to Dooley about Sissy and Rocky."

"Lester said you looked really hot. Like you were applying for a job there."

"Come on, Rhonda, do you think I'm moonlighting as a stripper?"

"You've got the body for it and they do make good money."

"Not good enough for me to wag my fanny in front of a bunch of beer-bellied old farts who've got more money than sense, no offense to Lester."

"None taken." Rhonda drummed her fingers on the Formica tabletop. She's a restless thing and I suppose that's how she managed to stay so thin. She doesn't have to spend her life at the gym as I do.

"So, tell me about the stranger. Who was he? Lester says the guy grabbed Dooley and flipped him to the ground—pow!" She slapped her palms together.

"That's true."

"Was Dooley trying to feel you up or something?"

"No. He threatened to kill me."

"Really?" Rhonda splayed a hand across her chest. "That's so exciting."

At the time, I'd thought it was terrifying. But thinking back on it, the incident *had* been stimulating.

"The guy. You never told me about the guy. Lester said he was wearing a cowboy hat and at first everyone thought he was a drunk."

"Did Lester do a play-by-play?"

"Basically."

"It was Conahegg."

"What?"

"The stranger. The guy who flipped Dooley Marchand on his butt, it was Conahegg."

"The sheriff?"

"Yes."

"The guy who gives you the hots but you claim you can't stand him?"

"That's the one."

"That's why you're so sleepy. You spent the night with him!"

"I did not spend the night with him." I wasn't lying. I hadn't spent the night with him. I'd left his place before one. I wasn't about to give Rhonda details about my sex life with Conahegg.

"I knew you and the sheriff were going to get together!" Rhonda smacked the table with a fist and her fork went flying. We tracked it as it flipped into the air, somersaulted twice and ended up in the oatmeal of a trucker sitting at the end of the counter.

He turned to glare at us.

Rhonda gave him her best Marilyn Monroe. "Oops, silly me," she said breathlessly. "I'm so sorry. Let me pay for your oatmeal."

"It's perfectly all right, little darlin'." The trucker returned her grin. "You don't have to pay for the oatmeal but as consolation, you could give me your phone number."

Giggling, Rhonda trotted over to him and wrote something on a napkin.

"You're a hazard to mankind, you know that?" I told her upon her return.

"Oh, pish, Ally, don't be such a stuffed shirt."

"That guy could be a serial killer, I can't believe you gave him your phone number."

"What kind of fool do you think I am?" she asked. "I gave him *your* phone number."

"YOU NEED TO GO VISIT Swiggly," Joyce told me when I arrived back at the office.

"He dumped me, remember. For a physical therapist named Gunther."

"Turns out he wasn't a physical therapist," Joyce explained.

"And he walked out of the house with thousands of dollars in religious art."

"You're kidding." This should keep Conahegg busy and out of my hair for a while.

"Nope. Not kidding. And Swiggly insisted he wants you as his nurse."

"Should I be flattered or horrified?"

"Go make the visit." Joyce shoved the chart at me. "He said he especially needs a back rub to ease his tension over the thefts."

"Horrified it is then."

I motored out to Swiggly's place with something less than joy in my heart. The man was as phony as a three-dollar bill and I didn't for one minute think he believed any of that stuff he spouted on television, especially after what Aunt Tessa had hinted to me. But I was a nurse and he was a patient, so I did what I was hired to do.

Esme bolted through the front door before I had a chance to ring the bell, her purse clutched so tightly in her hands her knuckles had gone white.

"Morning, Esme," I greeted her.

"Hello, Miss Ally," she said, "and goodbye."

"Are you going somewhere?"

She cast a glance over her shoulder. A look of disgust mingled with nervousness. "I'm going far from here."

"You're quitting?"

She nodded. "I never steal nothing in my life."

"Oh, course not."

I could see she was truly distressed, worrying her apron hem with her fingers, her hair flying haphazardly from her bun. "She say I do many bad things."

"Mrs. Swiggly?"

Esme nodded. "I don't know where to go. I don't know how to get another job. But I can't stay here no more."

"It's all right," I assured her. "You'll find another job. In fact, maybe I can help you." I thought of several of our patients who needed maid service as well as medical care while recuperating. I handed her one of my business cards. "Call me tomorrow."

"Thank you." Esme blinked back tears.

I patted her shoulder, then took a deep breath and went into the house, not knowing exactly what to expect. Confrontations with the maid, thefts by the sham physical therapist. Reverend Swiggly was excitable enough in the best of times.

"Hello," I called out, stepping into the foyer and shutting the door behind me. "It's the home health nurse, Ally Green."

I heard the sound of hard-soled shoes clopping against the terrazzo tile then Miss Gloria came into the room blandly attired as always.

"Oh, come on in. Ray Don needs your help in the bedroom. He's having a hard time putting that telemetry thingy back on."

"Telemetry?"

Miss Gloria frowned. "Didn't they tell you?"

"No," I ventured.

"He got so upset when he discovered Gunther was stealing from us that he started having those irregular heartbeats again. What do they call those? It's some initials."

"PVCs. Premature Ventricular Contractions."

"That's it," Miss Gloria said. "Anyway, he took off that box to take a shower and he can't get it back on by himself."

"It's called a halter monitor."

"I'll take you to him." She motioned for me to follow her.

We walked and walked and walked and finally ended up in the master bedroom. Swiggly was sitting on the edge of the bed in his silk pajama bottoms, his chest bare and his hair still damp from his shower. He was struggling with the monitor that was to record his heart patterns for the next twenty-four hours. He had the lead wires twisted in knots and his frustration level appeared to be reaching its peak.

"Thank the Lord you've finally arrived," he exclaimed when he spotted me. "Don't just stand there. Help me out with this thing."

"Sure." I smiled and set down my medical bag on the dresser. I accidentally knocked a small antique box to the floor, spilling its contents. Or rather, content. I stooped to pick it up.

A crystal earring.

Exactly like the one I'd found in the bathroom of Rocky's trailer.

A sudden chill ran though me. Nah. It couldn't be. Not the mousy preacher's wife. Why would her earring be in Rocky's trailer? She had no motive. Hell, as far as I knew, she didn't even know Rocky.

Then again… I stared at Reverend Swiggly. Hard.

I straightened. There was only one sure way to find out. If Miss Gloria could produce the other earring, then no sweat.

"This must be yours." I extended the crystal earring and the box toward Miss Gloria. "I knocked it off the dresser but I can only find one earring."

She snatched both the earring and the box from me and shoved them into the dresser drawer. "It's all right. They were cheap. I lost the other one over a week ago and I don't know where I could have dropped it."

CHAPTER TWENTY-THREE

GET OUT OF THE HOUSE, every cell in my body screamed. But my brain wasn't so smart. My mouth opened and words I'd had no intention of saying poured out.

"Hmm," I said. "That's quite odd."

"What's odd?" Miss Gloria asked. Her face took on a furtive expression. She formed her hands into half fists and cocked them in front of her breasts so that she resembled a curious prairie dog begging for treats.

"I found an earring like this one the other day and, silly me, I can't remember where. I'm wondering if it might be yours."

"Probably not," Miss Gloria said, one furtive hand went up to finger her naked earlobe.

"Hey," Swiggly interrupted. "Who cares about a pair of earrings? Help me get this damned thing back on."

"Ray Don." Miss Gloria sucked in her breath. "You said the *D* word in front of a guest."

"She's not a guest, she's a nurse and I'm sure she's heard the *D* word before."

"I've heard the *D* word," I assured him.

"You're going to hear it again if you don't get over here and strap this thing on me."

Not knowing how to make a graceful exit, and to keep Swiggly from turning the air blue with a plethora of *D* words,

I sidled over to him but still managed to keep a close eye on Miss Gloria.

What was her earring doing in Rocky's trailer? As far as I knew, she had no connection to the man. Unless Rocky and Swiggly had been lovers.

Maybe that's where Rocky had gotten the money he'd been bragging about—by letting Swiggly become his sugar daddy.

A pensive, dreamy expression came over Miss Gloria's face as if she was concentrating on something far away, a look not dissimilar to the one Aunt Tessa got when she morphed into Ung. The comparison made me nervous.

I pulled fresh lead pads from my pocket and bent to slap them in place on Swiggly's chest. When I raised my head, Miss Gloria had disappeared.

Damn.

Great. Now I was using the *D* word.

Hurriedly, I snapped the lead lines to the pads, stuck the monitor back into its pouch then hung the pouch strap around Swiggly's neck. "There you go."

I went to the dresser, anxious to retrieve the crystal earring, take it to Conahegg and have him compare it with the one I'd found.

"Wait a minute," Swiggly said. "Where you going? I need a foot rub. The doctor said that it was essential for me to relax."

"Just a sec." I raised one finger to silence him and slid open the dresser drawer with my other hand.

"Hey, what are you doing in my wife's drawer?" He had risen to his feet and was coming toward me.

"It's all right." I plucked the earring from among a stack of old-lady-style beige cotton panties.

Gak! Even her underwear was an off shade of brown. No thongs or high-cut briefs for our Miss Gloria. No silk or satin or lace. Plain and brown and nondescript like the woman herself.

I wondered if Miss Gloria ever got tired of being invisible.

"Are you robbing me?" Swiggly yelled, his face turning an interesting color of crimson. "I don't believe it. First Gunther, now you."

"I'm not robbing you, Reverend Swiggly. Please, take a deep breath and try to control yourself before you throw an embolus."

"A what?"

"A blood clot."

His breathing was ragged. He put a hand to his heart. "Maybe you're right."

"I wanted to compare your wife's earring to the earring I found."

"Why are you so concerned with my wife's jewelry? I'm the patient. You should be giving your attention to me." He jerked a thumb at his breastbone.

"And I will," I soothed, lying through my teeth. "Come on, pop back under the covers." I moved to the bedside, held up the top sheet and patted the mattress.

Reluctantly, Swiggly got into bed. "My feet," he moaned.

"Tell you what," I said. "Let me go get some hand lotion."

"In the bathroom," he said. "Get the aloe vera gel."

I slipped from the bedroom, but I had no intention of retrieving lotion to rub Swiggly's feet. I was getting the hell out of the house and over to Conahegg's office, pronto. But to keep from drawing attention to my plan, I had to leave my purse and medical bag sitting on Swiggly's dresser. Luckily, my car keys were in the pocket of my scrub pants.

With Miss Gloria's single crystal earring pressed in my palm, I tiptoed down the stairs as quickly and quietly as I could.

And I almost made it to the front door. My feet hit the terrazzo floor in the hallway, my soft-soled sneakers squeaking loudly.

"Going somewhere, Nurse Green?" Miss Gloria asked in a voice much stronger than any I'd ever heard come from her mouth.

I turned and saw her standing in the doorway of the living area.

She held a mean-looking shotgun in both hands.

Uh-oh.

I was scared. Very scared. If I hadn't developed excellent bladder control after years of Kegel exercises, I would have wet my pants on the spot.

What continued to perplex me, however, was motive. Why would a mild-mannered, unassuming woman like Gloria Swiggly kill a road toad like Rocky and risk losing her mansion on the hill? And kill him in such an exotic, erotic manner? It was completely out of character for her. The MO didn't fit the brown little woman with zero personality.

And then it occurred to me. Maybe Rocky and Miss Gloria had a thing going, not Rocky and Swiggly, although this was a little harder to imagine. Then, when pressured for money by Dooley Marchand, Rocky threatened to tell Swiggly about the affair. Maybe Miss Gloria paid him off and that was where he was getting the money he had bragged about.

Okay. That explained Rocky's sudden wealth, but not his kinky murder.

"Give me the earring," she said, extending one hand but keeping a steady grip on the gun with the other.

"What earring?"

"The one in your fist."

"Oh, you mean this." I held up the dangly earring. "The one whose mate you dropped in Rockerfeller Hughes's trailer house. What's the deal, Miss Gloria? Were you having an affair with him?"

"I don't have any idea what you're talking about," she denied.

"Then why are you pointing a gun at my head?"

"Give me the earring," she repeated.

I gestured to the front door a few feet away, so close and yet so very far. "I think I'm going to leave."

"You do and I'll blow a hole through you so big your Mama wouldn't recognize you."

I stared at her, bug-eyed and gaping like a catfish. Who would have thought she had it in her?

The doorbell chimed, playing "Lamb of God," and scaring the bejesus out of us both.

I could scream and get the attention of whomever was on the doorstep. UPS dude, Esme returning for her aprons, I'd even be happy to see Gunther.

Reading my mind, Gloria laid a finger over her mouth and shook her head. "Shh," she cautioned. "Don't say a word."

The doorbell sang "Lamb of God" again.

It was surreal. I was being held hostage by a gun-toting religious fanatic, listening to the door bell chime gospel music while my life ticked away.

I couldn't die. Not yet. I'd never traveled. I never learned to snow ski. I'd never dined in a fancy French restaurant.

I'd only had sex with Conahegg once!

Sweat popped out on my forehead. I stood frozen waiting for a brilliant idea to strike.

None did.

A knock this time, thankfully silencing "Lamb of God."

"Reverend Swiggly," a man called from the other side of the heavy oak door. "Sheriff Sam Conahegg. I'm here to investigate the thefts you reported."

Knock. Knock. Knock.

That's one thing I admired about the man. He was persistent as a bloodhound with the scent of jailbird in his snout. And more than anything in the world I wanted to wrap my arms around his neck and kiss him full on the mouth.

"Conahegg!" I shouted. "Help!"

"Shut up," Miss Gloria hissed, running to close the distance between us and shove her shotgun under my rib cage.

I guess I was expecting Conahegg to bust the door down using his big strong shoulder as a ramrod. It was a little anticlimactic when he simply turned the knob and walked right in.

"Ally." He stared at me, quickly taking in the situation.

"Close the door, Sheriff," Gloria said.

"What's going on here, Mrs. Swiggly?" Conahegg asked, giving her his best disarming grin. "You and Ally having a tiff? If you are, I can understand. The woman is so hardheaded she could win an argument with a billy goat. But violence won't solve anything."

Win an argument with a billy goat? That comment was uncalled for.

Gloria was not to be dissuaded. "Kick the door closed with your foot, Sheriff, and move against the wall, hands on your head. I'm sure you're familiar with the procedure."

Conahegg did as she asked. His flint-gray eyes met mine and welded there. *What in the hell is going on?* his gaze asked.

I arched an eyebrow and silently mouthed, "Rocky."

He frowned, not understanding my meaning.

"Turn around backward," Gloria commanded, favoring me with an excellent view of Conahegg's behind. Unfortunately, I was in no mood to appreciate it.

"Mrs. Swiggly, need I remind you that holding an officer of the law as a hostage is a very serious offense," Conahegg said.

"Shut up." She stepped over and removed his service revolver from the holster at his hip.

From behind us came a noise like a chain smoker scaling

Mount Saint Helens on a windy day. We three turned to see Reverend Ray Don shuffling toward us. He had thrown an expensive silk robe on over his pajamas and his feet were slippered in leather house shoes.

"They know," Gloria said.

"Handcuff the sheriff," Swiggly instructed his wife, relieving her of both the shotgun and Conahegg's thirty-eight.

She unhooked Conahegg's handcuffs from his belt and clicked them into place around his wrists. She turned back to Swiggly. "What about her?"

"Go get those heavy-duty zip ties from the pantry."

Gloria obeyed and disappeared.

The sound of Swiggly's labored breathing filled the room.

"Reverend Swiggly," I said, "are you all right?"

"No thanks to you. If you'd gotten that hand lotion and rubbed my feet like I told you," Swiggly lamented, "none of this would have happened." He shook his head as if I'd disappointed him deeply.

"If your wife hadn't been having an affair with Rocky Hughes none of this would have happened."

"Mrs. Swiggly was having an affair with Rocky?" Conahegg asked.

"No," Swiggly snapped. "You're wrong."

"So tell us what really happened," I coaxed.

"Shut up."

For a preacher, he could get really snarly. Miss Gloria returned and zip tied my hands together much too tightly.

"What are we going to do with them?" Miss Gloria murmured to her husband.

"Shh," he said. "Let me think."

Miss Gloria fidgeted while Swiggly cogitated. He whispered something to her, she disappeared again then came back with a set of keys on a red-and-white fishing bobber.

Swiggly ordered me and Conahegg to walk down the hallway toward the back of the house.

Without Swiggly to tell us where to go, we could have wandered through the house for hours and never found our way out. With his instructions, we reached the back door within a couple of minutes. We passed through the pool area where I'd met Swiggly and Gunther on my last visit.

But, we didn't stop at the pool. Swiggly and Miss Gloria marched us down an elaborate stone walkway leading to the river. Swiggly held the shotgun. Miss Gloria carried Conahegg's revolver.

To our left lay the large copse of blue spruce trees that separated Swiggly's property from mine. It was frustrating to realize that my own house lay no more than the length of a football field away. But with the trees and the stone wall blocking the view you couldn't even tell there was a house on the other side.

I closed my eyes and sent out mental vibrations and prayed Aunt Tessa's psychic antenna was tuned to my frequency, but I wasn't counting on it. Obviously, Conahegg and I were going to have to get out of this mess on our own.

We arrived at the river's edge, still out of view from the other houses on the water. Swiggly had constructed himself a nice little fortress, much to our misfortune.

"Keep going," Swiggly growled.

"You want us to walk into the water?" Conahegg asked.

"Out on the dock." He motioned with the shotgun. "Then get on board the boat."

We did as he said, stepping aboard the huge boat, that was this side shy of a yacht and far too big for the river.

"Miss Gloria," he said, keeping Conahegg far enough ahead of him so he couldn't lunge for the gun. "Put a couple of those cinder blocks into the boat."

We were going to die. Swiggly was going to take us out on the river, put a bullet in our brains, weigh us down with cinder blocks and toss us overboard. Our bodies wouldn't be found for a long time.

I gulped. Much as I love the river, I wasn't ready to lie with the fishes. Panic rose in me. Wild-eyed, I looked to Conahegg.

He was completely calm. Face expressionless, posture casual, as if he were out for an afternoon of pleasure boating rather than preparing to meet his maker. The man was too cool and I drew a modicum of strength from him. He must have a plan. I'd keep my eyes open and be ready for any signal he might throw my way.

Grunting, Miss Gloria hauled four cinder blocks into the boat.

"You drive," Swiggly said, tossing her the keys. "You two, sit down together in the stern."

We sat in unison on the cushioned seats at the back of the boat. Swiggly perched opposite us, the shotgun clutched in his lap.

Miss Gloria got in and rested Conahegg's thirty-eight on the dashboard. From where we sat you could see into the cabin below. A kitchenette complete with sink and stove. I supposed farther inside were sleeping quarters and a bathroom. I'd been to the Tarrant County Boat Show. I knew these puppies ran about a hundred grand.

The sun beat down relentlessly and before Miss Gloria could maneuver the boat from its slip, sweat was already cascading down my forehead.

In vain, I searched the banks for human life but it was ten o'clock on Thursday morning. Most of the residents were at work. Or they were housewives engaged in the latest episode of their favorite talk show while they dusted. Or they were retired fisherman who had been up before dawn checking their trot lines, had come inside for the day and were waiting out the heat with glasses of iced tea and central air-conditioning.

The damn plastic zip ties were cutting into my skin like shark's teeth and my fingers had gone numb. I wriggled them to keep the blood circulating.

Miss Gloria guided the massive craft through the narrow slough. I craned my neck at my house as we floated by. No sign of either Mama or Aunt Tessa. Although Mama could have been in the pottery shed. Still, even if she happened to see us, she'd probably wave and think how nice it was that I'd made pals with the Swigglys.

"So tell us, Reverend, how is it that you've arrived at this point in your life?" Conahegg asked as if he were making idle chitchat at a church ice-cream social.

"What?" Swiggly seemed distracted.

His fingers tightened on the shotgun. Through the material of his robe, I could see the outline of his halter monitor. He was sweating as profusely as I, a sheen of perspiration laying like a mustache across his upper lip. Not a drop of sweat marred any part of Conahegg's body. I was jealous.

Miss Gloria gunned the engine when we hit the main current and turned the boat upriver toward the direction of Sanchez Creek and the hidden underwater caves instead of the route most people with a boat this size took, which was downriver to Lake Granbury.

"You're a man of the cloth," Conahegg continued, "a very wealthy man with a reputation to uphold. Why are you risking everything?"

"My life is worthless." Swiggly glowered darkly at Miss Gloria. "My ministry is over. My wife has seen to that."

"It's not my fault you couldn't keep your pecker in your pants," Miss Gloria shouted, a woman transformed. Gone were any traces of her mousy countenance and in its place stood a woman pushed well past her limit of endurance. Her meek eyes had turned mad, her hair sprang like snakes from its tight coil.

If the situation hadn't been so dire, I would have laughed to hear the word *pecker* coming from her mouth. As it was, nothing seemed particularly funny.

"Did I tell you to kill that young man? Did I?" Swiggly shouted at his wife.

"I did it to protect you, Ray Don," she said. "You're all I care about."

"I was prepared to pay him off."

"He would have kept asking for more," Miss Gloria said, desperately trying to make her husband understand. "He was going to bleed you dry. I couldn't go through another humiliation like Louisiana."

"I wondered what happened in Louisiana?" I whispered to Conahegg from the corner of my mouth.

"Sex with an underage male prostitute," Conahegg whispered back. "Long time ago. Before his television ministry."

"What? You knew about his peccadilloes and didn't tell me?"

Conahegg shrugged as best he could with his hands cuffed behind his back. "It never came up."

I was miffed. He'd been holding out on me.

"Hey," Swiggly said, "you two quit talking amongst yourselves."

"I'm tired of playing the pious wife," Miss Gloria shouted above the engine, her hand pushing harder upon the throttle.

The boat shot through the water at an alarming speed. If she kept driving like a lunatic, we wouldn't have to worry about being gunned down by Swiggly.

"Er...you do know there are a lot of tree stumps on this side of the river, don't you," I asked her, leaning forward.

"Sit back," Swiggly commanded.

"Go ahead," Miss Gloria raved. "Tell them what you did. Let them see what I've had to put up with for thirty years. Show them the real Ray Don Swiggly."

"Shut up, woman."

"He likes young men," she sang out almost cheerfully. It was frightening the way she'd so completely changed. I began to wonder if her mental choo-choo had jumped the track. "The younger the better. And if that wasn't enough he takes up with that body builder Gunther and tries to pass him off as a physical therapist. Right under my nose. Ha! He thinks I'm an idiot. But that backfired on you, too, didn't it, Ray Don?"

So that explained Gunther.

"At least I'm not a murderer," Swiggly charged.

"I killed him for you. To save your reputation. To save your ministry."

"Is your wife admitting to the murder of Rockerfeller Hughes?" Conahegg asked Swiggly.

Swiggly looked pained. "Yes."

"But why?"

"Because that little weasel was blackmailing him," Miss Gloria interrupted.

She was whipping the wheel back and forth so violently I feared I might end up puking on Conahegg's shiny black boots. Swiggly didn't look so great, either. His skin was sallow, his breathing rapid.

"Rocky was blackmailing your husband?" I asked Gloria. "What for?"

"Go ahead, you tell her, Ray Don."

Swiggly squirmed in his seat. "There's no need for that."

"You're not too ashamed to do it but you won't talk about it." Gloria shook her head. "He was fooling around with that nice-looking young man. What was his name? Oh yes, Tim Kehaul."

And then suddenly, things fell into place. That night Conahegg had run over a naked Tim in my driveway I felt certain there had been someone in the bushes with him. It must have been Swiggly.

Tears glistened in Swiggly's eyes. "I never meant to kill him," he said softly. "I loved Tim."

"You loved everyone but me," Miss Gloria lamented. "Why, Ray Don, why?"

I exhaled sharply. Too deep for me. I scanned the water but rejected the thought of jumping overboard at this speed with my hands zip tied together.

"You strangled your lover, Tim Kehaul," Conahegg said, as if taking his official statement. That's a sheriff for you. He was about to be snuffed and all he cared about was getting the record straight.

"It was an accident." Swiggly was seriously sobbing, his tears mingling with the sweat on his cheeks. Whomever ended up reading his halter monitor tracing was in for a jolt. I imagine his heart was throwing premature ventricular contractions like drunken revelers tossing confetti at a New Year's Eve bash. "We were making love. I asked him if he wanted to try something new, something exotic."

"You and your exotic sex." Gloria turned her head and rolled her eyes. The boat bounced so high on the water it seemed we were flying. I clenched my hands into fists behind my back but it made the zip ties dig that much deeper into my flesh. "Whips and chains and costumes. Belts and ropes and hooks."

Hooks?

"It's better than being a dead fish in bed," Swiggly countered.

"I wouldn't be a dead fish if my husband didn't come home smelling of other men!"

Whew. We were really getting into it and I wanted out of

here. Pronto. I looked at Conahegg and struggled to hide the fear in my eyes. We'd been caught in the middle of a marital minefield, and I had the feeling that any minute a claymore was about to detonate.

"Things got out of hand," Conahegg elaborated for Swiggly. "And you pulled the rope too tightly around Tim's neck."

Swiggly gulped and nodded, crocodile tears rolling off his chin. If only his flock could see him now. They'd storm his mansion, raid his house and take back every cent he'd stolen from them.

But even though he deserved everything that was coming to him, I couldn't help but feel sorry for a man who'd spent his whole life living a lie.

"How did Rocky find out?" Conahegg asked.

I knew before Swiggly answered. The camera equipment in Rocky's living room.

"That's when he had the heart attack," Miss Gloria said, thankfully slowing the boat at long last.

The river narrowed and she had no choice. We weren't far from the pool and the underground caves.

"Rocky sent us a copy of the tape he'd made and I knew I had to do something," Miss Gloria continued.

"Tape?" Conahegg asked.

"A tape of Tim and Ray Don making love." Her voice caught.

"How did he get it?" Conahegg frowned.

"I don't know. Ray Don wanted to pay him off but I knew it wouldn't end with a hundred thousand dollars. That snake would keep crawling back for the rest of our lives, sucking us dry. So," Miss Gloria said. "I did what I had to do. I went to his house on the pretense of paying the blackmail money."

"That was Saturday night before last." Conahegg was so damned calm. He was acting as if he would be writing up his report rather than bobbing at the bottom of the Brazos very shortly. I had to admire his optimism. Me, I was wondering how Mama, Sissy, Aunt Tessa and Denny were going to make it without me.

"Early Sunday morning, really," Miss Gloria said. "Mr. Hughes told me I'd have to wait until after his girlfriend left." She looked at me. "It was your sister."

The expression in her eyes was so malevolent, I shuddered.

"Anyway, I went inside his trailer, which was a filthy hole by the way. It's a wonder he hadn't already died from some kind of poisoning. I told him that I had the money but first I wanted to get even with my husband by having sex with him." She glared at Swiggly.

"You really didn't, Miss Gloria, did you?" Swiggly's face blanched white.

"What's sauce for the goose is sauce for the gander. Don't you think it ripped my heart out to play the dutiful wife every Sunday morning on television when I knew that every Saturday night you were out with young men?"

"I'm sorry for hurting you." Swiggly reached for her but she pulled back.

"It's too late to make amends." She spoke to him, then to us she said, "Since everyone believed Tim's death was an accident, I figured I'd make Rocky's look the same way. I got him to drink a lot of alcohol and I gave him some of the Valium the cardiologist had prescribed for Ray Don. We got undressed and I crawled in bed with him."

The skin on my arms prickled. I glanced at Conahegg. He revealed no emotion.

Miss Gloria kneaded her forehead with her fingers as if warding off a migraine. "When he passed out, I put a pillow over his face and sat on him. It wasn't quite as easy as I thought it would be. He started to struggle."

Exactly the scenario Conahegg had depicted the day he called me into his office to give me Rocky's autopsy report, except the killer had been Gloria Swiggly, not my sister.

"I hit him on the head with a lamp and he stopped fighting. When he finally quit breathing, I tied a belt around his neck and the other around the bedpost. I was careful and wore gloves."

"Then I simply kicked him off the bed and left. And I would have gotten away with it if it hadn't been for those damnable earrings your aunt gave me." Miss Gloria glared at me.

My stomach squeezed and I fought a wave of nausea. The woman was capable of anything. I had no doubt she'd readily plug a bullet into me and Conahegg to preserve her way of life.

Miss Gloria took a deep breath as she realized we were staring at her. "I had to do it. I had to protect Ray Don. No matter what he's done, I love him." She had stopped the boat and turned away from the wheel. We were drifting along on the current coming closer and closer to the hidden caves.

"Ah, Miss Gloria, I love you, too." Swiggly hiccuped back his tears. He set the shotgun aside. I saw Conahegg eyeing the weapon. "Please forgive me my horrible sins against you. I suffer from a demon that eats my soul." Swiggly got down on one knee and reached for his wife's hand.

She touched his head. "Of course I forgive you. But first we have one more thing to take care of then our lives can go back to normal."

Swiggly and Miss Gloria both looked at us.

"Sorry," she said. "That's what happens to Nosy Rosies. I'm afraid you've got to die." Miss Gloria picked up the shotgun and peered down the sight.

"I'm willing to accept my fate," Conahegg said.

What? Had he lost his ever-loving mind?

"But I have one request to ask of you first," he said to Swiggly. "Please, if you're a man of God, if you do want to repent your own sins, then please grant me this favor."

"What's that?" Swiggly asked suspiciously.

Conahegg looked over at me. "Ally and I are madly in love."

Huh? We are? I stared at him, incredulous. Could he actually be in love with me? For a brief moment, my heart sang. Conahegg loved me.

Then reality set in. He had some kind of scheme in mind, some way to defeat Swiggly. He said he loved me for the preacher's benefit. Embarrassed that I'd jumped to such ridiculous conclusions, I shook my head.

Conahegg caught my eye. *Play along,* he said.

Okay, sure. Pretend I love Conahegg. Right. I could do it.

"Yes," I threw in, determined to do my part, "we're crazy for each other."

"I haven't had a chance to ask Ally to be my wife yet," Conahegg continued. At the word *wife* my silly heart jumped again. "But since we're about to die and you're an ordained minister, I was wondering if you'd mind marrying us first before you killed us."

CHAPTER TWENTY-FOUR

"DO YOU, ALLEGHENY Allison Green, take this man, Samuel Jebediah Conahegg, to be your lawfully wedded husband?"

"Jebediah?" I muttered under my breath.

"You're in no position to belittle someone's name," Sam mouthed right back.

He had a point. Somehow I'd never pictured my wedding day quite like this. Boat on a river. Intense July heat. Nursing scrub suit in place of a frothy white-lace gown. Homosexual televangelist minister and his mousy murdering wife with a shotgun in her hand.

Classic shotgun wedding. Call *Brides* magazine. I want to be on the cover of the next issue. And while you're at it, give *True Confessions* a ring.

Not too many blushing brides could claim such nuptials. Not even my family who boasted a long list of bizarre weddings from hot air balloon flights to circus freaks in a fern grotto—don't ask. Maybe I did have a little of that eccentric blood flowing through my veins.

"Do you?" Swiggly repeated. "Take this man?"

"Uh."

I stared at Conahegg. He peered down at me.

He looked quite handsome in his sheriff's uniform, his gray eyes hard as steel but strangely soft, too. His hair had grown out from the first time I'd met him two weeks ago and it looked sexier.

But the point wasn't to assess him for potential husband material, rather I should be stalling to delay our impending execution. Swiggly had been kind enough to untie us for the bogus ceremony and at the moment, my sweat-slick palm was clasped tightly in Conahegg's. He squeezed my hand. Firm, comforting, confident.

I caught my breath. For the first time since my father had died I had someone I could count on. Someone who could protect me. Someone I could lean on. It was a revelation.

"Hurry," Swiggly snapped. "We don't have all day. Do you want to marry him or not?"

"Yes," I finally said when I couldn't think of anything else to fill the void.

Miss Gloria burst into tears. "I always cry at weddings," she explained, dabbing at her eyes with a Kleenex, yet all the while clutching the shotgun in her arm.

"You may kiss the bride," Swiggly announced.

Conahegg wrapped his arms around my waist and quickly pressed his lips to my ear. "After I kiss you," he whispered, "I'm going to pitch you overboard. Swim for the caves."

There was no time to ask him what he planned. No way to know what was about to happen. My head whirled. My pulse pounded.

And then he kissed me.

As if he might never get to kiss me again. That kiss held the memory of last night's lovemaking. Tender yet hard. Wistful yet joyous. Hopeful yet desperate.

One minute those fabulous lips were pressed hard against mine and in the next minute I was flying through the air, legs windmilling like crazy, headed straight for the Brazos.

I had just enough time to inhale before the water closed over my head.

Without conscious thought, I started swimming. Terror

knocked on the door of my brain but I refused to let it in. I would not surrender to the fear threatening to strangle me.

Get to the caves.

But what about Conahegg?

I couldn't take care of him, couldn't make things right and that knowledge killed me. I was powerless to save him. He'd sacrificed himself for me and he was on his own.

I wallowed in guilt but only for a second. Instinct took control and I swam for my life.

A few seconds later I came up for air several yards from the boat. I heard a shotgun blast, saw pellets scatter through the water around me. I didn't have a chance to turn my head and see what was going on behind me or to try and locate Conahegg.

Blam!

Another bullet shower.

Blood pounding, I inhaled again and plunged down, down, down into the murky depths. I couldn't see more than an inch in front of my face. I kicked hard, going deeper still.

My temples throbbed. My entire body shook from the adrenaline rush.

More gunfire.

From a few feet under the water the sounds were muffled, less violent, as if the noises were on a distant battlefield.

I wondered how much ammunition they had. But how much did they need? It would only take two bullets. One for Conahegg, and one for me.

Blindly, I swam, heading for the caves and sanctuary.

A minute passed. Then two.

My lungs ached, stretched to the capacity of endurance but I was afraid to come up again.

When I could bear it no longer, I pushed to the surface and broke forth into darkness.

I gasped, drawing cool, musty air into my oxygen starved body.

I had made it. I was inside the cave, enveloped in complete blackness. I had no idea what was going on outside.

In the inkiness, I groped through the water, my hand outstretched until I hit the rough, rocky area.

It took more effort than I expected to haul myself from the water. I sat trembling on the stone ledge, my mind completely numb, unable to process the events that had transpired.

Gloria Swiggly had murdered Rocky because he'd been blackmailing her husband for accidentally killing Tim Kehaul in a very kinky game of slap and tickle.

And I had just married Sam Conahegg.

Who might very well be dead.

In a matter of minutes I'd gone from a wife to a widow.

I COULDN'T STAND IT. No matter what Sam had told me to do, I simply could not remain in hiding and wait without knowing what had happened to him.

By now the Swigglys surely had assumed I'd drowned. But they would probably keep searching for my body. Knowing that I carried their secrets, they had to make sure I was dead.

My predicament seemed hopeless. I certainly couldn't stay here forever. Especially when Conahegg might be injured and needing me. But I had no doubt the Swigglys were patrolling the river.

If only I had a weapon.

The cave was eerily silent. And cold. I shivered and wrapped my arms around myself. My scrub suit stuck to my skin.

I had to go back.

Taking several steps, I eased into the water and my sneaker slipped against something on the rock floor.

Curious, I reached down to see what it was.

A wooden handle. A metal blade.

My heart leaped with joy.

From the murky depths, the hunting knife Sam had lost when he'd rescued Denny on our camping trip. A knife matched against a thirty-eight and a shotgun wasn't much but it was something.

"Thank you." I whispered a prayer to the heavens.

Clutching the knife between my teeth so I could have my arms free for swimming, I dived under the water and swam from the cave.

The shift in lighting was immediate, going from total blackness to a murky haze which grew brighter as I got closer to the surface.

I came up as near the shoreline as I could manage. Feeling like an alligator, I took a quick, deep breath then submerged to my eyeballs and scanned the river.

The Swigglys boat bobbed not twenty feet away.

My heart lurched.

Both Miss Gloria and Ray Don were leaning over the opposite side of the boat and hadn't spotted me. The Reverend had an oar in his hand and was poking at something. When I realized what they were looking at all hope withered and died inside me.

Conahegg's body.

He was floating facedown in the water. A bloom of bright red blood trailing out behind him.

Instantly, tears filled my eyes and my upper lip began to quiver so violently, I was afraid I would drop the knife. My greatest fear was realized.

They'd shot Conahegg.

And I'd lost my lover.

A shudder ripped through me. I never imagined anything

could hurt so badly. The Swigglys had stolen Conahegg from me before I'd had a chance to tell him that I did love him.

No!

Guilt assailed me first. It was my fault. I should never have allowed Conahegg to throw me in the water. I should never have left him to face those hypocritical sons of bitches alone. He'd needed me and I had glibly swum away to save my own hide.

What kind of woman was I?

Then anger replaced my guilt. There was nothing I could do to correct my mistakes. Guilt wouldn't bring Conahegg back but I'd be damned if I'd let the Swigglys get away with murder.

I swam for the boat with revenge in my heart and not a plan in mind.

"Ray Don!" Miss Gloria's shout carried loudly over the water. "There she is!"

Miss Gloria swung around, the shotgun in her hand. She pulled the trigger, and the recoil sent her reeling. Lucky for me she was a shitty shot.

The pellets scattered a wide arc behind me.

Knife still clutched between my teeth, I submerged like a World War II submarine taking on the German fleet. I came up at the bottom of Swiggly's craft, grabbed onto the prop and began to rock the boat back and forth. It was a crazy, irrational thing to do. If they started the engine I was dead. But I was so filled with rage and grief over what they'd done to Conahegg, I couldn't think straight.

Miss Gloria screamed.

I let go of the prop and surfaced at the back of the boat, not sure what was happening. Treading water, I kicked back, preparing myself at any moment for a shotgun blast to the face.

Nothing happened.

Was she out of ammo?

I peered at the boat, which seemed to be empty, then I heard a loud keening sound of sorrow that matched my own anguish.

Then I saw the shotgun flying off to one side. Miss Gloria straightened. She'd been leaning over something in the bottom of the boat. I couldn't see Swiggly. I used the opportunity to snag the boat's ladder with both hands and pull myself aboard.

Swiggly lay on the floor like a landed tarpon. His face was beet-red and he was clutching his chest with both hands.

"Ray Don, Ray Don," Miss Gloria sobbed.

He was having another heart attack.

The nurse in me reacted before the potential murder victim in me had a chance to rationalize the situation. I stepped forward to see if I could help.

Miss Gloria heard me and she faced me, her eyes wide as if surprised to see me alive and well and back on board her boat.

"You!" she shrieked and grabbed for the pistol on the dashboard. It was closer than the shotgun.

But I was quicker.

Knife in my hand, I slashed her upper arm.

She screamed, dropped the revolver and clutched her wound. I grabbed the gun and turned it on her.

"Sit down, Miss Gloria." My heart was racing, my body exhausted, my emotions a wild tangle. "It's over."

Gloria dropped to her knees beside Swiggly, whose eyes had rolled back in his head. His respirations were extremely shallow, and he was sweating profusely.

"Please, you've got to help him. You're a nurse. It's your duty. You can't let him die."

"You killed Conahegg," I pointed out.

"Please," Gloria begged. "I love him. No matter what Ray Don's done. I'm begging you, don't let him die."

Every fiber of my body urged me to move forward, to do

what I could for Swiggly. But if I did I'd be leaving myself open to attack from Miss Gloria. I couldn't fend her off and tend Swiggly at the same time.

I stood frozen by my dilemma.

At that moment, the boat rocked heavily.

"He's stopped breathing," Miss Gloria shrieked. "Do something, do something."

I turned my head to the back of the boat. My pulse leaped with rapture.

Impossible.

Lazarus from the grave.

Conahegg pulled himself up the ladder with one hand. His expression grim with pain, his clothes saturated with water, a bullet hole in his right shoulder oozed blood.

I rushed to him. "You're alive, you're alive," I repeated. "You're alive."

"Just barely." He grinned and slumped against the seat, his face pale. To me he was the most glorious sight in the world. He waved a hand. "Give me the gun," he said. "I'll watch out for Miss Gloria, you give Swiggly CPR."

I knelt beside Swiggly and did what I do best. Conahegg had Miss Gloria get behind the wheel and drive the boat back to the Swigglys' mansion.

After a few minutes of CPR, Swiggly roused and blinked up at me, his color ashen. He whispered, "I never meant to kill Tim."

"It's over," I said.

"Don't judge Miss Gloria too harshly." His lips were dry. He coughed. "She did what she had to do."

"Shh," I said. "Rest."

To my surprise, we were met at the dock by a swarm of sheriff's deputies trailed by my mother. Her eyes were sharp, her posture erect. She didn't wring her hands or begin discoursing on some frivolous, unrelated subject. She'd shed her aura of perpetual dreaminess and seemed like any other concerned mother. Not since my father's death had she looked so capable.

"Mama?" I pushed aside my bangs which clung to my forehead like wet seaweed. If her body had been invaded by the pod people, I wasn't complaining.

The deputies closed in on Miss Gloria and Swiggly. Mama closed in on me. At some point, someone called an ambulance. I searched for Conahegg but he'd disappeared with one of his deputies.

Mama touched my shoulder. "Are you hurt?"

"Fine." I tried to say it lightly as if I hadn't almost died, but to my horror the word came out in a sob. Oh, no. I couldn't break down. Not in front of Mama. She needed me to be strong, to take care of her.

But I was wrong.

Instead, my mother took care of me. She wrapped a blanket around my shoulders and guided me over to Swiggly's cement picnic table. "There, baby," she murmured. "It's all right. Mama's here."

She sat beside me, put her arms around my shoulders and held me as she had when I was a little girl. I reveled in her attention, buried my head against her neck.

"Where's Denny?" I asked. "And Aunt Tessa?"

"Shh, stop fretting. Tessa went to pick Denny up at Braxton's. Don't worry. He's okay."

"Ally?"

I looked up to see my sister standing on the dock with us. Dressed in a blue jean jumper and a pink gingham blouse she looked like Rebecca of Sunnybrook Farm, not my wild child younger sister. Gone was the nose ring and the Dracula makeup. Even her midnight-black hair had been restored to its natural chestnut color. Beside her stood the priest from Saint Patrick's Episcopal church, Father Frank Turner, and he had his arm around her waist.

A huge lump formed in my throat. It was an emotional day. Hell, it had been an emotional two and a half weeks. Had only seventeen days passed since that night Sissy shot Rocky in our garage? So many things had changed, it seemed like a lifetime ago.

"What are you doing here?" I whispered. "The deputies were looking everywhere for you."

She reached out and took my hand. "I know." She smiled shyly at the priest. "Frank brought me home. I came to tell you what had happened with Rocky. I was ready to face the music."

"Face the music? But you didn't kill Rocky." I frowned, confused.

"No," Sissy said, "but I was involved in something else. I needed your help. I needed your advice."

"But you weren't here," Mama chimed in.

"I'm sorry," I interrupted. "I should have been here for you guys."

"No, don't apologize, let me finish. I had to call the police," Mama continued, smiling. "I handled everything for Sissy."

My mother's pride in herself was unmistakable. She'd accomplished something important without any help from me. I was proud of her, too. When the rubber met the road, she'd come through.

"You did a great job, Mama." I kissed her cheek.

"Thank you, dear."

"Where have you been?" I asked Sissy.

"Hiding out in my church." Father Turner stepped forward and offered me his hand. I shook it.

"You've been giving her sanctuary?"

"Yes."

I turned to Sissy. "Why didn't you call me?"

"I couldn't. Not until I could prove my innocence."

"Tell me what happened."

"Go ahead," Father Frank urged.

"I'm not proud of what I did," Sissy said. "But I'm the one who really found Rocky's body, Ally, not you."

"You already knew he was dead when I told you?"

"Uh-huh." She took a deep breath. Father Frank squeezed her hand. "I knew Tim and Rocky were up to something illegal. Rocky owed Dooley Marchand three thousand for the demo record and Tim had gotten in deep gambling. Tim borrowed money from Dooley and couldn't pay him. So he was performing sexual favors to pay off his debt, but I know he hated it."

Ah, I thought. So Dooley Marchand was the blond man Tim's neighbors had seen with him.

"Rocky asked Tim if he wanted to make a lot of cash and get Dooley off his back. Tim agreed. They targeted Reverend Swiggly for a blackmail scheme. Apparently, Darlene, who's from Swiggly's hometown in Louisiana, told Rocky he was gay. They plotted for Tim to have sex with Swiggly while Rocky would secretly videotape their liaison. Except no one expected Swiggly to get kinky with the autoerotic asphyxiation and accidentally kill Tim. But I didn't know any of this until after I found the tape."

"You've got a copy of the tape?"

Sissy nodded. "After I let Denny off at the house last Saturday night, I went back over to Rocky's and found him dead. I panicked and I touched the belt around his neck. He'd told me that in case anything bad happened to him that he had hidden a tape and if I viewed it I'd know who to blackmail." Sissy ducked her head. "I admit, I was going to go through with the plan and blackmail whoever was on the tape and keep the money for myself."

"What for?"

"I wanted to move out. Get a home for Denny and me."

"Really?" I stared.

"Well, at first it was to get away from your bossiness. At least that's what I told myself. But then I realized that as long as we stay here, I'm never going to grow up. I need to leave for my own growth."

And I needed her to go for mine. Where had she acquired this sudden insight? I slanted a glance at Father Frank. He smiled and I had my answer. "So what happened next?"

"Rocky said he'd hidden the tape in a safe place but he was killed before he could tell me where. Then I remembered he'd had a videotape with him when we went to Tim's funeral but that was the last I saw of it. I figured he'd stashed the tape somewhere in the church."

"And that's where I found her," Father Frank said. "In the chapel, searching for the tape."

"I didn't tell Frank what I was doing of course. Not at first." Sissy sent an adoring glance in the priest's direction. "But he was so kind. He gave me something to eat, let me stay in his house, eventually I told him everything and he helped me to see that blackmail was the wrong answer. Together we searched for the tape and found it. When we watched it and saw who had killed Tim, we called the sheriff's department and they told us Sheriff Conahegg had gone to Swiggly's house. When we went over to Swiggly's place and didn't get an answer, we came here. Mama called the deputies."

"Can I have a hug?" I asked, tugging off the now-damp blanket. I had some kind of green mucky seaweed stuff on my clothes, but Sissy didn't seem to mind. She hugged me like she hadn't hugged me in years.

"I was so scared," she said. "So frightened. I was so scared that you were dead. That Swiggly had killed you."

I put a hand on her shoulder and allowed her to cry. "It's all right," I said gruffly. I held her for the longest time, then a deputy came up to us.

"Miss…" He spoke to Sissy. "Would you like to come with me? We need your full statement."

"Where's Sheriff Conahegg?" I asked the fresh-faced officer.

"He's out front by the ambulance but he's refusing to go to the hospital."

"What?" I said. "Let me at the old goat."

"Ally," Mama said.

"Uh-huh?'

"Can I talk to you a minute?"

I wanted nothing more than to go to Conahegg but I couldn't ignore the change in my mother. "Sure."

"You know," Mama said, "Tessa and I have been talking. We think it's about time we got our own place, too."

I swallowed hard. "You mean leave the river?"

Mama touched my cheek. "You're the one who loves it, daughter. It's your home. Not mine. It really hasn't been since your father died."

"You mean I'll be living there alone?" Turns out I wasn't going to have to kick my family out. They were jumping ship on me. Honestly? It felt as if Atlas's boulder had rolled from my shoulders.

"We'll just be moving into Cloverleaf. Not far. Tessa's been eyeing a cute little house on Lee Street."

"How long have you been planning a move?"

Mama shrugged. "Since you met Sam. We figured as long as we were living here that you'd never have a life of your own. Sam's the right man for you. Ung told Tessa."

I stared at her, mouth open. It was a conspiracy, a plot.

"Go see about him," Mama said. "If anyone ever needed you, it's Sam."

"He doesn't need me! He doesn't need anyone."

"Oh yes he does. He's too stubborn for his own good and you're the only one I know stubborn enough to challenge him. Go, daughter."

"Okay, I'll go." Mama, Tessa and Ung might be certain that Conahegg was the man for me, but I wasn't so sure. Regardless, I stalked up the hill, trekked through the Swigglys' pristine palace and out the front door to the ambulance. Conahegg was leaning against the hood looking pretty tired, but when he saw me his face lit up.

"What's this about you refusing to go to the hospital?" I asked.

He rolled his eyes. "I didn't refuse to go to the hospital, I refused to go in an ambulance."

"How are you planning on getting there then, smart guy?"

"You're going to take me."

"I am?"

"Yes."

"Do you really think that's wise? You've got a bullet in your shoulder."

"The paramedics packed the wound. I won't bleed all over your car. Besides, I've had worse."

"I'll bet. You scared the life out of me. When I saw you floating facedown in the water I was sure you were dead."

"Did you miss me?" He quirked a corner of his lip upward.

"Yeah," I said gruffly. "I kinda did."

"I want to talk to you, Ally. Alone."

My heart kicked.

A patrol car went by with Gloria Swiggly in the backseat. Forlornly, she pressed her face against the window and stared at us.

Conahegg shook his head. "Sad case."

"What's going to happen to her?"

"All we have is the confession she gave us. The evidence is flimsy. Swiggly's rich. She could walk."

"What about Swiggly? He did kill Tim."

"Accidentally."

We stared at each other a moment.

"Sheriff—" one of the paramedics came up to us "—if you're not going to ride in the ambulance, we're going to leave and get the preacher to the hospital."

Conahegg nodded and stepped away from the ambulance. He swayed a little on his feet. I slipped my arm around his waist and pulled him close. It felt right.

Later in my Honda, I looked over at him. He had the passenger seat shoved back as far as it would go, his long legs still bent high, his neck lolling against the headrest. His eyes were closed.

"Are you going to be all right, Conahegg?" I asked, struggling to keep my voice on an even keel while a million different emotions slipped through my veins.

"Don't you think it's about time you started calling me Sam," he asked, opening one eye.

"Why should I do that and ruin a perfectly good adversarial relationship?"

"Because we *are* married."

I raised a finger. The thought of being married to Conahegg was the stuff of fantasies, but I wasn't going to let him in on my secret. No sense in further inflating that ego of his.

"We didn't have a marriage license," I pointed out. "Sorry to disappoint you, but it isn't legal, even if Swiggly is a preacher."

"But it was a good ploy to buy time." He closed his eyes again. "You've got to admit that."

"Yes," I conceded. "It was a stroke of genius. Good thing it worked."

"We're a pretty good team," he murmured.

"You didn't think so in the beginning."

We did make a good team. So good it was scary. Almost as scary as the new emotions overtaking me. Even though we'd been through a lot, had risked our lives, endured danger together, I couldn't get over how alive I felt.

"That's back when I thought you were a pretty, but nosy buttinsky," he said.

"You think I'm pretty?"

"Come on, Ally, don't play coy. It doesn't suit you. Sissy, yes, but not you. You're a damned fine-looking woman."

I mulled this over, then cleared my throat. "I'm pleased to hear you've revised your opinion of my supposed nosiness."

"Oh, I still think you're a nosy buttinsky," Conahegg said. "But a nosy buttinsky who knows what she's talking about."

"Thank you…er…I guess."

"You're welcome."

"So tell me, what happened after you threw me in the water?"

"I dived for the boat keys and knocked Swiggly over. He grabbed the pistol." Sam gestured at his shoulder with his left hand. "And he shot me for my troubles. I fell back into the water and decided it was a good idea to let them think I was dead."

"Lucky thing it wasn't Miss Gloria with the shotgun."

"She was too busy shooting at you." Conahegg sat up and looked me straight in the eye. "I swear, Ally, those were the worst moments of my life when I thought she might have hit you. You didn't surface and you didn't surface and you didn't surface. I would have swum after you if I could have. I was dying not knowing what had happened to you."

"I went to the caves like you told me."

"And you found my hunting knife. I really liked that bloodthirsty look in your eyes when you dived under their boat, my knife clenched between your teeth like Tarzan on a homicidal mission. You know," he mused, "I like my wives bold and bloodthirsty."

"We're not married," I insisted.

He grinned and winked.

What did he mean by that? And why was I getting a funny, fizzy feeling in the pit of my stomach.

"And by the way," I asked, "just how many bold and bloodthirsty wives *have* you had?"

EPILOGUE

AT TEN MINUTES after one o'clock in the afternoon on a cold day in early February, a jury of Gloria Swiggly's peers found her guilty of murder in the first degree and sentenced her to thirty-five years in prison, eligible for parole in seven.

A month earlier, after being released from the hospital following his third heart attack, Reverend Ray Don was sentenced to ten years probation for his role in Tim Kehaul's death. His ministry was ruined, his television show pulled from the airwaves. He sold the summerhouse next door and a nudist colony bought it but they hadn't moved in yet.

Conahegg and I left the courtroom together but we'd come separately. I hadn't seen him much since that day on the river. He'd been pretty busy cleaning out the sheriff's department of undesirable deputies and I'd been working.

He walked me to my car. "How's Sissy doing?"

"Fine." It was a blustery day. I turned up the collar on my coat and snuggled down into it. "She's still seeing Father Frank. Seems like it's serious and she's really changed a lot."

"That's good. Your mother?"

"Still painting her castles and trolls."

"Aunt Tessa?"

"Channeling away." I was leaning with my back against the door, trying not to shiver. Conahegg was standing in front of me, his cheeks red from the wind.

"And how's Allegheny? How are things with her?"

"Same old, same old."

His flint-gray eyes met mine. My jaw tightened. I wanted to say more but I didn't know what.

"Listen," we both spoke at once and then chuckled.

"You go first," he said.

"No you."

"When I was up there on the witness stand, giving my testimony, all I could think about was how glad I was to be alive to tell the story and how sorry I am that I hadn't done anything since about that spark between us."

My breath caught. I didn't know how to respond. It had been years since anyone had interested me in the way Conahegg did. On the other hand, I had never felt freer, more independent than I did now.

"Oh," I whispered.

"And, I wanted to apologize for not taking you seriously when you came to me with evidence. I had a lot of other things on my mind at the time but that's no excuse for poor detective work."

"No harm done. Everything turned out all right." My teeth were chattering but I was loath to go. I had a gorgeous sheriff apologizing to me. What woman wouldn't kill for such a moment?

"You're freezing," he said. "I'll let you get on home."

He turned to leave.

"Sam."

He stopped, looked back at me.

My heart was pounding to beat the band. "Why don't you call me sometime?"

"All right." His eyes shone with amusement and a smile curved his lips. He touched his forehead in a slight salute then walked away.

I got in the car, cranked the heater and the radio on at the same time. I let the engine idle and watched until Conahegg disappeared around the block, then I pulled away from the curb and merged into traffic.

I turned on my favorite oldies Motown station and found Areatha wailing her heart out. *Respect.*

I pumped up the volume and sang all the way home.

Everything you love about romance...
and more!

Please turn the page for Signature Select™ Bonus Features.

Bonus Features:

Signature Select™

BONUS FEATURES

SAVING ALLEGHENY GREEN

EXCLUSIVE BONUS FEATURES INSIDE

AUTHOR'S JOURNAL:

Good Girl's Guide to Murder

by Lori Wilde

Do wear red. It'll hide the blood stains.

Don't snog the hottie sheriff if he's convinced your sister is a murderer. He'll only think you're sleeping with him to change his mind.

Do throw away your diary. It won't prove you guilty, but the whole world will find out what you and Johnny Fishbeck did with that Dilly Bar behind the Dairy Queen when you were in sixth grade.

Don't change your name to Miss Scarlett. If your name is already Miss Scarlett, have it legally altered. Miss Scarlett is always guilty of *something.*

Do stay out of bars with lurid names even if the suspect is lurking inside. You don't want to get a reputation for being that kind of girl. Unless, that is, you *do* want to get a reputation for being that kind of girl.

Don't get your hairspray and your mace mixed up. Hairspray won't stop a two-hundred-pound psycho and mace sprayed liberally at your head in the ladies' room won't earn you any friends.

Do watch out for marshmallows. They can be surprisingly deadly.

Don't wear stilettos. It's hard to run from a killer while wearing Manolo Blahnik and even if you weren't a target to begin with, sleuthing in toe-pinching shoes that cost more than a set of steel-belted radials could qualify you as too-stupid-to-live.

Do expect the unexpected. Be prepared. You never know when an impromptu wedding could break out.

Don't use the alibi "I was home alone washing my hair." That excuse only worked for Rapunzel and cornrow aficionados with obsessive compulsive disorder.

Do maintain a sense of humor. But remember, misplaced sarcasm could land you in the pokey.

Don't admit you haven't got a clue. If push comes to shove, you can always buy one off eBay.

Alternate Ending

What could have been...

We asked Lori to write another conclusion to SAVING ALLEGHENY GREEN. *Lori didn't hold back at all—you're sure to be pleased by this quirky and delightful "alternate" ending.*

Enjoy!
MZ

ALTERNATE LAST CHAPTER FOR SAVING ALLEGHENY GREEN BY LORI WILDE

"I KNOW."

Don't ask me why I said it. In retrospect I should have been more circumspect, but suddenly everything made perfect sense. Rocky had been blackmailing Swiggly. That's where he'd gotten the money.

Clearly startled, Miss Gloria stared at me open-mouthed.

"You dropped the earring when you went to confront your husband's lover, Rocky Hughes."

"What!" Swiggly hollered. "That dumb punk wasn't my lover."

"No," Miss Gloria said through gritted teeth. "He was your illegitimate son."

"You're not gay?" I turned to Swiggly.

"Where'd you get a dumb idea like that?" Miss Gloria waved a hand.

Um, from Aunt Tessa. So much for Ung's powers of clairvoyant deduction.

"Ray Don's the biggest skirt chaser ever," Miss

Gloria said. "Although there was that one time in the French Quarter with that female impersonator."

"I swear on God's green earth, nobody would have figured her for a man." Swiggly pouted. "And there's no proof that Rocky twerp was my son."

"I caught you diddling his mama at that tent revival in Beaumont the year we were married. That's proof enough for me." Miss Gloria sank her hands on her hips.

"Wouldn't hold up in a court of law," Swiggly said.

"No," I interjected. "But DNA would. Is that why you killed Rocky? To keep him from going public about your relationship?"

"I didn't kill him." Swiggly snorted and glared at Miss Gloria. "She lost her earring at his place, she must have done him in."

"Believe me," Miss Gloria said, "if I'd wanted to murder someone it would have been you. I paid Hughes off to protect your ministry. And it's not the first time I've had to sweep your peccadilloes under the rug."

So apparently neither Swiggly nor Miss Gloria had killed Rocky, even though both had motive and opportunity. I was confused, not certain what to believe.

"How much did you give him?" Swiggly demanded. He threw back the covers and his feet hit the floor. His face was turning an unflattering shade of purple.

"Calm down, Reverend Swiggly," I urged. Illegitimate dad or not, murderer or not, I didn't want the man coding on me.

Swiggly ignored me and just kept ranting at his wife. "How much?"

"You know all that money you had in your secret account?" Miss Gloria smirked. "Drained it—every bit, gone. Gave it to your bastard son to silence him. Didn't think I knew about that hidden stockpile, huh?"

Swiggly called his wife a very ugly word and collapsed onto the bed. I hurried over and saw he wasn't breathing. Dammit.

"Call 9-1-1," I hollered at Miss Gloria.

I started CPR on Swiggly and by the time the ambulance arrived and hooked him up to the monitor, he was in sinus rhythm and breathing on his own. A car from the sheriff's department pulled into the driveway as the paramedics were loading Swiggly into the back of the ambulance. Miss Gloria climbed in with him and the ambulance took off.

I turned to the squad car. My heart leaped.

Conahegg?

But it wasn't Sam, rather it was Deputy Jefferson Townsend.

"Ms. Green." He waved at me, a serious expression on his face.

"Yes?"

"Sheriff Conahegg sent me to pick you up."

"What?" I was suspicious.

"It's extremely urgent, ma'am." He opened the back door.

I hesitated, remembering Conahegg had told me Jefferson could not have killed Rocky. But why would Conahegg send Jefferson after me when he suspected the man of stealing and dealing drugs? Why hadn't he already brought him up on charges or at least fired him?

Jefferson read my mind. "You're leery about me after you broke into my apartment and found all that stolen merchandise and drug paraphernalia. You think I've been stealing from the evidence room and dealing marijuana on the side."

I nodded.

"Let me reassure you, that's not the case. I've been undercover, acting as a dirty cop. Sam's been using me to infiltrate an electronics theft ring."

"Conahegg knows about this?"

"His idea."

So Sam had been lying to me. I clenched my jaw and knotted my fists. So much for intimacy and honesty.

"Sam didn't tell you the truth because he couldn't risk jeopardizing the operation. Not when we were so close to busting 'em."

I didn't know what to do. Trust my instincts or listen to Jefferson.

"Please, Ms. Green, get in the car. Sheriff Conahegg didn't want me to alarm you by telling you this, but that emergency I was telling you about? It's got something to do with your sister."

HEAVEN HELP ME, I got into his car. Sissy was the lure and I swallowed the bait.

"Where are we going?" I asked as Jefferson wheeled out of Sun Valley Estates.

"Sheriff's waiting for us," he said, not answering my question.

It dawned on me that I was in the backseat, behind bars, where they transported prisoners and Jefferson was my chauffeur, in total control of the door locks.

I was at his mercy. Trapped.

Oh God, I'd done it again. Let my concern for my family override common sense.

"Where are we going?" I repeated.

"I'm taking you to see your sister." His voice was calm. Too calm. A chill rippled over my spine.

I grappled in my purse for my cell phone. I should have called Conahegg before getting into the car with Jefferson. Why hadn't I called Conahegg?

Because you weren't speaking to him.

My pique seemed so absurdly childish now. I lifted the phone to my ear at the same time the back window slid down three inches.

"Throw the phone out the window," Jefferson said.

I looked up to see he had his duty weapon pointed at me through the cage. Our eyes met. I'd never seen such a cold stare on anyone's face.

"Don't make me shoot you," Jefferson said. "I'm not in any mood to swab your brains off the backseat of my car."

I had managed to stab in 9-1-1 on the phone before Jefferson brandished the gun. I heard the operator say, "What's your emergency?" as I slipped the phone through the narrow slit in the window.

"Now drop it." Jefferson cocked the hammer.

Reluctantly, I let go and I turned my head to see the cell splattered into a hundred pieces as it hit the pavement. So much for 9-1-1.

The window whirled up.

My heart thumped hard against the inside of my chest. "You did it. You killed Rocky."

"Ding, ding, ding," Jefferson said, driving me farther and farther away from Cloverleaf. "You win the grand prize."

"And Tim, did you kill him, too?"

"Yep."

"Why?"

Jefferson didn't answer. He pulled off farm-to-market road 51 and took a narrow, dirt lane toward the river. I realized we weren't far from Sanchez Creek, the place where Sam and I had taken the boys camping. We bumped across a cattle guard and I realized we'd entered the backside of the Triple D Ranch, miles from the ranch house.

Jefferson dragged me out of the car, his duty weapon pointed at my temple and made me put my hands behind my back so he could handcuff me.

"Walk toward the river."

"Come on," I said. "You have to give me something. Why did you kill Tim and Rocky? Did it have something to do with drugs? Did they double-cross you in a deal gone sour?"

"Shut up. I'm not one of those chatty killers who spills his guts just to give the heroine time to escape. There's no getting out of this one, so move it." He gave me a shove.

I stumbled and almost fell to my knees. "At least tell me why you're kidnapping me?"

"Because," Jefferson said, "you're my bargaining chip. Conahegg's breathing down my neck. He's about to arrest me. But now I have an ace in the hole."

"I'm your hostage."

"Bottom line, if the sheriff wants to see you alive again, he's got to promise me free passage over the border into Mexico before I'll tell him where he can find you."

"Oh man, you are seriously screwed. I mean nothing to Conahegg. He won't negotiate a deal."

"Wrong. He's in love with you."

"He's not."

"He doodles your name and I saw you coming out

of his cabin the other night and the next morning he was whistling around the station. He never whistles."

Conahegg had been doodling my name? And whistling over me? Ah, now why did I suddenly feel sappily hopeful about our relationship?

"Sam's not in love with me," I denied.

"You better hope you're wrong and I'm right," Jefferson said. "Otherwise your death is going to be very Edgar Allan Poe."

"What do you mean?" I asked, not really wanting to hear the answer. I stopped walking and turned to look at him over my shoulder.

"Keep moving." Jefferson nudged me with the end of his gun.

We hiked over a hill and when we cleared a copse of trees down by the water, I saw it.

My fate.

My blood froze.

There, in the middle of an isolated pasture, in the middle of a twenty-thousand-acre cattle ranch, sat a pine box that looked eerily like a coffin, and beside it, a mound of dirt, a gardener's shovel and a very deep hole.

Oh no way. I was not going to sit still for this.

I spun on my heels and took off at a dead run, but Jefferson anticipated my response. I hadn't taken two steps when he stuck out his leg and tripped me. I couldn't even put my hands up to break my fall.

Splat.

I hit the muddy earth face-first.

Jefferson grabbed me by the hair and dragged me to my feet. I'm afraid I did some blubbering. It hurt and I was scared.

Hey, I never claimed to be a badass.

He forced me into the coffin, with my hands still cuffed behind my back, and closed the lid. Darkness. The smelled of fresh-turned earth filled my nose and fear was an acrid burn at the back of my throat.

The situation was so bizarre I had trouble believing it was really happening. Jefferson slammed a lid onto the coffin and nailed it shut. I yelled until I was hoarse but it didn't deter him.

Then he pushed me, box and all into the hole he'd dug. The top of my head whammed into the end of the coffin. A few moments later I heard the sound of dirt being shoveled in on top of me.

Panic grabbed hold hard.

I couldn't die. Not yet. I'd never traveled. I never learned to snow ski. I'd never dined in a fancy French restaurant.

And I'd only had sex with Conahegg once!

How was I going to get out of this?

Face it, Allegheny, you're going to die.

I'd stupidly, idiotically gotten into the car with Jefferson Townsend because he told me my sister was in trouble.

Then another horrifying thought occurred. Where was Sissy? What if Jefferson had disposed of her the same way he was disposing of me? Was that how she'd disappeared?

Sissy, where are you?

I lay in the darkness of my tomb, listening to the sound of my heart beating, listening to the noise of my greedy breath desperately sucking in precious air.

That was when I realized dirt was no longer being thrown on top of the pine box.

I'd just been buried alive.

I FLOATED.

It wasn't sleep. It wasn't loss of consciousness. Rather, it seemed I'd gained a whole new level of awareness.

I'm only reporting what occurred. I have no solid explanation for what happened to me. My mind separated from my body, detached and rose up through the pine coffin, past the layers of dirt and beyond.

Suddenly, I was looking down at the mound of dirt that was my grave. I could see the area clearly. The river, the copse of oak trees, the expanse of field. Even a herd of white-faced Herefords. And I saw the tires of Jefferson's squad car billowing up dust as he sped back up the one-lane pasture road toward FM 51.

Was I dead?

Was this astral projection?

Is this how Aunt Tessa felt when she channeled Ung?

More than likely it was nothing more than hallucinations induced by hysterical hyperventilation.

But here's the cool thing. I felt more at peace than I ever had felt in my life. No matter what happened I knew everything would be okay. My family could and would survive without me. And while I would miss them, while I would mourn what I'd almost had with Sam and lost before it could even take root and bloom, I was no longer afraid.

Movement along the river caught my eye. I turned my head in the cosmic flow of ether and saw a small johnboat pulling to shore not far from my grave.

Calmly, I watched as the boat docked and a young woman got out.

She hurried up the slope. I studied her with detached curiosity as she grasped the shovel Jefferson had left behind. With fierce determination, she began to dig.

It was my sister. And for the first time in our lives, Sistine was rescuing me.

LATER, SISSY told me Sam had ripped the pine box open with his bare hands, never mind the nails. All I remember was that Sam's face was the first thing I saw and it was his arms that went around me and gently lifted me from the coffin.

I trembled in his arms and damn if Sam wasn't

tearing up. Sissy was jumping around all excited. It barely registered that we had a massive entourage. Mama was there and Aunt Tessa and of course three-fourths of the sheriff's department.

And in the back, over by a bank of squad cars with their lights flashing, waited Jefferson Townsend in handcuffs, a burly deputy with pistol drawn standing alongside of him.

"I saved you," Sissy said, and thumped her chest without one shred of modesty. "It was me."

I looked at Sam. He nodded. "Sissy's been working with me."

"What!" I blinked at him.

"I suspected Jefferson all along and when Sissy told me she thought she could get proof that he'd murdered Tim and Rocky, I gave her the go-ahead."

"You put my sister's life in jeopardy?" I scooted out of Sam's embrace quicker than if I'd just discovered he had a severe case of crabs.

"I assigned a man to look after her," Sam said, as if that was good enough.

"You told me Jefferson had an alibi. That he was on patrol the night Rocky was killed and that his partner had been with him the entire time."

Sam shrugged. "I lied."

"You lied to me?" I stared at him. I would never have expected an honorable man like Conahegg to tell a bald-faced lie. Especially after what we'd shared. My disappointment must have been written across my face.

"It was for your own protection," he said, a tad defensively.

I glared and crossed my arms over my chest.

"I was trying to keep you safe. I knew you'd go snooping around if I didn't throw in a red herring."

"And that worked out oh so terrific. If you'd told me the truth I wouldn't have gotten into the car with Jefferson."

My feelings were more than a little hurt that he'd lied to me and recruited Sissy to help him crack the case instead. What was I? Chopped liver?

"I'm sorry, Ally," Sam said and I heard remorse resonate deep in his tone. "I made a very bad judgment call."

"Damn skippee." I bit down on my bottom lip to keep from crying. I had to change the subject and pronto. "I don't get it. Why did Jefferson kill Tim?"

"A few months back Jefferson busted Tim and Dooley Marchand for making out in the park," Conahegg said.

As he talked, things began to fall into place. That night Conahegg had run over a naked Tim in my driveway. I had felt certain there'd been someone in the bushes with him. It must have been Dooley.

"But instead of running them on public lewdness charges, Jefferson, always the little entrepreneur, made them an offer. Make gay porn home movies using the equipment he'd confiscated from a high-tech electronics theft ring and he'd distribute the films. The cut was seventy-thirty. Seventy for Jefferson, thirty for Dooley and Tim."

I shuddered. Jefferson was even more of a creep than I'd guessed.

"Dooley and Tim went along with the scheme, more because they were afraid that Jefferson would trump up some bogus charge and have them thrown in jail than for the money." Conahegg took a deep breath. "This was all going on before I took over as sheriff of Cloverleaf."

"But of course." I met his eyes and he gave me a tight grin. I tried not to notice how sexy his forearms looked with his shirtsleeves half-rolled up like they were.

"The movies brought in a lot of money but Jefferson got greedy. He wanted more. When some lowlife dirtbag offered him a hundred grand to make a snuff film, Jefferson couldn't resist."

"Snuff films? You mean those porn movies where they kill people? I thought that was just a myth."

Conahegg shook his head. "Sadly, no. There's some sick bastards in the world."

I drew in my breath through clenched teeth and tossed a frightened look over at Jefferson. His face was stony. To think I'd been alone in the car with him and survived.

Just barely.

Sam saw where my gaze had gone. He reached out, drew me to him and squeezed me tight. Protecting me. "Jefferson knew he wasn't going to be able to blackmail Dooley into snuffing Tim on camera, so he decided to do it himself."

I slapped a hand over my mouth and willed myself not to throw up.

"He would have gotten away with it," Conahegg said. "If it hadn't been for Rocky."

"Rocky?"

Sissy looked at Conahegg and he nodded. "You can take it from here. You're the one who unraveled this part of the mystery."

My baby sister had been instrumental in helping Conahegg solve the case? Impressive.

"On the day Jefferson made the snuff film with Tim, Rocky saw his car in the yard and decided to go over and see if he could buy a lid of marijuana," Sissy said. "Jefferson didn't answer the door of course, he'd just killed Tim. He hid out in the closet, hoping whoever was in there would go away. But Rocky walked on into the house, found Tim's body and saw the camera equipment."

"Let me guess," I said. "He took the tape and used it to blackmail Jefferson."

"Yes, except he made a copy. He gave the original to Jefferson when he paid up, but then hid the duplicate. He told me if anything happened to him I was to get the copy and take it to the sheriff. But Rocky was killed before he could tell me who was on the tape and where he'd hidden it. I had no idea where to look for the tape. Then, I remembered he'd had a tape with him when we went to Tim's funeral, but that was the last I saw of it. I figured he'd stashed it somewhere in the church."

"And that's where I found her," Conahegg said. "In the chapel, searching for the tape. That's when she told me her half of the story."

"And you decided to use my sister as bait," I interrupted.

"Sam didn't use me. I wanted to do it. I wanted to catch him."

"Problem was—" Sam picked up the story again "—Jefferson figured it out. He knew I was closing in on him. He didn't show up for the rendezvous with Sissy. Instead he called me and told me that he'd buried you alive." Conahegg's voice cracked. "Ally, that was the worst moment of my life."

"Not too great for me, either. How did you know where to find me?"

Sissy grinned. "I'd been secretly following Jefferson and I'd seen him dig the grave a few days ago. I think it was originally meant for me. So you see, I saved you."

"Yes, you did." Then I started to cry and Sissy started to cry and we hugged each other tight.

Several minutes later we pulled away from each

other and I turned back to Conahegg and that's when I noticed he was bleeding.

"GOT A NEW PATIENT for you," Joyce said and plopped a folder on my desk. A week had passed since Jefferson had been arrested for burying me alive and I hadn't seen or heard from Conahegg. The last time I'd seem him he was being wheeled away on a stretcher. He'd neglected to tell me he'd gotten shot in the shoulder while taking down Jefferson. What was it with that man and his secrets?

I'd resisted the urge to call him. I was done hovering over people. The ball was in his court.

Groaning, I picked up the chart and chased after Joyce. "Hey, wait a minute. You've given me the last four new patients. I'm overworked and underpaid."

Joyce stopped and eyed me. "You don't want the case?"

"No."

"Fine then." She plucked the chart from my hand.

Something was up. That had been far too easy. I turned to go back toward my desk.

"I'll take him," Joyce said.

Joyce? Taking a patient? Something was most definitely up. I snatched for the chart but she held on tight.

"Who is it?" I demanded. I didn't like the canary-eating-feline expression on her face.

"You don't want the case."

"Joyce," I said, "Give me the chart or I swear I'll take you down at the kneecaps."

I must have looked as if I meant it because Joyce quietly passed me the chart. I held my breath and flipped it open.

Samuel J. Conahegg.

I suddenly felt very short of breath. I didn't know whether to throw the chart back at Joyce or immediately run right over to Sam's house.

"So what are you waiting for?" Joyce snapped. "Go already."

I flew.

Twenty minutes later I was standing on Sam's front porch, knuckles poised to knock, but unable to make that simple follow-through. What was I going to say to him?

"How long you gonna stand there?"

My heart took the express elevator to my throat and I whirled around to find Sam standing behind me, an amused smile lifting the corner of his mouth.

"I...um...you're my patient." I waved the chart. "I'm here to dress your gunshot wound."

"Uh-huh." He never took his eyes from mine as he trod up the steps toward me.

He looked so big and beautiful and...*nervous?*

I recognized the signs. He was clenching and unclenching his hands and beads of perspiration dotted his forehead.

It's August, you ninny.

August or not, ninny or not, something extraordinary was happening inside of me. My pulse blipped and a surge of pure joy rushed through my stomach, so strong it almost buckled my knees. Hope and a giddy happiness enveloped me. Elation. Exhilaration. Euphoria.

Oh, what was happening to me?

He reached out and took my hand and led me into his house. And I let him. It felt nice. Letting someone else be in charge for once.

"Ally," he said, guiding me to sit down on the couch. "We have to talk."

Talk? What was this about? He studied me and my early euphoria vanished.

His bigness and nearness was a bit overwhelming. Testosterone radiated out from him and it was almost more than I could handle. "What is it?" I whispered.

"There's something important I have to say."

I gazed over his shoulder so I wouldn't have to keep staring into those penetrating eyes. I wasn't sure I wanted to hear his confession. Was he married? Had he fathered four hundred children out of wedlock? Did he secretly like to dress up as a cartoon character when he had sex? My mind jumped to the stupidest conclusions.

"Hit me," I said, and cringed, prepared for the worst.

He squirmed. I grew more anxious.

"This is hard for me."

"Spit it out, man," I cried.

Sam took my hands in his. "Look at me, first."

I caught my bottom lip between my teeth, braced myself and gazed into his eyes.

He looked tortured. "I apologize."

"For what?" I eyed him suspiciously.

"For not calling you."

"Pffft. It's only been a week."

"And I've been thinking about you every damned minute."

"Really?" I liked how this was turning out. "So why didn't you call?"

"Because you're the best thing that's ever happened to me, Allegheny Green, and I'm so damned afraid of screwing it up." In that moment he looked so sweet, so damned adorable. "I'm not the easiest person in the world to live with. I can be arrogant and hardheaded."

"Don't forget demanding and uncompromising and secretive."

"That, too." He grinned.

"If this is your let-me-be-your-boyfriend sales pitch, it definitely needs some fine tuning. You're supposed to focus on your good points, not your bad," I pointed out.

He draped his arm across the back of the couch and leaned forward to gently stroke my cheek with his thumb. "This isn't a let-me-be-your-boyfriend pitch."

"It's not?"

"No."

"That's good, because like I said, it needs work."

"I was thinking of something far more serious."

"You were?" My voice came out all squeaky.

"Uh-huh."

"What did you have in mind?"

"This." Then he kissed me like I had never been kissed before.

And as I tore off his shirt and pulled him down on the couch, as mindful of his injured shoulder as one could be while locked in a lusty frenzy, I realized Samuel J. Conahegg had just saved me from myself.

Author Interview:
A conversation with LORI WILDE

Why did you name your heroine Allegheny? It's such an unusual name!

When I was a kid I used to collect unusual names. I used to keep long lists. (My mother thought I was really weird.) I ran across a singer named Allegheny and I loved the name so I added it to my collection. That was years ago, but when I started writing this book, the central character introduced herself as Allegheny Green.

How did Ally's story come to you? Had it been sitting with you for a while?

Actually, yes. For quite some time I'd wanted to do a story combining my nursing background with my love for life on the Brazos River, but it never seemed the right fit for my category books. I'd also been dying to write in first person. The book swirled around my head for several years before I wrote it.

How did you begin your writing career?
I wanted to be a writer since I was eight, but my father, a journalist, knew how difficult it was to make a living writing fiction. He urged me to become a nurse so I'd have something solid to fall back on. I became a registered nurse, but I never lost my desire to write. I took a job working double shifts on the weekend so I'd have Monday through Friday to write. I sold my first book to Silhouette Romance in 1994, four years after I started writing seriously.

Do you have a writing routine?
Oh yes. I write for a couple of hours in the morning, take a break for an hour or two, come back for another two-hour session, take another break, then come to the keyboard for a third two-hour session. I find it helps my creativity to break up the writing with spells of some mundane activity like cleaning house or exercise or running errands. I never watch television during the day, however. That makes me lazy.

When you're not writing, what do you love to do?
I enjoy exercising, believe it or not. I used to be a marathon runner and there are a lot of similar characteristics between long-distance runners and novelists. There's something about the discipline I find compelling.

What or who inspires you?

My husband inspires me because he's kind, funny, romantic and heroic. I'm so blessed to have found him. My father inspired me to become a writer in the first place. He infected me with his love of books and reading.

Is there one book that you've read that changed your life somehow?

One of the most emotionally charged books I've ever read is *A Prayer For Owen Meany* by John Irving. It's about the power of goodness. It made me understand that the external things we accomplish here are just that. It's what kind of person we are that matters, not whether we gain fame and fortune.

What are your top five favorite books?

A PRAYER FOR OWEN MEANY
LONESOME DOVE
THE THORN BIRDS
GONE WITH THE WIND
TOM SAWYER

What matters most in life?

Forgiveness.

If you weren't a writer what would you be doing?

It's hard to imagine not being a writer because it's all I ever wanted to do. But in a parallel universe I might be a chef. I'm a foodie and I love to cook. There's something rich and nourishing and inspiring about preparing a delicious meal for those you love.

Marsha Zinberg, Executive Editor, Signature Select™ met with Lori in the spring of 2005.

COMING NEXT MONTH

Signature Select Collection
BEYOND THE DARK by Linda Winstead Jones, Evelyn Vaughn and Karen Whiddon
Evil looms but love conquers the darkness in this collection of three new stories of otherworldly romance.

Signature Select Saga
COLBY CONSPIRACY by Debra Webb
While working to uncover the truth behind a murder linked to The Colby Agency, Daniel Marks and Emily Hastings find themselves trapped by the dangers of desire—knowing every move they make could be their last....

Signature Select Miniseries
WINDOW TO YESTERDAY by Debra Salonen
In this compelling volume containing two full-length novels, old regrets and buried secrets come back to haunt Ren Bishop and Claudie St. James, leaving them unprepared for the journey that lies before them.

Signature Select Spotlight
LEARNING CURVES by Cindi Myers
In the cutthroat business of network news, thin is in, and Shelly Piper's size-twelve curves are causing viewers to demand a thinner coanchor. But Shelly has come too far to lose her job—or a dress size.

Signature Select Showcase
THE STUD by Barbara Delinsky
Jenna McCue wants a baby and she wants Spencer Smith to be the father...or rather the donor. Spencer agrees, but on one condition: he "donates" the old-fashioned way. But getting pregnant will mean she'll never see him again. That's part of the deal. Or is it?

The Fortunes of Texas: Reunion
THE GOOD DOCTOR by Karen Rose Smith
Peter Clark would never describe himself as a jaw-dropping catch. So why is beautiful New York neurologist Violet Fortune looking at him as if she would like to show him her bedside manner?